Laura Jane Williams is a writer whose work has appeared everywhere from the *Guardian* to *Buzzfeed*, *Stylist*, *Closer*, the *Metro* and the *Telegraph*. She is *Grazia*'s former dating columnist, and the author of two previous works of non-fiction: *Ice Cream for Breakfast* and *Becoming*. *Our Stop* is her first novel.

Our Stop

LAURA JANE WILLIAMS

avon.

Published by AVON
A division of HarperCollins*Publishers* Ltd
1 London Bridge Street
London SE1 9GF

www.harpercollins.co.uk

A Paperback Original 2019

2

First published in Great Britain by HarperCollins*Publishers* 2019

ISBN: 978-0-00832-052-2

This novel is entirely a work of fiction.
The names, characters and incidents portrayed in it are the work
of the author's imagination. Any resemblance to actual persons, living or dead,
events or localities is entirely coincidental.

Set in Minion by Palimpsest Book Production Limited, Falkirk, Stirlingshire

Printed and bound in UK by CPI Group (UK) Ltd, Croydon CR0 4YY

MIX
Paper from
responsible sources
FSC™ C007454

This book is produced from independently certified FSC™ paper
to ensure responsible forest management.

For more information visit: www.harpercollins.co.uk/green

For anyone who, like me, chooses to believe
(despite all the evidence to the contrary)

1

Nadia

'Shit. Shit, shit, shit.'

Nadia Fielding launched down the escalator of the tube station, her new sandals flapping with force underfoot. If people didn't move out of her way because of the swearing, surely they would for the massive *thwack* she made each time a sole hit the step. She cursed ever having swiped up on the Instagram link, and she cursed the blogger who had made the black leather monstrosities look chic – and comfortable – enough to buy. They were giving her a blister already. *Fuck you, @whiskyandwhimsies*, Nadia thought to herself. *I hope your next sponsored trip to the Amalfi Coast falls through.*

Coffee held precariously in her hand, bag slipping from her shoulder, sunglasses beginning to slide off the top of her head, Nadia was a mess – but she'd be damned if she wasn't getting the 7.30. Today was the first day of The New Routine to Change Her Life, and The New Routine to Change Her Life meant catching the train on time.

She struggled with this. Midnight bedtimes after a night out with Emma or Gaby (she was healing a dented heart! Wine is so delicious!) and a general tendency towards being more of a night owl than an early riser (to think she knew people who did Super Spin before work!) both conspired to intensify Nadia's love affair with the snooze button. She only accomplished being on time for work about once a week, normally on a Monday. She thanked god she lived alone in a flat that technically her mother owned but that meant she didn't need roommates – no matter what time she got up, at least there was never a queue for the bathroom.

Monday was a perpetual Fresh Start – but often by the time Nadia put a Netflix series on that night, little had changed. She was always very conscientious between getting up and just before lunch, though. It was Monday afternoons that undid her. It couldn't be helped. The working week was just so agonizingly long, and she spent her whole life trying to catch up with herself. She was sick of being exhausted. A viral BuzzFeed article had called it 'Millennial Burnout'. But, that's not to say Nadia couldn't achieve big things when she put her mind to it – recently she'd polished off all seven seasons of *The Good Wife* in little under three weeks. Unfortunately, however, there was no way to leverage her binge-watching-of-American-lawyers-in-impossibly-tight-skirts-with-bizarrely-sassy-retorts-to-chauvinism skill into a salaried position. And so, life went on in a muddle. Well, until today. Today was the first day of the rest of her life.

Nadia's New Routine to Change Her Life wasn't to be confused with a Fresh Start, because obviously The New Routine to Change Her Life would not fail, like previous attempts. This time it would be different. *She* would be different. She'd become the woman one step *ahead* of herself.

The sort of woman who meal-prepped for the week in matching Tupperware, who didn't have to renew her passport at exorbitant cost the week before a holiday but instead recognized the expiration date with a three-month lead time and didn't get frustrated at the confusing form at the Post Office. She was to become the kind of woman who had comprehensive life insurance and a closet full of clothes already ironed, instead of crisis-steaming wrinkled & Other Stories dresses five minutes before she had to run for the bus. Nadia would become, when her new plan became her new reality, a beacon of Goop-like organization and zen. More *Namaste* than *Nama-stay-in-bed*. She'd be the Gwyneth Paltrow of Stamford Hill, with slightly wonkier teeth.

'Excuse me! Sorry!' she screeched, to nobody in particular and everyone all at once, as she approached the platform at speed. She normally hated the people that shoved her out of the way in tube stations and at bus stops, as if they were the only folks with anywhere important to be. On more than one occasion she'd shouted after an elbow-barger, 'EXCUSE YOU!' in pointed frustration. But today, this morning, *she* was the selfish oaf pushing through the commuting crowds, and she didn't have time to be embarrassed about it. The new Nadia was perhaps a little ruder than her old self, but goddamnit she was also more punctual. (She suddenly had an echo of the shrill soprano of her GCSE English teacher, who would intone, 'To be early is to be on time, to be on time is to be late . . . and to be late is absolutely unacceptable!')

'Wait! No!' she squealed. Nadia was four quick steps away from the train, but at the speed she was hurtling was about to go face-first into closed doors unless somebody defied Transport for London's rules and held them open.

'Waitwaitwaitwaitwait!' Her voice reached a pitch only dolphins could hear. As if in slow motion, a hand reached out and pinned the door back, meaning that Nadia could stumble aboard just as her knock-off Ray-Bans hit her face and she was temporarily blinded by their darkness. The doors snapped shut behind her. She'd made it. Just.

With a bit of practice, Nadia thought, suddenly smug, muttering a thank you and grabbing the only free seat to sit and slurp at her coffee, *I might be able to nail this new routine.* It had taken cajoling and effort, but so far, in the whole hour and half she'd been up, she was impressed to reflect that she'd stuck to her self-imposed rules. Ninety minutes on plan was better than ninety minutes off-plan, after all.

The New Routine to Change Her Life comprised several things besides making sure she was on the platform at exactly 7.30 a.m., to catch the tube from Angel to London Bridge. The other rules included:

- AT LEAST seven hours of sleep a night, meaning bed at 11 p.m. LATEST – and that meant lights out and eyes closed at 11 p.m., not getting to bed at 11 p.m. and spending three hours doggedly refreshing the holy trifecta of Instagram, Twitter and email and then wondering why it was so difficult to get up when the alarm went off the next day, whilst also fuelling the suspicion that everyone else's life was far easier and more beautiful than hers.

- Up at 6 a.m., to meditate for fifteen minutes, then lighting a soy-wax scented candle as she got ready for work with calmness and serenity, in the manner of Oprah, or perhaps the Duchess of Sussex.

4

- Swapping a station-bought, triple-shot, extra-large cappuccino that Nadia was sure gave her spots – she'd seen the trailer for a documentary about the hormones in milk – to make a bulletproof coffee in a reusable cup for the commute. She had heard about bulletproof coffees via a Hollywood star who documented her life and workouts on Instagram in real time and who added unsalted butter to her morning espresso to regulate her energy levels and poop schedule. ('That's like making a green smoothie with vanilla ice cream,' her mother had suggested in an email, which Nadia had, regretfully, no scientific retort for. 'At least I'm doing it in an environmentally friendly KeepCup,' she'd settled on, wondering if, actually, her mother was right.)

- Keeping faith in romance: just because her ex Awful Ben was, indeed, awful, it didn't mean she had to think all men were, and it was important to keep believing in love.

Nadia also planned on getting to the office before everyone else each morning. She worked in artificial intelligence, developing technology that could think for itself and replace basic human activities like stacking shelves and labelling boxes, with a view to eventually making the warehouse arm of her company totally AI-run. She intended to always get a head start on reviewing the previous day's prototype developments, before the inevitable meetings about meetings began, interrupting her every six to nine minutes and destroying her concentration until she wanted to scream or cry, depending on where in her menstrual cycle she was.

Her morning's self-satisfaction didn't last long, though.

The train stopped in a sudden, jerky movement, and hot brown liquid hurled itself from the lip of her KeepCup, soaking into the hem of her light-blue dress and through to her thighs.

'Shit,' she said again, as if she, a woman in charge of a team of six, earning £38,000 a year and with two degrees, didn't know any other words.

Her best friend Emma called Nadia's coffee addiction an attitude adjustment in a cup. She needed caffeine to function as a human. Groaning outwardly, pouting at the blemish she'd have to wear on herself all day now, she chastised herself for not being more sophisticated – she'd never seen Meghan bloody Markle covered in her breakfast.

Nadia pulled out her phone and texted her best friend Emma, wanting a bit of Monday-morning cheerleading.

Morning! Do you want to go see that new Bradley Cooper film this week? I need something in the diary to be excited about . . .

She sat and waited for her friend's reply. It was hot on the train, even this early, and a tiny bead of sweat had formed at the nape of her neck. She could smell BO, and instantly worried it was coming from her.

Nadia tried to surreptitiously turn her head and pretend-cough, bringing her shoulder up to her mouth and her nostrils closer to her armpits. She smelled of antiperspirant. She'd read about the link between deodorant and breast cancer and tried using a crystal as a natural alternative for three weeks a few summers ago, but Emma had pulled her aside and told her in no uncertain terms that it was ineffective. Today, she was 100 per cent aluminium – and sweat-free – in cucumber and green tea Dove.

Relieved, she looked around for the culprit, clocking a group of tourists arguing over a map, a nanny with three blonde children, and a cute man reading a paper by the doors who didn't look unlike the model in the new John Lewis adverts. Her gaze finally landed on the damp patches under the armpits of the guy stood right in front of her, his crotch almost in her eye. Gross. The morning commute was like being on Noah's Ark – wild animals cooped up, unnaturally close, a smorgasbord of odours akin to Saturday afternoon in Sports Direct.

She waited for her stop, staring idly around the carriage, trying not to inhale. She glanced lazily back at the man by the doors – the one with the newspaper. *Just my type*, she couldn't help but think, enjoying the way his tailored trousers danced close enough to his thighs to make her cheeks blush. Her phone buzzed. She pulled her gaze away to look at Emma's text, and forgot about him.

2

Daniel

Daniel Weissman couldn't believe it. As they'd pulled up at Angel she'd skidded around the corner and he'd held his breath as he'd held the door, like a Taylor Swift lyric about an innocuous beginning and a happy ending and love that was always meant to be. Not that Daniel meant to sound soft that way. He just got weird and jittery and soppy when he thought about her. She had that effect on him. Daniel found it hard not to let his imagination get carried away.

He tried to catch sight of her from his position by the doors – she'd snaked around to the middle of the carriage. He could just about make out the top of her head. She always had hair that was messy, but not like she didn't care about herself. It was messy like she'd just come from a big adventure, or the beach. It probably had a name, but Daniel didn't know it. He just knew that she was very much his type. It was so embarrassing, but in the sponsorship advert in between every ad break for *The Lust Villa*, there was a girl who looked just like her, and if Daniel hadn't seen her in a while even that – a bloody advert! – could make him nostalgic and thoughtful. It was shameful, really.

The Lust Villa was Daniel's summer reality TV fix, full of romance and seduction and laughing. Daniel acted like it bugged him that the TV had to be on at 9 p.m. every evening for the show, but he was always in the living room at 8.58 p.m., as if by accident, just settling down to his cup of tea in the big armchair with the best view of the widescreen. His flatmate Lorenzo pretended that he didn't notice the co-incidence, and they happily watched it together every night. Neither said it out loud – and nobody would guess it from Lorenzo's behaviour – but they were both looking for some-body to settle down with and it was quite informative watching what women liked and didn't like via a daily show that featured genuine relationships. Daniel used it as a way to get his confidence up, taking notes and learning lessons; last night, the bloke that was obviously there as a bit of an underdog had finally found his match, and now here Daniel was in this moment, today. He didn't want to be the underdog in his own life. That show made him feel like he owed it to himself to at least try with this woman. Just to see.

Daniel couldn't help but admire the serendipity of the morning. What were the chances she'd stagger right past him on the morning the advert got published? They'd only been on the same train at the same time on a handful of occasions, including today. He forced himself to breathe deeply. He'd done it – sent off the *Missed Connection* – to maybe, hopefully, finally get her attention, but he was suddenly terrified she'd know it was him. What if she laughed in his face and called him a loser? A dreamer? What if she told everyone at work – her work, or his work – how he was pathetic, and had dared to think he was good enough for her? Maybe she'd go viral on Twitter, or post his picture on her Instagram. On the one hand, he knew she was too nice to ever be so awful, but on the other, the tiniest voice in the back of his mind told him that's exactly what would happen. He shook his head to try and rid himself of the thought. Love was sending him crazy. Or was it that he was crazy in love?

'Mate, this isn't love,' Lorenzo had told him, not even taking his eyes off the telly to issue his damning verdict. 'You just wanna bang her.'

Daniel did not just want to 'bang her'. That wasn't it at all. He probably shouldn't stare at her silently and from afar, though. That was a bit weird. It was just – well . . . The politics of hitting on a woman seemingly out of the blue were so blurred and loaded. He could hardly approach her cold, like some train psychopath she'd have to shake by 'pretending' they were at her stop and then slipping out and onto a different carriage. But he also knew that if any blokes in his life told him they were trying to seduce a woman they'd never directly spoken to by putting an advert in the paper and then staring at her stealthily somewhere beyond Moorgate, he'd gently suggest that it probably wasn't the most ethically sound plan. He was *trying* to be romantic, whilst also saving face. He hoped he'd got the balance right.

In his head, the fantasy went like this: she'd read the paper and see his note and look up immediately and he'd be right there, by the doors, like he said, and they'd make eye contact and she'd smile coyly and he'd go, simply, 'Hello'. It would be the beginning of the rest of their lives, that 'Hello'. Like in a movie. And in that movie there wouldn't be five Spanish tourists in between them, crowded around in a circle, looking at a map, an indistinguishable babble punctuated occasionally

11

by the mispronunciation of 'Leicester Square'. Fuck. Where was she? Oh god, this was awful.

The train pulled into London Bridge and, after finally locating her as she steamed ahead through the crowds and towards the exit, the moment he thought might happen disappeared before his eyes. There was no bolt of lightning. No world slowing as their eyes met, not so much as a question but as an answer. She had barely acknowledged him when he held the doors and helped her get on the train – she'd been in a rush, and distracted, and her 'thank you' was more of a breathy 'ta!' as she passed by. As he tried to keep pace with her, Daniel realized he was disappointed in himself, and in the situation. He'd imagined this for weeks, and now . . . nothing.

She suddenly stopped in the middle of the departing commuters to read her phone, but it wasn't like he could slow down as well, let alone stand beside her, could he? So he kept walking and then waited by the exit. He wasn't sure what for. Just to see her, probably. To see her on the day he'd put himself out there, to remind himself it was real, that she was real, even if it hadn't gone to plan.

Later, when Daniel told Lorenzo how the morning had played out, he'd miss out this part – the part where he waited for her. What was he doing? He wasn't going to actually go up and talk to her. Again, she had a right to exist without him bothering her. He shook his head. *Come on mate, get a grip*, he told himself. He headed towards his office, his heart beating loudly and rapidly and disruptively in his chest.

He'd screwed it up.

He was gutted.

She hadn't seen it.

What a wasted gesture.

You bloody idiot, he muttered to himself, unaware that seeing the advert was exactly what was holding Nadia up back on the platform.

3

Nadia

Nads, not being funny but don't you think this sounds like it could be you?!

Nadia tapped on the photo Emma had sent through and waited for it to download, simultaneously bumping through the commuters heaving in the opposite direction to her.

The photo was a close-up of that morning's paper, specifically the *Missed Connections* section – the bit where Londoners wrote in about their commute crush and left hints about their identity in the hopes of landing a date with a stranger they'd seen on the bus or tube. Nadia and Emma were obsessed with *Missed Connections*. It was a mix of horror and awe – the same kind of compulsion that drove their love of reality TV.

The mating rituals of the sexes were a constant source of fascination for them both. Before she got the restaurant review column – a superb job for any best friend to have, since Nadia was frequently her plus-one – Emma used to be the dating columnist at one of the weekly women's mags, but most of her material was crowd-sourced from after-work drinks with Nadia and sometimes Nadia's work best friend, Gaby.

Romance and lust and sex and relationships were of endless interest for them all, and ever since they'd known each other, bad dates were almost worth it in order to have an outrageous story to share the next day. They'd had four-fingers-in-his-bum guy, and the divorced chap who'd disclosed on their first date that his wife had left him because he 'couldn't satisfy her – you know, sexually'. There'd been 'Actually-I'm-in-an-open-marriage-my-wife-just-doesn't-know-it' man, and also the one who picked at the eczema behind his ear and proceeded to eat it in between mouthfuls of his pint.

Emma once accidentally had three dates with a man Gaby had previously dated – Gaby had dumped him because he refused to wear a condom, and Emma found that out only after she'd dumped him for . . . refusing to wear a condom. For some reason all three of them had dated more than a handful of men called James, who ended up being referred to by number: James One, James Six, James Nine. The most memorable bloke was Period Pete, a friend of a friend who liked performing oral sex on menstruating women, and who the three collectively decided must have an undiagnosed iron deficiency.

Nadia, Gaby and Emma had talked about them all, trying to understand the puzzle of men-kind. Well, except for the one who said he'd be too busy to have a girlfriend 'for the next five years, at least', who Nadia had simply never texted back again. He was a riddle not worth trying to solve. She didn't want a man she had to teach kindness to.

Nadia wondered if it would change if any of them ever

got married – if they'd stop telling each other everything about their sex and love lives. She hoped not. She hoped that even in marriage or after fifty years with her hypothetical guy that there would still be romance and mystery and tension that she'd want to gossip over with her girlfriends. She'd heard on an Esther Perel podcast that that was important. For a woman who historically hadn't been very good at it, Nadia spent a lot of time researching love.

The image Emma had photographed cleared into vision and Nadia saw that it said:

To the devastatingly cute blonde girl on the Northern line with the black designer handbag and coffee stains on her dress – you get on at Angel, on the 7.30, always at the end nearest the escalator, and always in a hurry. I'm the guy who's standing near the doors of your carriage, hoping today's a day you haven't overslept. Drink some time?

Nadia stopped walking, causing a woman behind her to side-step and mutter, 'Oh, for god's sake.'

She reread the note.

The devastatingly cute blonde girl on the Northern line with the black designer handbag and coffee stains on her dress. She spun around to look back at the train she'd just disembarked. It had already left. She dropped her hand to run a finger over the brown mark on her dress. She looked at her handbag. She WhatsApped Emma back.

!!!!!!!!! she typed with one hand.

And then, *Um . . . I mean, lol but maybe?!*

After a beat she thought better of it: *I mean, the chances are slim, right?*

She mulled it over some more. She and Emma weren't

17

even sure that *Missed Connections* was real. It made her initial reaction seem increasingly off the mark. Nadia and Emma didn't care one way or the other – if it was real or made up by the weekly intern at the paper as a creative writing exercise – it was the fantasy of a stranger searching for somebody they felt a fleeting connection to that was fun. It was like Savage Garden knowing they loved you before they met you.

It was romantic, in a you're-a-blank-canvas-I-can-project-my-hopes-and-dreams-on sort of way.

In a fantasies-don't-have-problems-so-this-is-better-than-real-life way.

An our-love-will-be-different way.

Missed Connections felt full of more romance than messing around on Bumble did. Although, any time either of them doubted that sort of love existed, the other would bring up Tim, Emma's brother. He'd gone out to Chicago for a couple of weeks for work and used a dating app to meet a local who could show him around, maybe even partake in a fling. Through that app Tim had met Deena, and legend had it that when Deena went to the loo Tim pulled out his phone, deleted the app, and within three months had transferred out there to live with her. They'd got married that spring. *Miracles do happen*, Tim had said in his speech. *I searched the whole world for you, and there you were, waiting for me in downtown Chicago, in a restaurant window seat.*

Emma texted: *Question: are you sporting a coffee stain this morning, and did you get the 7.30? It's Monday, so I presume yes.*

Nadia replied with a snap of her outfit from above – the splodge of butter-laden coffee clearly visible – very obviously on her way to work.

But, Nadia thought . . . surely there were a million women

on the Northern line spilling coffee and carrying fancy bags that family members had sourced at discounted designer outlets. And nobody ever did things on time – not in London. Loads of cute blondes – *devastatingly cute* blondes – probably missed their intended train all the time. And yeah, she'd never really thought about how she instinctively always turned left at the bottom of Angel's escalator and walked towards the end of the track there, but that *was* something she did. Who else did? Hundreds, surely. Thousands? It was the longest tube escalator in London, after all. It could hold a lot of people.

Right then, Emma sent back, love heart emojis before and after her text, *I think we've got some investigating to do, don't you?*

I'm dying, Nadia wrote back. *It's totally not me. I'm grateful to all the other women out there who can't take a coffee cup on a train without spilling it, though. Makes me feel better about myself, lol.*

Could be you, though . . . Emma said.

Nadia considered it. *I mean, there's like a 2 per cent chance*, she typed. And then: *If that.*

Then it hit her: the man by the train doors, reading the paper. There'd been a man there! Was that him? Men must stand by the door and read the paper all the time, what with being male and commuting and picking up a newspaper on the way being statistically quite high. Nadia looked around the station, to see if she recognized anyone as the man she'd been near. She couldn't even remember what he'd looked like. Blonde? No. Brunette? Definitely handsome. Oh god.

A weird feeling of hope that it *was* her came over Nadia, whilst she simultaneously realized that hoping for that was kind of non-feminist too. She didn't have to wait to be chosen by a mystery man to date and be happy. Did she?

But – also – in The New Routine to Change Her Life, Nadia was supposed to believe that luck was on her side. And if luck really was on her side, maybe this was for her, and maybe this guy wouldn't be an insecure loser. Awful Ben, her last boyfriend, had had a weird fragile masculinity – he was emotionally manipulative and made her think *she* was in the wrong until he'd undone her confidence. And he did do that – he did undo her confidence. It had really bruised her, because for the six months they dated she almost came to believe there was something wrong with her. She still didn't understand why somebody would do that: say they'd fallen in love with you and then decide to hate everything that made them say that in first place. She was only just starting to feel like herself again.

Nadia shuddered at the bad memories. She thought about Awful Ben every day still, but when she did she always thanked the heavens that she was now out of that dire situation. She couldn't believe what she'd let herself put up with. Occasionally she set her web browser to private and typed in his Instagram handle to check he was still as much of a difficult, pretentious arse as ever. He always was.

But now, months after their break-up, Nadia was equal parts bruised and in need of an emotional palette cleanser. A romantic sorbet. Somebody new to think about. A man to be a bit nice to her would do, as if that didn't place the bar too low. Perhaps her own newspaper ad would read, *Wanted, man: must actually seem to like me.*

Oh, who was she kidding? Her advert would say: *Wanted: man with strong sense of self, capable of having a laugh, healthy relationship with mother. Must love romance, reality television, and be ready to champion and cheerlead as a partner through life, in exchange for exactly the same. Also must understand the importance of cunnilingus and pizza – though not at same time. I cum first, pizza comes second.*

Was she expecting too much? She thought of Tim and Deena. Surely she could have that too.

2 per cent is higher than 0 per cent, typed back Emma. *So, game on.*

Nadia laughed as she finally made her way to the escalator, emerging in the early-morning summer sun at the top. *Whatever you say*, she typed back. And to herself she thought, *But I daren't be too hopeful.*

'Emma has already texted me,' Gaby said, catching Nadia as she headed down to the lobby for an 11 a.m. break. The coffee cart in their lobby served an amazing dark espresso blend. 'And I reckon it's you as well.'

Nadia was astonished.

'Ohmygod. Worst thing I ever did was introduce you two to each other,' she replied, laughing, before saying to the guy behind the counter, 'double-shot espresso topped up with hot water, please.'

Gaby pulled a face. 'What happened to a full-fat cappuccino as a political statement?'

'I'm pivoting. I did one of those bulletproof coffees this morning, to see if it keeps my blood sugar regulated and also, have you seen this acne on my jawline? It's a menace. I think it might be too much milk – like, apparently milk is just cow hormones not meant for people – so I'm giving up for a bit. These little fuckers hurt, you know.

Nadia craned to see her own reflection in the glass of the skyscraper they worked in. Having acne made her really self-conscious. When she was in the middle of a flare-up she tended to dress in darker colours, as if she didn't want to be noticed. She needed a permanent filter to follow her around – it didn't look half as bad when she was on Instagram Stories and could use the crown filter to smooth everything out. She'd try anything to get rid of the angry red boils under the skin of her jaw, including sacrificing her daily cappuccinos.

'So,' she went on, 'I'm experimenting.'

Nadia thanked the barista and the pair walked from the lobby coffee stand to the lifts of RAINFOREST, home to two thousand Research and Development employees for a world-wide delivery service for everything from books to toilet cleaner to marble-top tables. This was where Nadia did her artificial intelligence work. Gaby was her work BFF. They'd met at the summer party two years ago and hit it off talking about AI and its role in a Good Future or Bad Future: what if they accidentally developed technology that turned on them, like in a horror movie? Gaby worked on what was called 'cloud computing' for the company, their biggest revenue-generator, selling pay-as-you-go data storage to everyone from start-ups to MI6. Nadia didn't really understand it, but she knew Gaby was about thirty times cleverer than her, and scared half the people in her part of the office.

'And, anyway – can I tell you about The New Routine to Change My Life?' Nadia hit the lift button. 'Because, I dunno. I guess I feel finally purged of Awful Ben and want to switch my energy up or something. I feel like I just came out of mourning. Like literally, this weekend I got my mojo back.' The lift arrived. 'And today I'm trying to be deliberate about keeping it. I'm taking my wellbeing and mental health seriously, beginning now.'

'That's great!'

'Thanks!' The lift button flashed '0' and the doors opened. The pair got in and Nadia hit the buttons for their respective floors.

'You know, if you want to get some endorphins going to keep your high, what about coming to spin before work tomorrow?'

Nadia rolled her eyes.

'No!' Gaby continued. 'Don't pull that face! It's so good. It's really dark in there and the instructor says positive affirmations and you get to scream because the music is so loud nobody can hear you.'

Nadia shook her head, watching the lights of the different floors ping brightly as they passed through. Spinning was her worst nightmare. She'd done exactly one SoulCycle class when she went to LA for work and spent forty-five minutes on a bike next to Emily Ratajkowski, wondering how a woman so tiny could peddle so fast. She'd hated it.

'Absolutely not. I don't do morning workouts. I'm happy with my evening body pump class, back row, two left feet but doing my best. Only psychopaths work out before noon.'

'Urgh. Fine. Also – we're getting sidetracked.'

'I'd hoped you hadn't noticed.'

'It really does sound like you, you know.'

Nadia raised her eyebrows, partly amused, partly sarcastic.

'It does! Literally you are cute and blonde and chronically late and you spill stuff. And –' Gaby suddenly seemed to connect some mental dots '– and today is the beginning of your New Routine to Change Your Life! So, energetically speaking, the exact day something like this *would* happen. It's like the stars have aligned. Today would be a great day to fall in love.'

'I can't tell if you're being earnest or teasing me.'

'Both,' Gaby deadpanned.

Nadia rolled her eyes good-naturedly again, afraid to give herself away.

'Emma says you might write an advert in response.'

'I'm toying with it, yes. If I decide the advert is really meant for me. Which . . . I'm not sure. I half want it to be. And I half think I'm insane for giving this more than two seconds' thought.'

'Do you have any idea who he could be? If it is for you? Is there a cute man on your train every day?'

Nadia looked at her friend. 'This is London! There are hundreds of cute men, everywhere, all the time. And then they open their mouths and become 200 per cent less cute because . . . men.'

'Ever the optimist, I see.'

'I'm just being realistic.'

'Never met a woman protecting her heart who didn't claim the same,' said Gaby, smirking.

Nadia said nothing, knowing full well that Gaby was right. She found herself doing that a lot: making sweeping statements that damned men to their lowest denominator, acting as if she didn't need or want one. She *was* protecting herself, she supposed, at least out loud. Of course, her friend could see right through that. Because Nadia was, in the same breath as saying all men were pigs, hoping that this one, the Train Guy, wasn't. Or, at the very least, that one guy, somewhere out there, wasn't. All morning she'd been having little fantasies about the advert being for her, and seeing him on the train, and falling in lust and love somewhere on the Northern line between home and work. She wanted that for herself. She wanted it for herself so hungrily that it scared her a bit, truth be told.

The lift arrived at Gaby's floor, and like they did whenever they rode the lift together, Nadia stepped off with her to finish the conversation.

'There is this one thing, though,' Nadia said. Gaby turned and looked at her, willing her to go on. 'Well. The thing my brain can't understand is that if a guy sees me on the train every morning, why wouldn't he just say hello?'

Becky from admin walked by on her way to the photocopier, and Nadia interrupted herself to throw up a small wave and say, 'Hey, Becky!'

'Nice shoes!' Becky said, as way of reply, disappearing around a corner.

Nadia continued: 'Why concoct some elaborate plot that involves a newspaper and relying on me – or, whoever, because it might not be me, like we've established – actually seeing it?'

'It's fun!' Gaby said. 'Cute!' She thought about it some more and then added, 'Plus, if some rando came up to you on your commute, would you honestly even give him the time of day?'

Nadia smiled. 'No. I'd think he was a creep.'

'Me too.'

'Urgh!' Nadia exhaled. 'I'm just trying to manage my romantic expectations, you know? I don't even know if I could stand another first date . . .'

Nadia made a noise that was like a gag of repulsion, summing up the many emotions of a serial dater in as succinct a way as any. But, even as she did that, her heart skipped a little beat. When a first date went right, it was the most magical, hopeful feeling in the world. A feeling of the gods smiling on her, of recognizing herself in somebody else. She once heard that love shouldn't be called 'falling', because the best love roots you, and makes you grow upwards, taller and stronger. She'd seen that happen with her mum and step-dad, after her biological father had left. Her old colleague and friend Naomi and Naomi's husband Callum embodied it. Her direct boss in her first job, Katherine, was the most charismatic, well-adjusted woman Nadia had ever had the honour of being mentored by, and Katherine often said she had got to be where she was at work because of the team she was part of at home. All of them said they knew early on that they'd met the person they wanted to spend their lives with, and committed, together, to making it work. Tim had said that about Deena, too.

'No – you couldn't stand another *bad* first date,' said Gaby. 'But what if this was the last first date you ever had, because it was so *good*?'

Nadia was grateful that Gaby was playing to her more romantic inclinations, because she was enjoying imagining what would happen if she met the love of her life through a newspaper ad. How they'd laugh about it, and be forever united in their appreciation of big gestures and taking chances. But Nadia was suddenly suspicious too: Gaby was usually sceptical and pithy about love, priding herself on dating man after man but not needing any of them. It wasn't like her to coax anyone into believing fairy tales were real.

'What's made you such a romantic all of a sudden?' Nadia asked, eyes narrowed. 'You're supposed to be my cynical friend.'

Gaby shrugged, non-committal. 'What are you working on today?' she said, by way of reply.

'Now who's changing the subject!'

'Don't get smart with me, Fielding.'

Nadia made a mental note to follow up with Gaby later

on her sudden softening. Something was different about her, now she thought about it. Nadia was a tart for her work, though, and so was seduced by her own vanity into talking about it.

'It's crunch time on the prototypes for the fulfilment centres soon. That newspaper exposé really damaged the stock price and John wants actual humans out of the role as soon as possible to get the whole thing boxed off as an HR issue. Which sucks for the thousands of people who don't know they're going to be unemployed by Christmas . . .'

'Oh, that's hard. That's really hard,' Gaby said.

'I feel bad, yeah. I'm building robots to replace humans, and . . . well. It's so conflicting, you know?'

The lift pinged back open, and seeing that it was going up, Nadia stepped in.

'To be continued?' said Gaby.

'To be continued,' said Nadia. 'I'd like to maybe brainstorm ideas about making sure everyone gets jobs elsewhere? I'd like to help.'

'Sure!' Gaby said, adding: 'Maybe over lunch this week? Wednesday? I've got a lunch meeting tomorrow. We've not been across to Borough in ages. And we're not done talking about this missed connection.'

'Stop talking to Emma about my love life!'

Nadia could hear Gaby giggling even as the lift went up.

4

Daniel

'You've been infatuated with her for months, mate. Today is a big day!'

Lorenzo had called him at work, despite being asked not to. But Lorenzo hated his job and got bored easily and liked winding up his flatmate and also feigning busyness at his own desk, at a publishing house north of the river. Plus, he was charming enough to persuade the receptionist, Percy, to connect the call, even though Daniel had given Percy numerous and explicit instructions not to. Lorenzo enjoyed practising his charm and getting his own way. Reaching Daniel at his office was another way for him to show off.

'She's not bloody seen it, though,' Daniel hissed down the phone.

'Can you change the adjectives and send it again, for somebody else you've spotted? Throw enough shit and something will stick,' Lorenzo said, and Daniel was about 70 per cent sure he wasn't joking. Lorenzo *said* he wanted a relationship, but from what Daniel had seen his requirements for dating were that she had a pulse, and didn't talk too much. It was very Lorenzo of him to suggest simply trying the same tactic with another woman.

'Go and sell some books,' Daniel retorted.

'Can't be arsed, mate. Still on a comedown.'

Daniel hated that Lorenzo did coke Thursday through Sunday. He never did it at home, Lorenzo promised, but Daniel was still the one made to put up with his mood swings as he scaled the walls and then festered on the sofa for the first half of the week – even if he did watch great telly as he did it. Lorenzo was a good bloke, but didn't half make some choices that Daniel couldn't help but think weren't exactly sound. It was so frustrating to be witness to. They'd ended up living together through a SpareRoom.co.uk advert Lorenzo had put up, and Daniel had his suspicions from the beginning that they were a bit chalk and cheese, but the location of the flat and the rent price were basically perfect, so Daniel had made a decision to largely overlook their differences, not quite becoming friends, but certainly becoming more than just strangers who lived together. They had forged their own, very particular, double act, and until Daniel had a place of his own, it did the job.

'I'm going now,' Daniel said. 'I've got actual work to do. I'll see you at home.'

Lorenzo was still talking as he put the phone down. Not seconds later, Daniel's mobile flashed with a message. It was Lorenzo.

Well done on having the balls, mate, it said. That was Lorenzo's way of saying, *I know you hate it when I'm a twat but I can't help it*. Daniel double-tapped it and gave it a thumbs-up.

Daniel resumed idly scrolling through the emails on his desktop, trying to focus on the day ahead and not on the morning that had been. He couldn't. He couldn't stop thinking about her. He couldn't stop thinking about the day they first met.

Not long after Daniel's father had died, just after Easter, Daniel had begun to force himself to leave his desk whenever he felt claustrophobic, or uneasy, or like he might cry. In his grief – the word 'depression' still sort of stuck in his throat a bit, sounded a bit wet – his therapist had said that being outside, in nature, would always help.

Christ. He couldn't believe he had a *therapist*.

'Keep using your body, make sure you engage with the world, take a stroll around the nearest park, even, just to get the energy moving differently,' she told him at one of their first sessions together, when he'd said about panic attacks that grabbed him by the throat and made him feel like he couldn't breathe.

He'd had to pay sixty-five pounds an hour to go private because the NHS waiting list was too long, his situation too dire to wait because he could barely function, and he wondered, not unkindly, if this was the kind of advice he could expect for two hundred plus quid a month. Anyway. Walk he did, at the very least to feel like he was getting value for money, and she'd been there, Nadia (of course, he didn't know that was her name then), in the courtyard tucked away off Borough Market. A random Friday. Poof. At his lowest, in a moment of pure emotional desperation, this positive, engaged, clever woman had appeared and her verve – her very essence, her aura – was like sunshine, solar-powering everyone around her. It had knocked Daniel sideways.

Daniel knew exactly which day he'd first seen her because

31

it was two weeks after the funeral, and five weeks after he'd started his six-month consulting contract at Converge, a petroleum engineering firm. It was the day his mother had rung when he was in a meeting about the design flaws of a submersive drill, and he'd excused himself in time to pick up in case it was urgent.

She'd said, 'He's here.'

'What do you mean, Mum?' Daniel had replied. 'Dad's . . . Dad died, remember?'

He'd held his breath as he waited for her to realize she'd used the wrong word, said the wrong thing. He held up two fingers to the guys on the other side of the glass partition, signalling two minutes. He just needed two minutes. They were impatient, needing his sign-off before lunch, and suspicious of an outsider coming in this late in the project and pissed off that he'd been pushing for a pivot on the next steps. He didn't care. He wanted to make sure his mum was okay. He wouldn't be able to handle it if she had dementia or memory loss or something. He'd just lost his dad – he couldn't lose her too.

'Daniel,' she'd replied, level-headed. 'I know he's bloody dead. It's his ashes. They've just been dropped off.'

Daniel exhaled loudly in relief. She wasn't crazy. Well. Any crazier.

'But it's a bloody bin bag's worth! He's so bloody heavy I can't shift him anywhere. So he's just here. In the kitchen with me, by the back door. All his ashes in a heavy-duty bag that I don't know what to do with.'

Daniel closed his eyes and pinched the bridge of his nose, stunned. His dad's ashes. Because his dad was dead.

'I'm having a coffee and telling him – your dad – about Janet Peterson's new Vauxhall Mokka – they had it in gold, can you bear it! Gold! And you know, I say new but obviously it's good second-hand. Cars lose money as soon as you drive them off the forecourt – but anyway, it's a bit creepy. Your dad. Can you come by after work and help me?'

Daniel could almost have laughed. In fact, he did laugh, and told his mum he'd be across to Ealing Broadway at about seven, and in the meantime to go hang out in the living room to watch *Loose Women* instead. She'd been so strong since the funeral that it made him feel ashamed to be the "weak" one. He was about to go back into the meeting – literally had his hand on the door knob to push back through – when his throat closed up and his shirt collar felt tight and he had a vague notion that he might be sick, because his body was remembering, all over again, that his dad was gone. His best mate. His loudest champion. Dead from a ruptured brain aneurysm.

They'd been drinking pints in the pub together before Sunday lunch, his dad telling Daniel he could help him with a flat deposit and not to worry about it, it wasn't a loan it was a gift, he wanted to see him sorted and London property prices were so crazy now he'd never be able to do it alone. It was weird for a thirty-year-old to have a flatmate, his dad said – he'd had a kid and a wife by that age. Daniel had said he'd think about it, that he was a bit proud to accept a handout, that it was normal to be thirty and have a flatmate in London, it was an expensive place, he liked the company, and living in Kentish Town, and that afternoon, before he could accept and say, 'Dad, I love you, cheers for looking out for me', over the spicy bazargan at home his sixty-two-year-old dad had keeled over and had never woken up. In a single hour, everything was different and nothing was the same and Daniel had lost the man who'd made him.

Daniel made a break for it, after that phone call, turning on his heel with his head dipped down to cover his face, a face that was ashen and streaked with tears. He took the back stairs, all twenty-three flights of them, down to the ground floor, and pushed out of an emergency exit onto the street. He stood with his back against the wall, panting. He didn't realize he'd started walking until he flopped down on a circular bench in the sun, drenched in sweat, somewhere off the market. He sat, closed his eyes, breathed deeply, let the tears and sweat dry, and thought about his dad, thought about how lonely he was, thought about how badly he'd been sleeping and how the insomnia might be the thing to drive him truly mad.

On the bench he'd had his back to her, at first. He'd been staring at nothing in particular, just sort of letting the sun be on his face and closing his eyes to do a bit of deep breathing, reminding himself that he would be okay. He didn't call it a 'mantra' as such, but when he missed his dad in his bones he'd say in his head, 'Be alive, and remember to live. Be alive, and remember to live. Be alive, and remember to live . . .'

He became vaguely aware of a voice just over his left shoulder getting louder and louder, and he tuned his ear into it like a radio dial finding a signal on a country road, until he could hear a woman's voice clearly saying:

'. . . Because it's going to be built anyway, right? So it needs to be built by people who come from lower-class or lower-income families . . .'

That was what had made Daniel pay particular attention. He was the first in his family to go to university. His family was very modest. His dad had missed only three days of work as a postman in his forty-year tenure, putting Daniel through a degree with hardly any debt. It had been important to him that his child had the opportunities he hadn't. The woman's voice continued: 'The only way artificial intelligence will ever look after poorer people is if people from these underprivileged communities are the ones programming it.'

As an engineer, Daniel had a small amount of knowledge of artificial intelligence, but not much. 'The next industrial revolution,' one of his undergrad professors had declared, but Daniel had preferred the known entities of maths and equations and building things for the now, not the future. Daniel craned over his shoulder a little to see who was talking. There was a guy – suit trousers with no belt, obviously fitted by a tailor to the exact drop of his hip, narrow pinstripe instead of plain black, shoes so shiny you could see your reflection in them – giving the girl a sort of wry look. A smirk.

'I'm not sure about that . . .' the wry-smile guy said.

Daniel didn't like him at all. He looked like he was from the gang at university for whom everything had come easy. The good-looking guys with the athletic frames who didn't play football or rugby but played tennis or lacrosse. They got pretty average grades but were the first ones to get above average jobs, because their families all knew other families who could put in a good word. Daniel had friends at university – good ones, who he still knew now – but they'd all grafted, all been the working-class kids whose accents got mysteriously broader in the company of the posh boys, as if to hold up their class difference as a shield instead of bowing to the pressure to act like they were from somewhere they weren't. A small 'fuck you' to privilege.

Most posh boys were amused by it, and a couple even tried to befriend Daniel, but he always felt like it was a game to them. That them being 'unable to see class' meant they could acquire a friend from a working-class family who spoke with different vowels and it be a testament to their own character. But anyone who comes from very little money knows never to trust a bloke who says money doesn't buy happiness. Money buys food and electricity and pays for a school jumper without holes in it so you don't get picked on, and you can't be happy without that.

The woman talking was smooth. She wasn't losing her temper as she explained her theory to this loaded rich guy, but she was passionate. Cared.

'We need kids from underprivileged communities being recruited directly so that they take this technology in the right direction. Otherwise it's just a bunch of rich people making rich-people decisions that continue to screw over millions of people for not being rich – like literally, the gap between the haves and have-nots will get to the point where there will be a minimum net worth a person has to have to even be alive. It's sickening. Sickening! But we can absolutely do something about it.'

Daniel loved what he was hearing. He loved this woman, with her unbrushed hair and crazy arms and rice burrito and big ideas about social responsibility. He thought, *My dad would like her*. He positioned himself at a bit more of an angle so he could see her.

The rich man held up his hands. 'Okay, okay. Jesus, Nadia, you can have the fund. We'll do something. I hear you.' He shook his head, laughing. 'I'll talk to the board. Give me a month or so.'

Nadia – *so that was her name* – laughed too.

Daniel had stood up at that point, his Apple Watch buzzing on his wrist to remind him that he had a conference call with the Cape Town office in ten minutes. The geologists had analysed the surface structures of the new site and he needed their input to know what to do about the drilling problem. He knew he couldn't miss it if they were to come in under budget – and Daniel's USP was that he always under-promised and over-delivered. That's why he could charge the day rate he did. He felt much better now anyway. Now that he knew this woman existed.

He made eye contact with her before he left. It felt like the bravest thing he'd done in months. She was beautiful and untamed. He stumbled a little, backing away from the pair, unsteady on his feet. She half watched him, looked at him for what could only have been half a second but felt like a full minute to Daniel, and then she turned back to Rich Man. Daniel felt like he'd been slapped by the Love Gods, and it wasn't his dad he thought about as he walked through the doors of his office, but the woman.

'She just had this . . . *spirit*,' he said to Lorenzo, later on. 'And no ring on her finger either. I checked.'

Lorenzo had laughed. 'This is the first time you've seemed even vaguely excited by something since your dad, mate. I'm pleased for you.' And then, in a lower, more serious voice: 'You'll never see her again, though, of course. Don't get too carried away.'

5

Daniel

When Nadia got on Daniel's train before work two days after he'd overheard her speak at the market, first he gave a word of thanks to the universe, or maybe his dad, or whoever was up there doing him this very solid favour, and then sent a swift gloating text to Lorenzo.

Had she been on the Northern line this whole time? (Yes.) Why was he only just noticing her now? (He had been in his own, grief-fuelled world.) He knew he had to do something about it. He hadn't stopped thinking about her, and had even gone back to the same lunch spot the next week to see if she was a regular, which was a bit much but true nonetheless. She hadn't been there, of course. It was a lot to expect she would be.

Seeing her on the train felt like being given a second chance at a first impression. He looked out for her the next day, and the day after that, and the day after that – greedily, he wanted his third chance, and his fourth. The tube trains were huge and there were so many people on the platform and he couldn't be sure, obviously, that she hadn't got on one of the others whizzing through the underground every morning. She could have been on the 7.28, or the 7.32, or the 8 a.m. or 6 a.m. People didn't always stick to the same schedule like he did. Daniel was anally retentive in a lot of ways, and thrived off routine and certainty. But for Nadia to be on the same train as him, even that once? He decided to hold onto that as a sign.

In total he'd seen Nadia (though he actually couldn't decide in his head what to call her. Nadia was her name, after all, but having not been formally introduced it seemed presumptuous, even in his imagination, to refer to her like that. But then, why would he call her 'woman on the train' when he knew her name? It was confusing, and mostly meant he just imagined her face and didn't really call her anything) seven times, always around 7.30, always seeming a little frazzled in a 'Working Woman with A Lot To Do' kind of a way. Three of those times she'd been in his carriage, once he'd seen her on the platform at Angel, and three times he saw her on the escalator at London Bridge. Twice he thought he'd seen her in and around the general Borough Market area, but it hadn't been her, it had only been wishful thinking.

When he did catch her, she always had her phone in her hand, but unlike a lot of other commuters, she didn't wear headphones to listen to music as she travelled. Daniel knew if he spoke to her one day, out of the blue, at least she'd be able to hear him. But then, he didn't want to screw up his one shot at getting to know her. He worried that simply striking up conversation on a crowded tube – a place notorious for how anti-conversation it could be, where even a smile could make you seem demented because it just isn't the done thing – he'd seem slimy and pervy. A woman had every right to get to work without fending off advances from men who thought she was hot. He knew that. He wanted to give her a nod of encouragement so she could let him know if she was interested as well. It was Lorenzo who had joked that *Missed Connections* was the place to do it. Lorenzo was kidding around, but as soon as he'd suggested it, Daniel knew that was how he wanted to get this woman's attention. He'd seen her reading the paper before. It could be just the ticket.

'But why this woman?' asked Lorenzo. 'I don't get it. You don't know her!'

How could Daniel explain to Lorenzo that, above all else, he just had this *feeling*?

6

Nadia

'Am I being crazy?' Nadia asked. 'I feel like I can't put a message in as a response because it might not even be me. Can you imagine? He's expecting bloody Daisy Lowe to respond, and he ends up with bloody ME?'

Emma was pushing a grilled peach around her plate, loading toasted hazelnuts and creamy goat's curd onto her fork. She had summoned Nadia to In Bocca al Lupo because, yes, she had to review it imminently after an RnB star and her Saudi boyfriend were spotted eating at the bar two nights earlier and it had immediately become The Place to Be and her editor wanted it in Saturday's paper, but also because, as she'd said in her text, *In Bocca al Lupo means good luck! In Italian! And your grandmother was Italian and you need some good luck! It will be a good luck meal for love!* It was a bizarre logic that suited only Emma's mental gymnastics, especially because the restaurant itself wasn't actually Italian, but Nadia couldn't be bothered to go home and cook and, truly, if a singer with

43

twelve Grammys and a sold-out arena tour was going to chow down on the wood-fired Torbay sole on a Friday evening, Nadia could sure as hell do the same thing the following Monday. Plus, Emma would be expensing it. It was something of a personal rule of Nadia's to never turn down a free meal. In The New Routine to Change My Life she should, technically, have been at home with a face mask on, eating a salad and meditating, but that didn't matter. She could do that tomorrow, and Monday had already been mostly a success.

'Listen,' Emma said, using her fork to gesticulate. 'Awful Ben. What a bastard, yes?'

Nadia scowled at the mention of his name. 'Yes,' she said, slowly.

'You deserve love, and happiness, and everything your heart desires. Yes?'

'. . . Yes.'

'Right then. You've got to make that happen for yourself. You've got to put yourself in the way of your own fate. You've got to write back – of course the advert was for you!'

They were interrupted by the delivery of a garlic, parsley and bone-marrow flatbread, from a waiter with dancing eyes and plucked eyebrows.

'Compliments of the chef,' he said, and Emma replied, 'Thank you, darling.'

She only ever called service people *darling*, sort of as a way to ingratiate herself into their favour and because in the reviewing industry nobody wanted a reputation as a miserable or rude customer. But also, Nadia thought, you could tell a lot about a person by how they treated service people: waiters and cleaners and doormen. Emma's manners were always impeccable, whatever the motivation, and it made Nadia like her friend even more.

'Uh oh,' Emma said. 'You seem grumpy. Why are you grumpy?' She used her hands to tear up the bread, and licked welts of seasoned oil off her fingers and wrists once she was done.

'I'm not grumpy!' said Nadia, too brightly. Emma raised her eyebrows, knowing the minor changes in her friend's moods better than she knew her own.

'I'm not grumpy! I just . . .' Nadia took a big gulp of white wine. 'Just don't bring up Awful Ben that way, okay? I can. You can't.'

Emma nodded. 'Fair enough.'

'And also, don't talk to Gaby about me. It feels like you're ganging up on me. I'm excited and I'm scared and I need to feel like you're on *my* team, not a team together.'

'Right,' said Emma, wide-eyed. 'I hear you. Though, let the record show we are all on a team together. Team Nadia.'

Nadia suddenly felt guilty that she'd said anything. That hadn't been the right moment to bring up Emma and Gaby talking about her. The two women finished the flatbread and emptied their glasses in silence. Hats off to Emma, she knew when to shut up and let Nadia have a bit of a wobble. And, at some point – not now, but at some point – Nadia would probably have to mention to one of them that sometimes how close Gaby and Emma had become bothered her.

It had been cool that the first time Emma came to after-work drinks she'd taken to Gaby so well. Emma was typically the jealous one, wanting Nadia all to herself. A typical only child, unpractised at sharing. But it was like the phrase 'house on fire' had been designed especially for Gaby and Emma. Nadia had sat there more or less mute as the two swapped outrageous dating stories and entered into a flirting competition with the wait staff. They'd never graduated to hanging out without her, but every time Nadia invited one out, the first question would always be if the other one was coming. Nadia knew it was childish to feel envious over how they'd clicked, but . . . well. She was envious at how they'd clicked. She'd been trying to see them separately just lately. Not that she'd made that clear out loud or anything. She didn't want to seem immature.

Nadia let her temper calm down so that by the time their starter plates had been cleared and Emma said, 'I still think you should put an advert up in response,' Nadia was able to relax into herself and smile. She knew her friend only wanted what was best for her.

'No!' Nadia said, laughing. 'Oh god! I just don't think I can!'

Emma was impatient. 'How are we going to find him then?'

'I don't know! Maybe I don't even want to find him!'

'Well, that's bollocks,' said Emma. 'You're a shit liar and I can tell that's a lie.' She poured them both more wine. 'I can tell you're gagging for it to be you. Look at you! Texting all *maybe it is me!* all day and then being moody tonight. You're afraid to be excited. I see you.'

'Oh shut up,' Nadia said light-heartedly.

'You're going to have to be on the lookout. Like, on that 7.30 train every morning, the end near the escalators. That's where you should start. Stake the joint out a bit. If it *is* for you, surely there will be a guy hopefully looking at you, all "Notice me! Notice me!"'

Nadia giggled. 'Well, yes. That I can do.'

She twisted at the napkin in her lap.

'And – I'm sorry for snapping about Ben. He really was just . . . awful. He used such horrible mind games to make me doubt myself, and make myself smaller. I lost myself to him. I'm glad that relationship happened because fucking hell I learnt so much, but . . .' She absentmindedly fiddled with the cloth. 'He ruined me. My head knows love is real and not all men are so horrible, blah blah blah. But my body. It's like muscle memory or something. I get tense just hearing his name.'

Emma nodded, understandingly. 'That's a thing, you know.'

'Getting tense at somebody's name?'

'Yeah. Muscle memory is a thing. We store trauma in our muscles and that's why we get pain in our bodies sometimes: it's old wounds in the fibres of our being.'

Nadia didn't really understand. Trauma in the fibres of her being? It wasn't like Awful Ben had hit her or anything; although, one night, in a rage, he had hit himself, and the sound of it – *thwack* – had scared Nadia into knowing that if she didn't leave she could be next. It started out as words, accusations and little niggles, but within a few weeks Nadia found she couldn't breathe properly around him, and yet still felt like she couldn't end it, that she was somehow bound to him. She was terrified to stay, but even more terrified to leave. She never thought she would be one of 'those' women, but it turned out there are no 'those' women – only 'those' men.

'Yeah, I know it sounds crazy, but there's stuff you can do to let your body release like, bad memories. Really, really!'

Emma was exposed to all kinds of stuff through the paper she worked for. She'd once been silent speed dating where she had to do a slow dance to classical music, with a stranger, the only points of their body touching being one finger and with eye contact unbroken. She said it was the most erotic three minutes of her life. Or, another time, she'd ended up at a New Year's Eve party with an ex-footballer who now sold bagels on the TV, and he offered her a threesome with his fiancée. Emma had said yes.

'Emma, if this involves a woman fingering me in front of an audience I will actually kill you.' That was another thing Emma had done – a Yoni love class that meant everyone had their vulva massaged by a teacher wearing a beaded kaftan and latex gloves. It was supposed to cleanse their energy and encourage deeper orgasms. Emma had orgasmed in front of an audience of six other women who'd paid £350 for the half-day workshop and who then afterwards took it in turns to hug her in congratulations.

'Oh god,' said Emma, 'I'd never do that again. I think it was her herbal steam that gave me that recurring thrush, you know. No. This is just lolling about on mats in our Lululemon, but it works! Denise at work did it and said she cried in class and then got on with her life. That she really felt her energy shift. In fact – let me text her for the name.'

Nadia had never known anybody as interested in the ridiculous and the sublime as much as Emma. That was probably why they got on – Emma encouraged Nadia to experiment more, to be a little braver, and Nadia made Emma a little more thoughtful. She smiled at her friend as she texted, and looked out across the restaurant. It was almost full, and she lingered her gaze on a table of City boys across the room. *It could be any one of them*, she thought, surprising herself in her hopefulness. *Literally, if it is for me, the guy who wrote it could be in this very room.*

'That guy could literally be anywhere, couldn't he?' she said, as much to herself as to Emma.

'I'm telling you,' Emma said, setting her phone back down on the table, screen-side down. 'Write him back! You've got nothing to lose.'

Nadia hesitated. She didn't. There was nothing to lose. Because if she wrote back and it actually wasn't meant for her, the only person who would know was him. And they were strangers. Nadia could even laugh it off and say she thought she was writing to somebody else too. And if the guy turned out to be an axe-wielding serial killer who lived with his mother and had voted LEAVE, Nadia could simply deny she was the author of any return note. She could blame Emma. Feign total ignorance.

Emma bent down to her bag. 'Hold on,' she said, rustling through her stuff. 'I've got an idea.'

She resurfaced with a notebook and two pens, victorious. Nadia watched her open it on a fresh page, and write in loopy cursive: 'TRAIN GUY ADVERT'.

'You're really going to make me do this, aren't you?'

'Yup,' said Emma, pen poised above the page. A waiter came and topped up their glasses. 'We'll have another bottle, please,' Emma said to him. 'I think my friend is going to need it.' Nadia smiled at him weakly.

'So. I'm thinking you should be direct about this,' Emma said. 'His advert contained a compliment, but wasn't too sickly, and that was cute, right? That hit the right note?'

'*If* it was for me,' Nadia said.

'*If* it was for you, his tone was just right, right?'

'Well, we're here still talking about it and thinking of writing back to him, so . . . yes. The boy did good.'

'The *man* did good.'

'Man, yes,' said Nadia, not realizing how good it felt to make the distinction between man and boy. She was twenty-nine. She *should* be dating men. 'And listen, I don't want to sound too desperate or anything, though, you know? That's important.'

'Well, you're not desperate, is the thing.' Emma seemed to have a flash of inspiration, and she held up a finger as if to say, *hold on!* 'What about . . .' Emma started to scribble something down, smiling to herself. The waiter delivered a new bottle and asked if they wanted fresh glasses. Nadia said no, eager to get rid of him, in the nicest possible way, so she could see what Emma was writing. Emma passed the paper over to Nadia, who silently read:

Hey sexy papa, your advert hit my heart so hard it hurt, and I can't wait for you to hurt me a little more. I'll bring the whips and chains, and you bring your dazzling charm. Friday night work? Love, the devastatingly cute blonde on the 7.30.

'Close,' said Nadia, laughing. 'Definitely a great start.' She took the pen and paper off her friend and turned to look out through the window for inspiration. She watched a couple a few years older than her, maybe in their mid-thirties, making out against a lamppost like teenagers. Summer did that to people. Made them act like they did the first summer they realized they fancied someone and that swapping spit could be a fun pastime. Summer released inhibitions.

'Hello? Earth to Nadia?' Nadia's gaze refocused on Emma. 'You're supposed to be writing, remember?'

'Yes. Sorry. I was watching those two people make out. They seem to like each other.'

Emma peered over her shoulder and said, 'Jesus. I want what they're having.'

'Hey,' Nadia said. 'Are you seeing anyone? What happened with that Tinder guy? I feel out of the loop. I haven't had an update in ages.'

'Dead in the water,' Emma said. 'Why do all men want a mother and a therapist and a best friend and a cheerleader, all wrapped up in the body of a Kooples model, and at best what they bring to the table is, like, they've never killed anyone and maybe they know how to make chicken in mushroom sauce?'

50

'Should I put that in my ad?'

'Your guy seems romantic! Or at least minimally above average. He's the one in fifty who are worth the effort, because *he* is making the effort. I think that's the ratio. For every fifty men, one is worth the hassle.'

'Okay, okay, I'm writing something back. What about:

I'm shy, and I'm often late, but I make great coffee and I think it's me you wrote to, to call cute? I can't figure out who you are on my train, but come talk to me! I won't bite. At least not at first.'

Emma laughed. 'That's . . . kinda fun!' she said.

'I am not actually serious.'

'You could be though! Or, what about:

Wine me, dine me, sixty-nine-me, train man: just let me know who you are by saying hello, first? Love, the devastatingly cute blonde with the amazing hair (you forgot to say about my amazing hair in your advert, but that's okay. Just remember it next time.)'

'You make me sound self-obsessed! OMG!'

Emma shrugged. 'I mean, you are, a bit. At least with your hair.'

'This hair costs me two hundred and ten pounds every twelve weeks. I think it would be a crime against hair if I wasn't proud of it, don't you?'

'Very true.'

'This is hard,' complained Nadia. 'What if I reply, and it's shit, and he loses interest?'

'Woah, woah, woah, friend – stop that before it starts! It

51

is NOT your job to seduce him. It is *his* job to impress *you*. Whoever the next guy is, he has to break the cycle, okay? No more simpering, pliable Nadia. Date like the Nadia we know! And love! Literally your state of mind cannot be to impress him. He'd be lucky to have you. Okay?'

'Okay.'

'And if he is the one in fifty who is worth being bothered about, you'll be lucky to have him too. And together, it will be lovely.'

'Okay.'

'Literally, one in fifty, okay? He has to prove he is one in fifty.'

'It's hilarious to think he's probably looking for his one in million.'

'It is. Nobody will ever win those odds. We're all only human, after all.'

Within the hour, a third bottle of wine had been ordered.

'Wassabout being flirt-y. FLIRT-Y,' slurred Emma, just enough to let Nadia know that she was as pissed as she was. 'I'm-the-best-flirt-y. I really am.'

Nadia nodded, sagely. 'You are. You really, really, really are.' She sank back in her chair, and smiled at her friend without showing her teeth – the smile of the drunk.

'I gotta go home,' she said. Picking up her phone from the table and hitting a button to make the time glow, she said, 'It's almost midnight! I-gotta-be-up in like . . .' She went quiet and used her fingers to help count from midnight to 6 a.m. 'Six hours!'

'I like your new routine thing,' said Emma. 'I couldn't do it, but I like you for doing it. Is proactive.'

Nadia nodded, her eyelids drooping. 'Me too,' she said. 'I'm-no-very good every day but I try,' she said.

Emma paid, getting a receipt so she could expense it, and they feigned a more sober demeanour as they walked the flight of stairs to the reception area, not speaking except to say a strident 'Goodnight!' to the two stern-faced women in short black dresses and sleek ponytails on the desk.

'Uber,' said Nadia outside. 'I need an Uber.' She figured she could justify the expense of it since she'd not spent anything all night, even though The New Routine to Change My Life limited silly mid-week expenses like taxis. She paid her mum a good chunk of money every month, almost like rent, so that eventually the flat would be in her name. But the chunks of money needed to be bigger if she was going to own the deeds before she was 75. She poked around on her phone and ordered a cab.

'Three minutes, it says.' She glanced up in time to see Emma looking further down the street at something, and instinctively followed her best friend's gaze to see Gaby – work BFF Gaby – waving. Nadia looked back over from her to Emma, who looked slightly panicked, and then shouted, 'Gaby! Is that you?'

Gaby walked towards them, looking fabulous in what Nadia knew, even with her wine goggles on, was a date outfit. Hadn't she said she wasn't dating?

'Hey, guys!' she said, brightly. 'What are you two doing here?'

'We just sent an advert to the paper . . . for Train Guy,' said Emma, smiling brightly.

Nadia corrected her, 'Well. Didn't send it. *Wrote* it.'

Emma shifted her eyes from side to side, mischievously. 'Yeah. What she said.'

Nadia suddenly felt nauseous, as well as a lot more sober. 'Emma!' she said, as if addressing a naughty puppy who had peed on the carpet.

'No,' said Emma, giving nothing away. 'I mean yes. No. Maybe!'

A white Prius pulled up alongside the three women.

'Nadia?' said a guy through the driver's window, and Nadia looked down at him, waiting for him to say something else before realizing he was telling her that he was her ride.

'Oh, I – this is me,' she said, offering her cheek to Gaby to kiss it, and then to Emma. 'Tell me everything tomorrow?' she said to Gaby, alluding to her date dress. 'I knew you were seeing somebody!'

And then to Emma she said, 'You had better be joking about that advert! I swear to god, Emma.'

Emma smiled as if butter wouldn't melt, helping her into the car and closing the door behind her. 'Of course I am,' she said, as Nadia wound down her window to hear her. 'I wouldn't send it without permission.'

'We love you!' Gaby shouted through the open window, holding onto Emma's waist as the pair waved her off.

'I love you both too,' Nadia slurred, before telling the driver, 'Hey – can you put something nice on? Some music? Something romantic. Something about love.'

The cab driver switched on to a station that seemed to play love songs on repeat, and Nadia left Emma and Gaby in the middle of Soho, her head filled with thoughts of the man on the train lusting after her, arriving home just as the last chorus of 'Endless Love' finished. She went to bed without taking her make-up off, dreaming of trains and duets and newspapers. And, of course, totally forgot to set an alarm.

7

Daniel

Daniel had had Percy block out the last hour of his Tuesday as a meeting in the diary, and slinked off from work early. He was headed to his mother's for tea, and was in the perfect state of mind to get fussed over. He'd never be too old for his mum. He'd not told her about the advert – the only person who knew was Lorenzo, what with it being his idea. It was literally yesterday's news, anyway. He wanted to forget about it. What a stupid, dumb, pointless thing to have pinned his hopes on. He felt like a right twat.

Daniel passed by security on the way out, and a man with a walkie-talkie called, romantically, Romeo, held up his palm for Daniel to high five.

'My brother, my man,' Romeo said, turning the high five into a sort of fist grab, pulling Daniel's right shoulder into his right shoulder so that they bumped in a way Daniel had seen American sports players and some rappers do. Romeo wasn't American. Romeo had been born in Westgate-on-Sea.

'How's it going today? You're looking shaaaarp.' Romeo spoke as if he was the comic relief cousin in a Will Smith movie about a comedy bank heist done in the name of love, but was white with blue eyes and blond hair scraped up into a man-bun, and had a degree in Landscape Architecture. ('Turns out I don't like being outdoors much,' he'd explained, with a regretful shrug.)

Daniel tugged on his own collar, jutting it upwards like John Travolta. He'd worn a jacket with his suit trousers today, which wasn't expected in the office and which the weather was about ten degrees too warm for, but he'd wanted to look nice because it lifted his mood. He liked to take care of himself, liked to spend money on clothes. He liked feeling as though he was putting his best foot forward – it bolstered him. And after yesterday, he wanted to feel bolstered.

'I try,' Daniel said, attempting to make Romeo laugh. 'I try.'

The suit was navy, a colour he had always bought his formal wear in, ever since his first suit at twelve, which his mother had insisted be navy: 'Because that's what Lady Di likes Charles in.'

Romeo frowned instead of laughing. 'Okay, cut the bullshit, man. What's up?'

On Daniel's second day back after his dad's funeral, Romeo had found Daniel around the side of the building. He'd been crying, spinning around in small circles, pinching the bridge of his nose, trying to stem the flow of tears so he could get back to his desk without anyone questioning if he was back too soon. Daniel had never been rude to Romeo, but he had never gone out of his way to be friendly to security, either. He'd never ignored anyone on the door, but hadn't extended courtesy beyond a mumbled 'Hello' each morning. After Romeo gave him a hug – two men, hugging, around the side of one of London's most prestigious buildings in the middle of the day – and told him to let it all out, whatever it was – well. Daniel started to stop and chat to his new buddy in the evenings, when he was on shift, asking after his day or dissecting the Arsenal game the night before, and on one more memorable occasion listening to the merits of a dream-interpretation workshop Romeo was undertaking, until now it was one of Daniel's most treasured moments of the day. It felt like normalcy. It felt like he'd found a friend.

Plus, Daniel particularly respected how Romeo hadn't brought the crying up since, and didn't pry as to why he'd been in such a state that day. He just carried on minding the door and greeting everyone who walked by, and that was a classy move, to Daniel. A real classy move.

'You know what . . .?' Daniel started, and he trusted Romeo to tell him the whole sorry thing. That he'd seen this woman and thought it would be cute to do a *Missed Connection*, and that he felt pretty stupid that it hadn't worked. He thought he'd wanted to forget, but he didn't: he wanted to talk about it, to be sad out loud.

'What! Well, that's damned cool of you!' Romeo exclaimed. 'It's here, in this newspaper?' He reached behind the reception desk and rifled through a stack of papers – it looked like a collection of the past week's. He flipped through them, looking for yesterday's. 'Ah – got it!'

'Oh god . . .' said Daniel, but Romeo was already flicking through the pages with lightning speed.

'Well, I'll be damned!' Romeo said. '*To the devastatingly cute—*'

'Don't read it out loud!' Daniel said. 'Jesus!' Daniel held up his palms, in surrender. He knew the thing off by heart:

he'd laboured over it for three days before he finally hit 'send' on the submission email. He didn't need the agony of having Romeo read the whole monologue out to him.

Romeo gave a hoot of laughter and read the rest under his breath, only muttering the odd word.

'Smooth,' he said in conclusion, closing the paper and putting it back where he'd found it. 'Really smooth, bro.'

'Well,' said Daniel. 'Not really, though. She was in my carriage and didn't look up once. She'd not read it. She was texting!'

'Coulda been texting about the ad,' Romeo said.

'No,' Daniel replied. 'I could just tell. She hadn't seen it. She'd have at least looked around the carriage if she had.' It then occurred to him: 'Unless she *did* read it, but didn't realize it was for her. Maybe I wasn't specific enough?' He threw up his hands, exasperated by himself. 'I've been like this all week,' he told Romeo. 'Self-obsessed and neurotic. I hate it.'

Romeo stroked his chin, leaning back against the reception desk.

'You know, I met a woman called Juliet on my first day of training for this job, and thought we were destined to be.' Daniel watched his friend talk. Romeo met a Juliet? He wasn't sure if this was true, or if Romeo was about to hit a punch-line.

'She'd give me the eyes across the table, hot as shit even under that fluoro lighting they have, you know. Every day for a week she'd catch my eye, and on the last day I thought, damn, I gotta make my move.' Romeo was wistful as he spoke, and Daniel understood what he was saying was, as implausible as it sounded, genuine. 'But on the last day, she didn't come. I never saw her again. I think about her, you know? Because I think we could've been something.'

Daniel didn't know what to say. 'I'm . . . sorry?' he settled on, making it a question. A near-miss in love was a special kind of disappointment.

'I just mean,' Romeo said, snapping out of his reverie, 'at least you went for it. You don't have to regret it, you know? Good for you, man. You said something.'

'Yeah,' said Daniel. 'But to reiterate: she didn't see it. Or doesn't care. So.'

Romeo nodded. 'She beautiful? Your woman?'

Daniel smiled. 'Yeah.'

'She kind?'

Daniel nodded. 'I think so.'

'She work around here?'

Daniel narrowed his eyes, wondering if there was some sort of security-person network that meant Romeo could track her down.

'Yeah,' he said. 'No idea where, though. Something to do with artificial intelligence maybe? I heard her talking about it the day I first saw her.'

Romeo offered his hand to Daniel so that they could shake goodbye.

'If she works around here, maybe she'll surprise you yet. Not to sound woo-woo or whatever, but I think it's not enough to love – you've got to have faith.'

'Faith,' Daniel repeated, appreciating that Romeo was taking his plight seriously. 'Okay.'

'I'll keep everything crossed for you, bro. I think you did a cool-ass thing.'

Two mornings later, faith wavering but still intact, Daniel had read almost the whole paper by the time the train whizzed through Angel, and Moorgate, and then Bank. When he got to the *Missed Connections* section, right at the end, he wasn't going to read it, because what would be the point? But two words jumped out at him: *devastatingly cute.* That's what he'd called her – Nadia. He looked up and around the carriage, suddenly sheepish and exposed. His body knew what he was about to read before his mind did. The hairs on his arms prickled in excitement and he felt the back of his neck flush and redden.

It's creepy that you're watching me when you could be saying hello, but maybe you're trying to be romantic. I just want you to know that I won't bite until at least the third date, so don't be shy. If you think I'm devastatingly cute then be brave with it: kind, romantic and bold? That's my love language. From the girl you wrote to with coffee on her dress, on the 7.30 at Angel x

Daniel smiled, and looked up and around the train again. Was she there? Was she watching him, like he had watched her? He couldn't see her from where he always stood, by the doors. He was grinning like an idiot and couldn't stop. He opened the paper again and reread what she had written. He liked that she'd called him out for being a bit creepy, because intellectually he knew it was borderline bizarre that he was being so dramatic, and making a joke out of it felt . . . intimate. Like, that was cool, that she could poke fun at him. You had to be comfortable with yourself to poke fun. And to say the thing about the biting and the third date – that was flirty, and cheeky. She'd complimented him, too, which was kind of key. He'd put himself out there, and she was telling him it was okay. It was good – it was an encouraging and funny and kind response. Just the right level of provocative. If he could see her, he'd march right up to her and tell her: drinks, tonight, 6.30.

But she wasn't around. The train pulled into London Bridge and Daniel stuffed the paper into his bag. He searched the crowds for her face. He kept his eyes and mind alert as he walked through the station, all the way to his own office.

'Daniel! My man! How's it going today, brother?'

Daniel fished the paper out from his bag, and said to Romeo, 'Dude. Check this out! Check it out!' He opened the paper on the *Missed Connections* page and pointed at the response. 'She wrote back, man! Can you believe it?!'

Romeo took the paper from Daniel and read the small section meant for him in silence, his eyes growing bigger and bigger in admiration.

'Well, she's a feisty one. Congratulations!'

Romeo held out a hand for Daniel to shake, and Daniel beamed at both the advert and his mate in front of him who knew this was a massive thing for him. He felt a funny sense of accomplishment. Accomplishment, and also slight dread because: what now?

'You gotta figure out a way to get this newspaper connection off the page and into real life,' Romeo said. 'She's asking you to!'

'Yes, I do,' said Daniel, nodding. 'I mean. Surely I wait for her to be on the train and then just . . . go up to her and say hello, right?'

'Sure,' said Romeo. 'Sure.'

'Sure?'

'Well. Or, you could amp it up a little, you know. Sounds like she's a gutsy one. Maybe you could build the tension a little bit.'

'Uh huh. Yeah. Totally.' Daniel nodded. And then he shook

his head because he actually didn't know what Romeo meant. 'I mean – like how?'

Romeo folded the paper and handed it back to him. 'Write her back, man. Make this a thing. If you build up the anticipation, the climax will feel all the better – for both of you. Girls love that shit!'

Daniel nodded. 'I'm not a girl, and I love that shit too! Romance is nice, right? The thrill of the chase and all that?'

'You got this, man,' said Romeo.

Daniel nodded, understanding. 'So if I write back, it needs to be flirty, like she has been, but also – well, you know on the dating apps when people say "I don't want a pen pal"? I don't want it to seem like I'm playing a game where it's more about the letters than actually getting to meet.'

'That's smart thinking, man,' Romeo said. 'You're absolutely right. So maybe what you want is some kind of like, riddle, yeah? A clue that she has to solve. You said she's clever, so I bet she'll love that.'

'A clue she has to solve, but nothing that makes her think she has to impress me.' Daniel's face darkened with a memory. 'My mate Joel always did this thing at uni that he'd read about – do they call it negging? Where you like, make a woman want to impress you by making out that she hasn't already?'

'Negging, yeah,' said Romeo, disapprovingly.

'That's some weird psychological crap,' Daniel said. 'I like her, and now I know she likes me . . .' Then it occurred to him. 'Oh. Well. Actually that's not quite true. She likes the idea of me – we don't know that she's identified who I am. She hasn't even been on the train since Monday, so . . .'

Romeo held up his hands. 'Do NOT tell me that you're doubting if she'll fancy you,' he said. 'She will, man. I like girls and all, but I'm confident enough in my sexuality to tell you that you're a handsome bastard.'

Daniel smiled, chuffed, already standing taller for Romeo's compassionate words. 'Cheers.' His dad's face flashed into his mind. His dad had always made him stand taller, always believed in him before he believed in himself.

Romeo held out a hand, and as Daniel met it he pulled him in for one of his half-hugs, half-shoulder-bump things.

'You're inspiring me to get a bit romantic myself, truth be told,' he said. 'I've had two dates with a woman I like, you know? Maybe I'll text her and wish her a good morning, just because she's on my mind. Nothing wrong with that, is there? If you feel it, say it, and all that.'

Daniel nodded. 'That's a nice thing to do for people we like,' he agreed.

Romeo held out his fist so that Daniel could knock against it with his own, as a goodbye gesture.

'We're a right sort, aren't we?' Romeo said, and Daniel couldn't help but agree. Love was in the air, and he was thrilled about it.

8

Nadia

'I am going to fucking kill you,' Nadia said in a voice note to her best friend. 'I can't believe you sent that! You total . . .' Words failed her. She could not *believe* that Emma had sent in an email to *Missed Connections* on her behalf. 'This hangover cannot process this. You've made me sound . . . cheap! And like I'm some sort of sexy temptress! What the fuck is the thing about the biting? Nobody has made that joke since the nineties, and even then it was always someone's pervy uncle. I said it ironically, but you've not bloody used it ironically. Oh god. If I get approached by some weirdo seventy-year-old who looks like Piers Morgan and has his hands down his pants, I will actually kill you. I just threatened to kill you, but I need you to know I will actually slaughter you.'

Nadia was an hour late for work, and in a foul mood. She'd been on time for work once this week, on Monday, but had forgotten to set her alarm twice after that. Last night she'd had a cocktail after work with her team, and then met her old colleague Naomi for dinner and they had talked so late that she was basically asleep by the time she fell into bed at midnight – again forgetting to set an alarm. That meant she'd woken up this Thursday morning with a start, had to rush to shower, and hadn't had time to fully assess if her outfit actually looked like an outfit or was mismatched in a way she couldn't pass off as cool. She'd have to start The New Routine to Change My Life again tomorrow. Or maybe on Monday.

'Don't act like you're mad!' said Emma, when she eventually called back in response to the scathing voice note. 'It's a cute advert. I did you a favour! And I promise I didn't do it when we were drunk. I saved it in drafts and only sent it yesterday, when I was sure it was a good one.'

'It's not a good one! It's awful!' said Nadia, determined to give her a hard time for doing it without her permission. *I don't bite*?! What was Emma thinking?

'No! It *is* a good one! I 200 per cent know in my bones he will approach you. You'd be talking to him right now if you'd been on time for work! That's how good it is!'

Nadia had a weird twinge in her tummy at the thought of it – that if she had gone into the office on time, on her regular train, she could be talking to her future right now. But her future could wait twenty-four hours. Couldn't it? She could use today to build her courage. Suddenly she was less angry and more excited.

After talking to Emma, Nadia picked up the paper again, open on the page with *Missed Connections* on. She took a breath and reread it, carefully unpicking it sentence by sentence.

It's creepy that you're watching me when you could be saying hello, but maybe you're trying to be romantic.

Okay, well. That bit was actually okay, if she was totally honest. It was a sort of warning that he had better not be an actual creep, stalking her or something. She could deal with that. The line between big romantic gesture from a stranger and weird stalking was, actually, pretty fine, and probably rested on how handsome and well-adjusted the author of the letters was. Nadia had once read a Twitter thread about a girl whose date had known to come to the back door of her house, not the front, and brought a bouquet of lilies for her, because he knew she liked lilies. The woman said she'd never told him to use the back door, and that her favourite flowers had never come up in conversation; and to some it might have seemed like she was overreacting, but this woman said she knew in her stomach something wasn't right. Two weeks later, the guy was arrested for masturbating onto her car bonnet at three o'clock in the morning.

I just want you to know that I won't bite until at least the third date, so don't be shy. Bloody hell. That bit really was awful. Horrid, horrid, horrid. *I won't bite until at least the third date?* Emma was insane for including that. It was provocative in all the wrong ways. If Nadia had written it, she would have said something like . . . well. She wasn't actually sure, off the top of her head. That's why she'd delayed writing her own response – it was tough to get the tone right! But just because she hadn't got around to it herself didn't mean she wouldn't have done it in the end. Probably. Maybe.

Hmmm. Nadia started to acknowledge the edges of a feeling that maybe Emma had done her a favour. Would she have ever decided on the 'perfect' response? Maybe it was like Pilates: you could put off doing it, or you could just go and get it over with and admit the flood of endorphins felt incredible after.

If you think I'm devastatingly cute then be brave with it: kind, romantic and *bold? That's my love language.*

Hmmm. That bit was nice. Nadia could deal with that. It sort of stated her values and she liked declaring out loud that kindness was key. Kindness without being wet. Kindness that meant he knew to let other people off the tube before he got on, and that if he came to the pub and Emma was there he'd let her rant on a bit and then tell her she was absolutely right, no matter what she was ranting about. That was something else her old boss Katherine had told her: that when her husband was still just her boyfriend, he'd been out with her friends and listened sympathetically to a break-up story that went on and on. Katherine had thanked him afterwards for listening, for being as good a friend to her BFF as Katherine tried to be.

'If she's important to you, then I want her to be important to me,' he'd explained to her.

Katherine said that was when she knew she wanted to marry him. Nadia had loved hearing that story. She loved knowing when men had been good and caring. She carried around a mental storybook of all the tales the women in her life had told her, that she opened in her mind when she felt herself begin to go down the all-men-are-the-same path. They weren't. The good ones existed. Maybe not all of them were good, but perhaps Emma had been right when she said one in fifty was good. Katherine and Naomi had both won in those odds. Nadia forced herself to believe that she could too.

If she had to score the ad out of ten she'd begrudgingly give it an eight and a half. Emma lost a point for the biting thing – Nadia wouldn't ever forgive that. But. Maybe, possibly, *potentially* it could have taken Nadia weeks to do it herself, and so at least something was out there.

She allowed herself a little smile.

He could be reading it right now, she thought to herself. *He could be thinking of me as I am thinking of him.*

The idea of it wasn't unpleasant. In fact, it felt oddly comforting.

What would he say in return?

9

Daniel

'I really am going to have to ask you to piss off,' Daniel said to Lorenzo as he poured boiling water into his favourite Arsenal mug. 'I am *not* reading a *dating guide*. Absolutely not.'

He manoeuvred around his flatmate to the fridge, pulling out the plastic carton of milk and doing a double take as he realized that it was weirdly light. He looked at it, pointedly, sighing dramatically.

'Lorenzo, did you put an empty milk carton back into the fridge?'

Lorenzo looked from the carton to Daniel's raised eyebrows.

'It's an emergency stash day,' Lorenzo said with a shrug, opening the drawer where they kept the single-portion pots of UHT milk that they made a game of stealing from hotels and buffet breakfasts. Daniel wasn't sure how it had begun, but there was now a specific drawer for them, for these long-life UHT milks, which had more recently come to involve UHT milk sachets too.

'There's a trend for them,' Lorenzo had acknowledged knowingly once, as he returned from a weekend wedding in Edinburgh with ten sachets. 'The sachets are much easier to open. More environmentally friendly too.'

Some weeks they didn't buy proper milk at all, living off the UHT drawer. What was weirder was that Daniel and Lorenzo didn't even really talk about it. It was just a thing that they did. No milk in the fridge? Time for the milk drawer, then. It normally happened at the end of the week, on a Friday, so at least today they were consistent with their milk-buying inconsistencies.

By way of a mild apology it was an easy-open sachet that Lorenzo handed over now. Daniel took it, shaking his head. It felt like there was a 'Joey and Chandler' dynamic between them sometimes – and that probably wasn't a good thing.

'I'm just saying, have a glance at it,' Lorenzo said, taking a milk sachet for himself and ripping it open with his teeth. He drank it down, on its own, in one gulp.

'It's for girls!' Daniel said. 'Presumably girls who want to pick up boys! I don't want to pick up boys!' He held his tea by the rim of the mug, deciding it was too hot and switching it to the other hand to hold by the handle. 'If I was a girl picking up boys it looks like a mighty fine book, but as I am not, I shall proceed on my own, book-free,' he said, adding defensively, 'I don't need a book to tell me how to chat a woman up.'

Lorenzo picked up the copy of *Get Your Guys!* from the table where he'd left it out for Daniel the night before.

'All I'm saying,' Lorenzo intoned, 'is that everyone at work was equally as sceptical as you, except the woman who commissioned it. And one by one, she passed it out to the 5 girls on the staff and, one by one, they all had stories about trying what –' he glanced down at the front cover to remind himself of the author's name '– Grant Garby says, and now most of them are engaged.'

'But,' Daniel said, closing his eyes as if very, very tired. 'They are women. Hitting on men.'

Lorenzo shook his head. 'Well, you see, I thought I should take a look at it, you know, as research, and it *is* my job to PR books, even if I wasn't PR-ing this one. Know the market and all that. And he's fucking genius. Grant Garby. He has this whole YouTube series and everything. It's been a slow grower, but since it came out and word has spread, he's sold like, one hundred thousand copies. Chicks swear by him, but he reckons blokes should be reading his stuff too.'

Daniel finished his tea and put the empty mug in the sink, where it would live for two days until he'd finally cave in over his dishwasher stand-off with Lorenzo and empty it himself, thus making room for a kitchen full of dirty crockery and the whole cycle could start over again.

'Why do you need help hitting on women? It's literally the only thing you're good at.'

'Rude,' said Lorenzo, only half insulted. 'And, my friend, this is what makes me so clever: continual practice.'

'Continual practice.'

'Continual practice. Christians don't go to church once, and then say they're Christian forever. They go to church every Sunday, to keep practising their religion. I'm no Casanova because I got lucky with girls a few times – I'm called The Closer because I practise the skills needed to be The Closer.'

'That's disgusting,' said Daniel, looking at his watch. 'Nobody calls you The Closer.'

'I call myself The Closer.'

'I repeat: that's disgusting.'

Lorenzo moved to block Daniel's exit from their shared kitchen. 'Listen to me. I fucking care about you, man. I care that this works out for you. Okay? And I'm telling you – read the book.'

Daniel made eye contact with his friend, who instantly, in a fit of embarrassment at being so candid, looked away and moved aside. Theirs wasn't an easy relationship, but Lorenzo had definitely stepped up after Daniel's dad had died, and he figured that's what he was getting at: that Lorenzo wanted Daniel to have something work out in his favour. Lorenzo was caring in the only way Lorenzo knew how.

Daniel took the book.

'Fine,' he said. 'I'll look at it.'

Lorenzo clapped his hands, thrilled to have charmed yet another person into bending to his will. Daniel wondered if that's where he'd learned to do it – from the book.

'Chapter six, buddy – that's the one. I double dare you to try it.'

'Chapter six,' Daniel said. 'Fine.'

As he travelled to work, Daniel felt like there was a huge spotlight on his backpack illuminating the fact he had a dating guide in his possession. He'd be mortified to be caught with it, and worried one wrong move could see his bag slip from his shoulder and its contents splay out for the judgement of everyone else on the underground. What if she saw it? Nadia? His paranoia was so great that he'd almost managed to convince himself that The Dating Guide police were going to search every carriage, demanding anyone with a dating guide on them step forward. He had visions of having to declare to everyone, including Nadia, that he had a hardback copy of *Get Your Guys!* and he'd never be able to get on the tube again. He'd got the guide to help with Nadia, but if she saw he had it he would lose her before it had even begun, he was certain.

He was relieved that she wasn't actually on the train today.

'My man, how's it going today?' Romeo asked him, as he slipped through the glass doors of his office tower.

'I HAVE A DATING GUIDE!' Daniel declared, desperate for somebody – anybody – to know. He couldn't carry the guilt. He needed to be absolved.

'Good for you!' said Romeo, totally unfazed by Daniel's non sequitur. That was the thing about Romeo: he was just happy to be alive, and happy that everyone else was alive too.

Daniel fumbled around in his bag, pulling it out for Romeo to see. 'It's called *Get Your Guys!*' he said, panicked. 'Lorenzo forced me to take it.'

'Oh,' said Romeo, taking it. 'Have you got to chapter six? My sister read this and said chapter six changed her life.'

'Chapter six? No, no, I haven't read chapter six. I haven't read any of it!' Daniel shook his head. 'I don't need to read a dating guide!'

Romeo shrugged, thumbing through it. 'Well then, what harm can it do?' he said, not unreasonably. 'If you don't need it, why are you freaking out about having it?'

Daniel scowled. 'I have to go,' he said, taking the guide and slipping it into his bag again. He leaned into Romeo and lowered his voice.

'Tell nobody,' he said, walking off.

Waiting to find somebody you like to flirt with is like waiting to go on stage to learn your lines, chapter six told him. Daniel had sat at his desk for ten minutes before asking Percy to book him a meeting room – the most private meeting room, in the corner, where nobody would walk by its glass front on the way to somewhere else. That's where he sat now, nursing the guide. The introduction had explained that it was a book meant for heterosexual women, but that in actual fact Grant Garby worked with men as well, because at the root of all connection is humanness, and we are all human.

Except for Lorenzo, Daniel thought darkly, which in turn made him feel guilty.

Chapter six was basically a long list of tips on how to flirt, and what's more, how to flirt with strangers. Daniel was engrossed, in spite of himself.

When you haven't dated in a while, it can become easy to think that there is a dearth of men out there to date, the book said. *But opportunity to make friends out of strangers is everywhere – you just have to have the nerve to talk to them.*

The first tip was simple: make eye contact. Daniel weighed this up. Catching the eye of people was actually quite a bold thing to do: typically, Daniel would keep his head down and get to where he was going, barely conscious of who might be around him on the way. Wasn't that . . . normal?

Okay. I can do that, Daniel thought to himself. *Eye contact. Easy.*

He slipped the book onto the chair beside him, piling some papers he'd brought with him on top of it, and flipped the sign on the meeting door to 'occupied'.

He headed for the staff kitchen at the far end of his floor. The book was right – his instinct was to keep his eyes fixed on his shoes as he walked, or maybe firmly ahead, on his destination. The book had asked how friendly this must make him seem, or how approachable. *Valid point*, Daniel reflected. *Okay.* He got to the kitchen, pretended to look for something for a minute, decided on getting a glass of water, and then turned on his heel, heading back towards the meeting room – but this time at a slower pace. He forced himself to let his eyes roam, which felt vulnerable and exposing. But then his gaze met Meredith's, a perky thirty-something who had a similar role to him, but on a different team.

Gah! thought Daniel, looking away quickly. *Eye contact!*

The book had said to smile, to not be afraid to acknowledge the other person, and maybe say hello. That in itself wasn't a radical idea – essentially Grant Garby was advocating politeness – but it felt exposing. Like holding up a sign that said 'Single and Looking', which was a turn-off, wasn't it? Daniel kept walking. He sneaked a glance over his shoulder, but Meredith had gone. At least she wasn't staring after him, thinking what a freak he was.

Okay, the next person I make eye contact with I will smile at, Daniel coached himself. He looked up to Percy staring at him. Daniel smiled broadly.

'What are you doing?' Percy said.

'I am . . . smiling,' said Daniel.

'Why are you walking up and down the office like you've only just realized you've got legs?'

'No,' said Daniel. 'I'm not, erm . . . I'll . . .'

Percy looked at him, trying to understand what Daniel wasn't saying. Meredith walked past them both then, and coyly said, 'Hey Daniel,' as she went by.

'Hey,' said Daniel, to the back of her head. She turned around and looked at him over her shoulder, and then she was gone.

Percy looked at Daniel and back to Meredith.

'Weird,' he said, under his breath, moving to answer a ringing phone.

Daniel went for his lunchtime walk to the market with the sole purpose of Making Eye Contact. He'd not even done it properly with Meredith – he'd forgotten to smile! – but she'd made a point of seeking him out to say hello later. Daniel understood the idea behind it now – if he could practise being brave around women, when it came to finally talking with Nadia he could be more sure he wouldn't screw it up. Making eye contact and smiling at strangers – and, chapter six said, finding the courage to make chit-chat with strangers too – was all a way of building the Flirting Muscle, so that it was strong for the person who might go on to mean something.

It's like the gym, but for flirting, Grant Garby had written, and Daniel was starting to see why his book had sold so many copies. It wasn't radical. It was a really well-reasoned argument for putting yourself out there in a way that was natural and well-meaning.

Daniel held his chin high, almost demented in his quest for eye contact as he walked to the burrito place. It wasn't until he held the eye of other people that he realized, once again, how often he didn't. And it was incredible, the effect that it had on people. He could see women – and he didn't discriminate between younger or older, conventionally attractive to him or not – respond immediately to him. Nobody shied away or accused him of being a pervert or chased him off, waving their handbag at his head. It felt friendly. He wasn't being sleazy or gross, just friendly. The way these women smiled back at him made Daniel feel like the most popular guy in London. There was a bravery to seeing people, but a bravery to letting himself *be* seen too. Making eye contact was like taking up space in the world, and to take up space he had to believe he was worth the space. He'd never thought of himself as shy, but the eye-contact thing was making him feel confident, and he definitely hadn't felt that way for a while.

Fine. Chapter six. You were right, Daniel texted to Lorenzo.

Yes mate!!!! Lorenzo pinged back. *Have you done the 'asking advice' bit yet? It fucking works every time!*

Then, after a second, Lorenzo also said: *If you need emergency condoms because of this, my side table near my bed is always packed with them. Extra-large tho.*

Daniel knew what Lorenzo was talking about – about the advice, not the condoms. Daniel could source his own condoms, should he need any. Which wasn't the point of today. Today was just about exploring this confident feeling. He liked it. He liked how confidence felt.

The book suggested that the way to move from a smile to talking to a stranger was best practised in a queue at a café. The book said to ask the person behind you a question, like which cupcake flavour to pick, because you couldn't decide – thus opening up the floodgates of possible conversation.

It's an invitation to get talking, the book decreed, *with no obligation to keep going on either part. If you turn to the man behind you and say, 'Would you get the lemon or the chocolate? I can't decide,' he can answer the question and that's it. Or, he can answer the question and you can use it as a way to rank muffin flavours, or the merits of frosting. Initiating conversation doesn't mean you are proposing marriage, it simply means you are a person capable of chit-chat, of connecting. And if it doesn't work, that's not because you aren't worthy: it's because the other person didn't want to chat. That's all. So try again.*

The book also said chit-chat was a great time to introduce some light teasing too. *If he answers blueberry, don't be afraid to tell him, 'Oh, it would never work out between us! Who chooses blueberry when chocolate is on offer?' It plants the seed that there could be an 'us', and challenges him to act, if he is interested. Suddenly he might declare, 'Well hey! Don't write me off that easily!' and then, before you know it, he's asking for your phone number.*

Daniel wasn't sure about the mind games behind that, but he was willing to try, since even simple eye contact had made him feel more prepared for coming face to face with Nadia. He stood in line for his burrito behind two women in suits, presumably from one of the offices near his own. It was about a half square mile of offices, including, somewhere, Nadia's.

Daniel scrutinized the board. A burrito was a burrito, so there weren't many options to have to choose from. He'd have to pick between meat or veggie mince, or perhaps ask for an extra side of sour cream.

The queue pushed forward. There was one bloke in front of the women, and it would quickly be their turn. He had to say something soon, else he'd lose his chance, and then what? He'd rejoin the back of the queue so he could work up his courage with somebody else? No. *That* was weird. The book said this was all supposed to be super natural, super chill. Whatever, man. It's all good.

He ended up leaning towards the women in front of him and saying, 'So what do you think, ladies? Avocado or extra avocado?'

They didn't hear him, and carried on talking. The taller woman said to her shorter companion, 'You see, that's why

80

you have to get them heeled *before* you wear them. It's like high-heel insurance.'

'That's so smart,' the other woman said. 'I shouldn't cut corners.'

Daniel coughed a little, involuntarily.

'What do you think?' he tried again, making his voice a little louder this time. 'Avocado,' he said, even louder, 'or extra avocado?'

One of the women turned around and looked from Daniel to the extra space beside him. It looked like he was talking to himself.

'Oh,' said Daniel realizing. 'No, I . . .'

The woman turned back around. Daniel stared at the back of her head.

'DO YOU THINK I SHOULD GET EXTRA AVOCADO?' he bellowed, at which both women turned around.

The women looked at each other, the penny dropping that he was talking to them.

'Or . . . just a . . . normal amount?' Daniel squeaked, his palms suddenly sweaty and his face colouring purple.

Slowly, her eyes darting confusedly from side to side, the taller woman said, 'Well, do you really like avocado?'

Daniel nodded. 'Yes.'

'Get extra then,' she said, to which Daniel issued a sort of *pffffffft* noise between his lips.

'Extra avocado? Wow. I could never date you, then,' he said, before he even really knew what he was saying.

'Excuse me?' the taller woman said. Daniel's mouth flapped open and closed like in *Finding Nemo*. 'Date me? I'm three feet taller than you and about six times as hot. A date isn't really on the cards, is it?'

Daniel just stood there, wishing desperately that he could

simply turn on his heel and run, forever, until he reached Greenland.

'What an arsehole,' the shorter woman said, shaking her head and steering the elbow of her friend so they both turned back around, before stepping forward to give their order.

Daniel cast his gaze around him, humiliated, figuring out if anyone had witnessed what had happened. He didn't mean to say that – to be unhinged that way. He panicked! It was his first time trying out the advice! It had all nose-dived! A teenager sat by the window eating his food looked away quickly as Daniel turned his head. His shoulders were shaking slightly, like he was laughing at him. Daniel lowered his eyes so that he didn't have to look at the women as they left. The shorter woman barged into his shoulder as they passed. Daniel let her.

'What can I get you?' the man behind the counter said.

'Meat burrito,' Daniel replied, quietly. 'Extra avocado. Thanks.'

'Hey, is this yours?' Percy said, as Daniel walked back through into the office. He was holding up a copy of *Get Your Guys!*

Daniel stuttered slightly. 'Mine? No. No way. Absolutely not.'

Percy looked confused. 'It's just it was in with your things in the meeting room,' he said. 'Meredith found it.'

'Meredith found it,' Daniel repeated.

Percy smirked.

'No idea who it belongs to,' Daniel said, striding past Percy's desk and towards his own. 'None at all.'

'Sure,' Percy said. 'Well, I'll leave it in my out-tray in case you change your mind,' he added.

Daniel scrunched up his face. 'I won't,' he said, accidentally giving the game away. 'It's shit.'

He silently lamented that he hadn't just stuck to what he knew worked: writing notes in the newspaper. He was much slicker in writing than in faux-flirting. He sat down at his desk, pulled up the submission box for *Missed Connections*, and began to type.

10

Nadia

Over the weekend Nadia had checked the *Missed Connections* part of the paper, both days, desperate to see if Train Guy had written back. She was about 75 per cent convinced that what Emma had written was too gauche, too provocative, too . . . much, to warrant a response from him. And yet, still she hoped.

Even though she'd not quite made the 7.30 again on Friday, she'd still held out hope that Train Guy would be in her carriage today. She let herself get really carried away, waiting the whole ride for somebody to make eye contact, to smile, to invite conversation because, yes, he had put the advert in the paper, and yes, it was about her, and why didn't they bunk off work together – here, today, now?

Over the weekend she'd bolstered her confidence and by Sunday night found herself wondering if – one full week on from his first advert – tomorrow she'd meet her man. She hadn't realized how much she'd been looking forward to Monday morning again until it was 9 p.m. on Sunday night without a hint of the Sunday Night Scaries settling in. Whereas normally she'd feel a sinking feeling deepening in her stomach as the evening wore on, this weekend she'd been positively giddy at bedtime looming ever closer, knowing that the closer bedtime was, the closer Monday morning was.

Nadia fantasized that they would get off the train – on the morning they met – head to the river, and walk alongside the water. It was that funny kind of early-morning light in July – the sort that shines a certain way, highlighting problematic female moustaches and chin hairs – so the two of them would probably find a shady spot, where the sun could come from behind Nadia and give her a sort of halo that he'd find seductive and disarming, and would make her look biblical, in a way, and less like a woman transitioning into a werewolf because the moon was full. Nadia knew that one way to get any two women impassionedly bonded was to casually mention a sudden necessity to tweeze a thick, wiry chin hair – where did it suddenly come from? What made it hide in plain sight until one day a foot-long black twig could poke any bystanders in the eye? It was one of the many mysteries of being female.

As they strolled on their imaginary date, Nadia would be tempted to bring up her horrible ex, to plead with Train Guy not to hurt her like he had done, to not make her anything less than herself, but before she could he'd say something funny and she'd laugh, and her laugh would make him laugh more, and she'd forget. Oh, how he'd make her forget.

On this Monday morning, though, the fantasy shifted, because there it was. He had written back:

Coffee Spill Girl: So what, you don't like big romantic gestures? I thought you might appreciate the time it takes

to craft an advert witty enough to get chosen for publica-
tion . . . (although, I see that in writing back you're more
of a romantic than you're letting on ☺) Anyway, I've got
dark hair, my mother thinks I'm 'quite handsome, but
must shave properly', and am always in the last carriage,
because it's the least crowded. I promise to say hi in person
if you do. From Train Guy x

Nadia smiled, instantly looking up to see if anybody was trying to get her attention. It was a *great* note – he was flirting! He wasn't afraid of her! Well, of Emma, anyway. He'd seen the humour in what Emma had sent in and was showing her that he knew how to spar a little too. That was super-hot to Nadia. She loved a little verbal rough-and-tumble.

Her eyes roved around the carriage, waiting for the moment that would change everything. Maybe this really would be the morning they bunked off, that they took that walk.

It seemed more crowded than usual. The reason Nadia had resolved in the first place to get up earlier and get to the station for the 7.30 tube was that it didn't usually get properly busy until after eight. How was she supposed to figure out who the author was when everyone was shoulder-to-shoulder, crammed in like beans in a can?

She scanned the faces she could see.

What would Emma tell me to do? she asked herself. Emma would tell her to swallow her pride and be brave. That's why they were friends, after all – Emma brought out that side of Nadia.

Right, Nadia thought to herself. *Brave.*

Nadia pushed back her shoulders and inhaled and lifted her face so that it faced the carriage, fully. She decided to stand up from where she'd taken the last empty seat, and move towards the doors. The guy said he was normally beside the doors, so that's where she'd go.

Her heart beat so hard in her chest that she thought it might launch out of her body and fall at her feet.

Hmmm, she thought, blood pulsing in her ears. Somebody had already slid in under her – before she'd barely finished standing – to steal her seat. She looked left and right. *But does he mean the far single door at either end, or the big middle doors?* She decided on the big middle doors. Nadia folded the paper as she walked, swaying into people's armpits, but hoping that in keeping it under her arm, the page turned out at the *Missed Connections* page, it might act as a bit of a sign. A good omen.

Two men nearby could fit the description of 'dark hair, handsome if shaved'. Holding onto the poles above her head for balance, Nadia peered through the suspended arms, and as a few people trickled out at Moorgate she found the room to manoeuvre next to one of the men. He was tall, and broad, and actually probably didn't need to shave in order to be handsome. He had the sort of aesthetic that wouldn't go amiss on the BBC at 9 p.m. on a Sunday, the sort of look of a man who knew how to live in the Amazon for three years with only a pocket knife and a piece of string, or who would look good in a bobble hat with snow in his eyelashes, somewhere in the Arctic, saying soothing things about penguins.

Nadia steadied herself. He was *gorgeous*. Like, properly gorgeous. Was this her guy? She took in his pressed shirt and dark suit and shiny shoes. He was super corporate-looking – she wouldn't normally go in for a guy who looked like he had a housekeeper who did his ironing – but that was no reason to totally dismiss someone. She racked her brain for something to say, for a witty and kind opening line – the kind that he'd incorporate into his speech when they married, and everyone would agree, 'Oh! That's so Nadia! Of course he loved her right from the start!'

The man shifted his gaze and looked in her direction, half smiling. Nadia realized she'd been staring. She grinned manically back, and then saw the glint of gold above his head, where he was holding onto the pole. Third finger. Left hand. He was married.

Nadia looked away.

Not him, she thought, pressing down the thought that a) she was disappointed, and that b) his marriage was inconvenient, but not wholly problematic.

Yes, it bloody is, she coached herself, internally. *Stop self-sabotaging. No more married men – not what after happened with John.* She fleetingly let herself feel the heartache of when she'd fallen in love with her boss at twenty-two. Nothing had ever happened, but they worked enough late nights together that it could have done, if they'd been different kinds of people. Last she'd heard, he'd ended up telling his wife that he hadn't been happy for years, and that he'd had affairs with several co-workers – and apparently he now lived in Portsmouth as a part-time single dad who wrote a weekly Modern Masculinity column for the *Guardian* and ran fishing retreats for men looking to get in touch with their emotions. She hoped he was happier now. She really had been fond of him – but then, of course, so had many of the women in her old office.

Nadia started to let her mind drift into a spiral of shame-talk, berating herself for not having standards higher than Is Not Already Married, when she remembered she had spotted two men in the carriage. Two possibilities. So if it wasn't the married man – where was the other?

There.

He'd moved across to a seat the other side of the glass partition, and was reading the paper.

That's him! Nadia thought, staring at the top of his head. *I can feel it, that's him!*

He was younger than the other guy, and his beard wasn't expertly manicured like Married Man, but a bit more scraggly and unkempt. She could see what his mother meant by how a bit of a tidy-up would nudge him a few points higher on the Handsome Scale. He looked a bit student-y still, despite definitely being closer to thirty than twenty-one.

He wore suit trousers with New Balance trainers, and a shirt that was open at the neck, no tie. He didn't look corporate so much as maybe designery, like he was less likely to work at a finance firm and more like he worked in media. Nadia couldn't think which media companies were at London Bridge – weren't most of them in Leicester Square, or Soho? Not that that mattered. She'd find out all that, if she rose to his challenge and said hi in person.

Nadia wove through the bodies in the middle of the carriage and approached where he sat, positioning herself so that she faced the glass partition, and could easily lean across and speak to him without scaring him.

'Your mother is right,' she settled on, bowing down so that her voice landed squarely in his ear, in a way she thought was suitably sexy and provocative. 'You would be handsome after a shave.'

She thought she sounded flirtatious and that it was fun to allude to the self-effacing joke he'd made at his own expense. She imagined he'd look up and he'd concede that his mother was a clever woman, and then Nadia could say something about how attractive it was that he respected his family that way. Or something. She hadn't figured out the details – all of this was new, and a tiny bit scary. She hadn't wanted to overthink it. So that's why she'd just said it. Said the first thing that came to her. *Your mother is right.*

The guy looked up. 'I beg your pardon?' he said, his brow knitted together in confusion.

Ah, shit. She had led with the wrong thing. She tried to back-pedal.

Nadia forced a giggle. 'No, I don't mean that,' she said. 'I meant . . . Your mother is obviously certifiably mad.'

The man's eyebrows shot up now, from above his nose to below his hairline.

'Well, maybe not certifiably mad,' Nadia countered, feeling hot at her neck. 'No, just, you know, she probably means well. Mothers, hey! Ha!'

Oh god, oh god, oh god, she thought to herself. *You are fucking this up, royally!*

'You're very handsome,' she continued. 'Probably even more so with the beard.' Her words tumbled out over each other in a nervous pile-up. 'And very romantic. Well done. You are handsome and romantic. That's . . . the . . . jackpot! Handsome and romantic is the jackpot!'

'Ma'am,' somebody beside her said. 'Are you okay?' The voice turned away from her. 'Is she okay?'

The man was looking up at her, and Nadia had a nauseous feeling in the pit of her stomach that told her something was wrong. Very wrong.

'I'm just nervous, is all,' she said, her voice squeaky now. 'I don't normally . . . you know . . . go up to men on public transport, and—'

The man stood up. The tube was pulling into London Bridge station, her stop.

'Get the fuck away from me,' the guy said, leaving her to stand staring at the space he had vacated, hot with humiliation. She came to just as the doors were beginning to close, realizing she had better get off as well. She hoped it didn't look like she was following him.

An older man with grey hair and white sticky bits of dried spittle at the corners of his mouth, a man who Nadia couldn't be certain had brushed his teeth that morning, or any morning, actually, tapped her on the shoulder as she stood to catch her humiliated breath and, as she turned around, stood there hopefully and said, 'I'll go out with you.'

Nadia's jaw dropped. 'I . . . No, thank you,' she said, scurrying off towards the escalator, wanting nobody in the history of the world to ever talk to her ever again.

'Whore!' the man shouted behind her.

Nadia's phone buzzed as she crossed the road to her office.

Anything? said Emma.

Nadia sent back a sad face emoji. *I just hit on the wrong guy*, she typed. *Well. At least I hope it was the wrong guy. If that was the right guy I definitely blew my chance.*

What happened?????!!!!

Oh god, I can't. I'll tell you later.

There had been a moment when Nadia saw a woman with a blonde bob and a fake Louis Vuitton bag in her carriage, and her imagined narrative was interrupted by the worry that maybe *she* was the devastatingly cute blonde.

No, Nadia thought, *no way. She's got press-on fake nails!*

Nadia hated that – that she'd been reduced to making another woman the competition and thinking bad thoughts about her. Even if the woman was wearing an awful lot of winged eyeliner for that early in the morning. Nadia had so wanted this all to be true – for this to be her romantic moment. She hadn't understood how hungry she was for it until the temptation had been waved in her face, and it had appeared it had made her territorial. She wanted to protect what she thought of as hers.

Gaby was waiting for her in the lobby at work.

'Anything?' she said, handing her a tall black coffee, which was lucky because Nadia had already given up on her KeepCup. It was too much of a faff to make coffee before she'd had coffee, ironically.

'You will not believe the arse I just made of myself,' Nadia cringed. 'I hit on two men, neither of whom were Train Guy.' She took a sip of the coffee Gaby had handed her. 'Thank you for this, by the way.' She took another sip. 'I say neither were him – at least I hope they weren't. I made such a twat of myself that I'm not sure I can ever get on the underground again. I looked like a desperate, man-hungry old bag with no life. It was awful.'

'Oh god,' said Gaby laughing, and then, realizing laughter probably wasn't the best response given how genuinely upset Nadia seemed, said, 'I mean. I am laughing in solidarity with you. Love makes fools of us all!'

'I'm sad about it!' Nadia said, laughing too, now. 'I waited all of last week to see if he would write back, and he finally did, and then I couldn't find him!'

'It was a cute advert – I saw it.'

Nadia looked at Gaby, who shrugged.

'I am a tiny bit invested in this,' Gaby said. 'And I am glad you are too. I wasn't sure which way it was going to go at first.'

Nadia took another gulp of coffee. 'Oh shut up. You know as well as I do that I love love, and would *die* if a man put an ad in the paper for me. I'd decided to hope this was all going to be gloriously romantic and a story I told for years to come until I started to hump the leg of any thirty-year-old with a beard on the commute. It's shameful!'

'Nadia, you are hilarious.'

'I'm pathetic!' Nadia laughed. They got into the lift together and rode up to Gaby's floor.

Gaby checked the time on her phone. 'I've got an 8.30 a.m.,' she said. 'Which is so inconvenient. Meetings should be afternoons only. It fucks my whole morning up when I have to take time out. I hate it!'

'I'm just in the lab all day,' Nadia said. 'Where I belong. I can't degrade myself in front of robot code.'

The lift opened. They both registered him at the same time. A man in a navy suit stood in front of the reception desk, his back to the two women as he leaned forward towards the receptionist, seemingly deep in conversation. Even though she could only see him from behind – or perhaps *because* it was from behind, his bum pert and round in his suit trousers – Nadia lowered her voice and whispered, 'I'd let him fuck *my* morning up.'

Gaby swatted at her arm.

'Nadia!' she giggled. 'I won't be able to concentrate now! I think that's my meeting!'

'I hope it is . . .' Nadia said, as Gaby got out. 'Bloody hell.'

Gaby turned and shot her a dirty look and the doors closed, and Nadia laughed. The laugh forced the man at the reception desk to turn in her direction, his profile becoming prominent over Gaby's shoulder.

Oh! Nadia thought, racking her brain. *I know you!*

The doors closed before Nadia could place him. Up the lift went.

11

Daniel

Daniel waited in the lobby of the twenty-first floor for his 8.30 meeting – a favour to a friend he knew through a 'City Professionals' networking group, designed to get mid- and high-level workers to talk to each other across disciplines, because you never knew when it might come in handy, especially when everyone had shifted into a 'gig' economy or portfolio career these days. When nobody had true job security – nor a desire to stay with one company for too long – it helped to keep everyone connected.

Daniel had been roped in to sitting on the social committee, and had been sent to a fellow member's office to discuss the numbers for the next networking event. It was to be held in the basement of the Marriott off Grosvenor Square, and had somehow ended up costing one hundred and twenty-five quid a ticket. Daniel thought that was outrageous ('Who has a spare hundred quid for NETWORKING!' he'd said to Lorenzo, ranting about it one night. 'Well, to be honest with you mate, if I didn't get off my tits every weekend, I would,' Lorenzo had unhelpfully replied.)

'Daniel?' said the woman walking towards him down the corridor. He shifted his gaze to the left of where he'd been looking, towards the elevator. He thought he'd heard somebody laughing, and it was such a joyous, child-like giggle he felt compelled to see who it belonged to.

The woman calling his name continued: 'I'm Gaby.'

'Gaby,' said Daniel, reaching out a hand in greeting. 'Michael has said such great things about you,' he lied, smiling.

Gaby laughed, and motioned for him to follow her.

'We both know that isn't true,' she said.

Daniel said nothing in response, sensing danger, as he was led into a corner meeting room. The only noise was the shuffle of their feet along the cheap office carpeting, until the maze of glass partitions ended in Gaby's office. It took up a huge corner of the building, with a north-west view that looked out across the River Thames and towards Parliament.

'So, I gather we've got a little problem,' Gaby continued, barely taking a breath between her welcome and getting to the point of the matter. Her bum hadn't reached the seat before she'd launched in. She looked like a newsreader, with the city splayed out behind her that way.

Daniel laughed. 'I don't deal in problems, Gaby, I'm a solutions man.' He smiled widely. 'So I come in peace.'

Gaby visibly softened.

'Right,' she said. 'Sorry. Yes. God, Michael warned me you were charismatic.' She smiled, but barely. It was coy and controlled. Daniel briefly wondered if she was flirting with him.

'I just think,' he said, 'let's move it to The Flying Pig and keep it under twenty-five quid a head, and make the focus the actual networking: not how flashy it is.' He saw a dark cloud pass over Gaby's face. 'With all due respect, of course,' he added. Now he understood why he'd sensed danger before: this was a woman used to telling people what to do – not being told.

'The Flying Pig?'

'Yeah, by the Barbican? Nice and central, still has white tablecloths . . . I used to go to school with the bar manager there. If it's on a Monday, he can do us a deal.'

'A deal,' Gaby repeated, somewhat amused.

Daniel smiled again, sensing she was coming around. 'I'm a man who knows a man,' he said, shrugging. 'And that man can make this actually affordable to those of us saving for a flat deposit.'

Gaby laughed. She said she got his point.

They sat in the meeting room for twenty-five minutes, hammering out the logistics of the event and dividing up the tasks. Gaby was good at delegating, and fired off emails from her phone as they talked, ticking things off her list as quickly as she added them, and together they switched their plan, making it more cost-effective, but keeping the roving magician. Tickets would be thirty-five pounds, with an in-built donation to a charity they would decide on later.

'Well,' Daniel said, looking at his watch. 'We've made fast work of this. It's 9 a.m., so I've got to get across the road to my office, but I'll cc. you in on an email to Gary once I've got the numbers from the caterer, and then leave the rest to you.'

'Great. Thank you,' said Gaby, adding, 'and Michael was right: you put the right perspective on this. I don't know what I was thinking with the ticket price. I suppose I just wanted my first shot on the team to make a mark, is all.'

'No worries,' said Daniel. 'I just, you know, I like a bargain, is all.'

Gaby smiled. 'Sure thing.'

'How do you know Michael, anyway?' Daniel couldn't help but ask her, mostly because the twitch in her eyebrow earlier told him they must have dated. With all *The Lust Villa* he'd been watching he fancied himself as an amateur romance psychologist.

'We're very different people,' said Gaby, not quite answering the question. Daniel didn't say anything. He'd learned, again from *The Lust Villa,* that if you wanted somebody to tell you their secrets the trick was to stay silent so that they'd go on to fill that silence. It worked. Gaby added, 'By which I mean, we're exactly the same. Both pig-headed and stubborn and always right, so, together it was always asking for trouble.' Gaby shrugged. 'We went out for a bit, and then we stopped going out.'

Daniel laughed.

'But he's a clever bastard, I'll give him that. I really do think what he's set up here could be beneficial to a lot of people. And at the very least, a bit of fun four times a year.'

'Yes, absolutely. Nice excuse for a piss-up,' Daniel replied, kindly. And then, 'And I understand that. About you and Michael. My ex and I were too similar too. Both indecisive. Couldn't even go to the cinema without a four-hour discussion beforehand. Makes sense to date an opposite, in a way.'

Gaby smiled. 'I've never had that problem. Every woman I know has cultivated decisiveness as part of her personal brand.'

Daniel laughed again – he enjoyed this woman with the ballsy attitude and straight-talking. 'God bless the fourth wave.'

'Ahhh,' said Gaby, standing to end the meeting and usher him out of the door. 'A man who knows his feminism!' They walked back the way they'd come, towards the lift.

'Well, I don't know about that. When I was growing up my dad told us it was just called respect.'

'Music to my ears. Not a strong mother raising a strong boy, but a strong father setting the example.'

'Yeah, my dad was a hell of a guy.'

'Was?'

Daniel nodded. 'A few months ago. Brain aneurysm.'

'Oh, I'm so sorry. He sounds like he was a wonderful, feminist man.'

They reached the twenty-first floor reception area, slowing to an eventual stand.

'Thank you. He was. I mean, I'm not sure he'd self-iden-tify as feminist, but he was definitely the guy you'd want in your corner.'

Gaby narrowed her eyes. She liked this man in front of her, doing his friend a favour and being so open and consid-erate about the ticket prices and Nadia *had* said she thought he was cute earlier – or, well, she'd said it bit ruder than that but the sentiment was the vaguely same.

'This is a weird question,' she said. 'And I am totally not hitting on you – I'm seeing somebody, actually – but . . . are *you* seeing anyone right now?'

Daniel crinkled his brow in response, half embarrassed and half intrigued. He sort of fancied Gaby herself, in a way – it was a slight ego dent that she was complimenting him whilst also saying she had a boyfriend.

'I mean, no,' he said, wondering why on earth she'd ask. 'But . . .' How could he explain he'd seen a woman on a train he was hoping to get to know? He couldn't.

'There's a staff party – for clients too – at the Sky Garden, this week. I don't feel unprofessional asking you because you seem cool, and it could be good for you to meet some of the guys here, if you want, but – there's somebody I'd love for you to meet. A woman. Do you think you'd like to come?'

'There's a woman you want me to meet?'

Gaby laughed. 'I know *we* just met, but – my friend, she works a few floors up and saw you when she walked me off the elevator earlier. She said you were cute. And I can vouch for you being clever, and you seem like not a dick?' Gaby closed her eyes and shook her head a little. 'I sound unhinged, don't I? I'm just trying to do her a favour, is all. You guys would get on. I can intro you to the wider team too – engineers have to network, right?'

Daniel shrugged.

'It's an open bar,' Gaby added, playfully.

'Right,' he said. He felt backed into a corner, somehow. That he couldn't say no. Did he want to? He couldn't say he wasn't intrigued. It didn't feel right, but also, he could hardly pledge emotional allegiance to Nadia. They hadn't even spoken! And still, saying yes felt disloyal. He didn't know *what* to say.

'Okay. Sure,' he settled on. 'Do you want to text me the details?' He reached into his top inside pocket for a business card. If she texted, he could always text back backing out, once he'd figured out an excuse. 'I don't know if I can quite say I trust you, but . . .'

'Oh, you can trust me,' Gaby said. 'You are just the kind of guy my friend would love, and I get the sense you're just the kind of man who'll know what to do with her.'

Daniel smiled. Were it not for Nadia, he'd actually quite enjoy the adventure of attending a business meeting with a beautiful woman, only to be set up with another, presumably equally as clever and pretty, woman. But then, he couldn't hold back on account of her, could he? That was . . . ridiculous.

'Is she okay with you matchmaking on her behalf?' Daniel said.

'Oh god no – she'd kill me,' giggled Gaby, and suddenly Daniel did trust her. Just like that. Because of how gently and honestly she admitted it. 'But I know she'll forgive me once you've met. I just have a feeling you're perfect for each other.'

12

Nadia

'And he's super cute,' Gaby said, over a quick burrito lunch in Borough Market. 'He has this sort of dopey English gent vibe about him, all very Ben Whishaw – you know, the one who builds the cars in James Bond – but he's . . . nice. He's really nice.'

Nadia rolled her eyes as she stuffed her extra order of avocado into the second half of her meal. 'Just because I dated an arsehole last doesn't mean I now want "nice",' Nadia complained. 'I know what nice means.'

Gaby shook her head as if to say, *what?*

'Nice means . . . wet.'

'Nooooo!' said Gaby. 'That's the 2012 definition of nice. Today's definition of nice is like, woke. And kind.'

'As opposed to woke and . . .?'

'Woke and using it to get into your knickers. I appreciate that there is no man to be trusted less than the one who has feminist in his Twitter bio.'

'This is true,' said Nadia, giggling. 'The man with feminist in his bio is the one who tells you how much he likes women, at the same time as telling you he doesn't have the gag-reflex to go down on you.'

Gaby hooted with laughter. 'Ha! Yes. The man with feminist in his bio doesn't *mansplain*, he passionately defends.'

Nadia nodded in agreement. 'The man who has feminist in his bio reads a bell hooks book and then lets YOU know the ways in which YOU'RE oppressed!'

'He pushes the men in his life away in disgust, leaving the women in his life to do his emotional labour!'

'He asks *permission* before sending a dick pic!'

'This is a fun game,' Gaby said.

'Yeah,' said Nadia. 'Hashtag not-all-men.' That was enough to make them both burst out laughing again. They expected any man to be a feminist in the same way they expected any man to like oxygen and breathing. Of course they did. They just didn't need to wang on about it, was all. Feminism was an ongoing act, not a chat-up line.

'But seriously, I'm giving you a head's up that cutie patootie from reception this morning is coming to the summer party, and I'd like to introduce you to him. I just . . . I have a feeling.'

'A feeling.'

'Does a realm of possibility exist in which you can trust me?'

Nadia narrowed her eyes. 'Fine. Yes. I will come, and I will meet him.' She popped the last chunk of her lunch in her mouth and thought about it.

'Although I did actually feel like I'd seen him somewhere before. Maybe on Bumble? Or Tinder or Hinge?'

Nadia tried to conjure up an image of him in her mind, but she'd only seen him in profile before the lift doors closed.

It had been a millisecond of recognition. On the other hand, Nadia absolutely had a type, and several times a day she could find herself having her head turned by yet another dark-haired, tall, suit-wearing bloke with stubble. She was unimaginative that way. She liked to stick to the classics.

'Hey,' she said, thinking how much her best friend would like the opportunity to meet the men at her company too. 'Shall we invite Emma?'

Gaby flushed pink and said, 'Actually, um, I already did.'

'Oh,' said Nadia. 'Well . . . that's cool.' Her tone implied that, actually, it was anything but cool.

It bothered her that Gaby had gone over her head to ask Emma to come. Emma had never been to a RAINFOREST work event before, so it's not like it was a given that Nadia would've asked her. Nadia only had the idea because she'd need a wingwoman as much as anything, and Emma was an excellent person to be stood beside when chatting up men. She knew exactly when to stick around, and exactly when to excuse herself to go to the bathroom and not return.

'I just, I figured you'd ask her anyway, and we were chatting on Instagram this morning, so . . .'

'Yeah, totally,' said Nadia. 'When this guy ends up being a dud, at least I'll have my dancing partners.'

'He is *not* a dud,' said Gaby, emphatically. 'I am willing to stake my full-price Gucci belt on it.'

'God, I love that belt,' Nadia said. She'd long wanted one herself. 'Well, in the meantime . . . I'm going to write back to Train Guy again. Then I'm not putting all my eggs in one basket. I'm going to meet your guy, and that takes the pressure off Train Guy, who, let's face it, could still be Quasimodo. Or worse, a Tory. So. That's sensible, I think.'

'Babe, there's no pressure anywhere, at all. This is supposed to be fun! Just have fun with it! And anyway, you're not even going to want to send an advert to Train Guy once you've met *my* guy. I have a sixth sense about these things. He is absolutely the man for you.'

Gaby glanced at the time on her phone.

'Okay, shoot, I gotta go. I'm in another meeting in five.' She gave Nadia a kiss on each cheek. 'You can name your first child after me, yeah? You and Daniel?'

Nadia rolled her eyes. She loved her friend's thoughtfulness – and enthusiasm – but she felt a small stab of guilt for the man on the train she'd spent all this time thinking about. It was the right thing to do, though. That's what they say, isn't it? Not to put too much weight on the idea of one man too soon? That's what Emma used to say when she had the dating column, anyway. And not that she would say as much to Gaby, but Gaby really did have a weird ability to nail people's characters. If she said Mr Cute Bum was also Mr Cute Personality, Nadia should at least put on some lipstick and go meet him. And to increase her odds, she really would reply to Train Guy's advert as well. She'd read in Emma's copy of *Get Your Guys!* that it was wise to spread your hope, so that you felt less pressure and could enjoy each interaction for what it was, instead of what it was in your head.

Back at her desk, then, she pulled up the submissions page for *Missed Connections* and typed in:

Thanks for leaving me high and dry, Train Guy: I basic- ally proposed marriage and a shared mortgage to a man who would be handsome if he shaved, and it wasn't you! I wanted it to be you. Don't tell anyone, but you're right: I love a grand romantic gesture. Ball is in your court now, friend. Make yourself known. Love, Coffee Spill Girl.

13

Daniel

'Mate, come on – you're going to need back-up. I'm a great wingman! You know I'm a great wingman!'

Lorenzo was wafting his buttered toast around as he stood in the kitchen wearing nothing but boxer shorts. He was uninhibited about being half-naked. He was uninhibited about being fully naked, actually. When Daniel had first moved in, he'd found Lorenzo sat stark bollock nude in front of the telly one Saturday afternoon, without even the smallest hint of embarrassment when Daniel passed through to the kitchen. Daniel had put his foot down on having bare skin on any of the furniture after that, which Lorenzo had protested against but ultimately conceded to. If Daniel had ever found a rogue pube on the coffee table he'd have happily strangled his flatmate, quite sure the law would be on his side. How could it not? Shared spaces were not for bare arses.

'But I'm not going because I actually want to be set up,'

Daniel explained, for the seventh time, as he reached for his keys. 'I'm going because this woman, this Gaby, was very persuasive, and I don't want to reflect badly on Michael by being rude. In fact, Michael himself might actually still be able to make it in time, so I already have a wingman.'

He walked towards the front door, checking his reflection in the mirror on his way. Lorenzo followed him. Daniel tried not to think of the crumbs he was making.

'Isn't it ruder to go and blow off this girl than to not go at all?' Lorenzo said, with a full mouth.

'Don't say girl. She's a grown-up. She's a woman.'

'Shut up. Girls are . . . girls. And I'm coming. I'll come pick you up from work at about six? Okay?'

'I'll text you,' shouted Daniel, as he closed the door behind him. 'Let me think about it.'

He had no intention of thinking about it.

It was the day of the party, and Daniel felt weirdly anxious. He was committed to seducing his rush hour crush, not this woman at the party. Whenever he felt sad about his dad he tried to imagine what he would tell him about her, about Nadia, this woman on the train, and their notes to each other – and he'd sort of have a conversation with him in his head, one that was nice and positive, rather than feeling miserable that he was gone.

And he couldn't wait to tell his mum something nice, something a bit exciting and hopeful, rather than all of their conversations being about something neither of them could control. Daniel often wished he had a brother, a dude to figure out this family stuff with. But he didn't. The closest thing he had to a brother was his cousin Darren, who was fed up with what he called 'rainy and fucking miserable' England and had gone to Australia on an under-thirties visa and met a bloke that he went on to marry. They lived in Sydney and posted pictures on Facebook of weekend cookouts where they were both muscly and bronzed and had matching sunglasses which suited one of them (Darren's husband) but not the other (Darren's head was a bit narrow for sunglasses like that).

It was a funny day, and on the walk to the underground station and then as the tube sped through to Angel, Daniel found himself thinking that he'd only be able to get out of the party if she was there, on the train. He decided that would be the sign to gather his courage and at least make eye contact, and if he could do that, then he could simply not turn up to the party. But then he didn't see her on the platform, and she certainly didn't get into his carriage, and so by the time he got off, ready for work and certain he hadn't got his nudge from the universe or some larger being, he messaged Lorenzo to say, *Okay fine, meet me at six.*

Lorenzo texted back immediately, with the two beers emoji and a smiley face.

Romeo wasn't on the door this morning, so Daniel didn't have an excuse to slow down and sound out his love life with the man who increasingly was the only person who talked sense to him about . . . well, anything, really. The pang of disappointment he felt reminded him that he hadn't seen his mates from university – the ones he used to have a beer at the weekend or get dinner with – for a while either. He was thirty, almost thirty-one, and everyone he knew apart from Lorenzo had left the immediate area of London to start a family – or at least start thinking about maybe thinking about starting a family.

He'd stopped going to weddings every weekend – that had tapered off about two years ago, when he'd had his last serious relationship, with Sarah, who'd left him for a guy at work who wore a waistcoat unironically – and now spent a lot of time at christenings and first birthdays in the Cotswolds or Kent or, for his friends Jeremy and Sabrina, Milton Keynes. But never just at the pub, after work.

His group had, in a lot of ways, moved on without him.

For ten years, they'd called each other brothers and swore it was 'bros before hoes'. Daniel reflected that it might have been poor taste to call the women they dated hoes, but nothing rhymed with 'young women with dreams, hopes, aspiration and quite a good sense of humour'. In his twenties, his group of mates swore to one another they were family, but in the space of a few years, maybe even less, everyone except Daniel had peeled off and built actual families, recognized by the state. Sam's wife had even taken his name, which had caused a weird rift between her and the other WAGS of the group. They'd all said it wasn't feminist, but then Rashida had screamed at them that her feminism was about choice, and they needed to take a look in the mirror if they were going to tell her what she should and shouldn't do. Daniel wasn't sure what to think. He didn't have a wife to worry about.

On his way up to the office, he took out his phone to text the lads' WhatsApp group, saying, *All right, guys, we've gotta get together soon, man. London, one Saturday afternoon? Or maybe even an Airbnb somewhere?*

Over the course of the morning he got a stream of messages that concluded six out of the other guys in the thread were up for it. Daniel asked if it was crazy to say this weekend. It was rare to be able to do anything spontaneously now they all had responsibilities. But Terrence said his missus was on a hen weekend for her youngest sister, so everyone could crash at his place, and that made it easier. Some could make it just for the Friday, and some just for the Saturday, but all in all six of them was a bloody good show.

Daniel's mood was lifted enough to start looking forward to the night's party. Things could be good, he thought, if he let them be. He went out at lunch and got his hair-line tidied up and splashed on some Hwyl perfume at the Aesop store: he'd read on the *GQ* website that it was the scent every hipster should be wearing. He thought to himself how much better he felt for being proactive in his own happiness. He didn't know a lot of people who went after the things that made them feel good – he knew a lot of people who sat around and waited for life to happen to them. Romeo seemed proactive: that's why he liked him. It was apt he was in the lobby on his way back in from lunch. Daniel was pleased to see him.

'Looking good, my friend,' Romeo said, which was almost word-for-word what he said every day. And then, 'And smelling good – is that the Aesop stuff?'

'You know it,' Daniel said, bumping his fist as he walked by.

'You've got a spring in your step today, huh?'

Daniel stopped and turned around. 'Romeo, I've decided today is a great day.'

'That's the spirit, Daniel. Man, are you right. You inspire me, man!'

Daniel winked at him. He was feeling inspired himself.

'And she wrote you back, I saw. Might that have anything to do with this wonderful mood?'

Daniel spun on his heel to look at Romeo. 'What? I didn't see the paper today. I was so busy looking for her on the tube that I didn't think to look for her in the paper!'

Romeo flung a copy of that morning's newspaper from the welcome desk over to Daniel, who thumbed immediately to the right page, read her note, and then stood, grinning, at Romeo.

'Daniel?' Romeo said, eventually.

'Yes?' Daniel said, dreamily. She'd looked for him! On the train!

'Don't just stand there – go write her back!'

Daniel smiled even wider, if that were possible.

'On it,' he said, pointing a finger at Romeo with his thumb in the air, which he bent slightly like a trigger. 'ON. IT.'

He went back to his office and wrote back to Nadia, first-time perfect:

> *You're funny. Do you get told that a lot? Funny and cute. How lucky am I?! Listen, if you ever made the train on time I'd happily make my move. I'm pretty eager to meet you properly. Love, Train Guy.*

He read and reread it several times, and with a nod of satisfaction hit 'Send'.

Daniel's good mood lasted until just after 7 p.m., when he stood in the middle of the Sky Garden, London's highest public garden, in a huge tower in the shape of a walkie-talkie, with views across London.

He was surrounded by strangers, vaguely aware of Lorenzo telling his somewhat embellished story about the time he spent as a stripper to pay for his Master's degree, and how he once got his penis stuck in the trunk of the elephant sewed to the front of his G-string. The girls – women, although they all seemed quite young, maybe

114

twenty-two or twenty-three – were lapping it up, laughing loudly and touching his arm and teasing him so that he retold parts, making them laugh even more. As Daniel was wondering which of them he was trying to sleep with, knowing that with Lorenzo he wouldn't have limited himself to just one, Gaby pulled on his sleeve.

'You made it! I'm so pleased!' she said, going in to kiss both of his cheeks.

'I did,' Daniel said, issuing air kisses back. 'Though I'm afraid it looks as though my plus-one is more popular than I am.' They both gazed in Lorenzo's direction, where he had moved on to telling his joke about the crab at the bar, and as he reached the punchline his audience collapsed, once more, into flirtatious giggles. One of the women, holding her throat as she tipped her head back, made eye contact with Daniel as she regained her composure. She held it for a moment, pointedly, and then just as quickly looked away.

'You'll be popular with the only person who matters, though,' Gaby said. 'The woman of the hour should be here any minute. She was going to walk from the office to get her steps in.'

'Very sensible,' said Daniel, not sure of what else to say. The pair stood, suspended in the awkwardness of not really knowing each other, and not really in the mood to feign wanting otherwise. Drink. He decided on drink. 'I'm going to go to the bar – can I get you anything?'

'No, no,' Gaby said. 'I just need to go say hi to someone over there. 'I'll come find you in a minute. I'm so glad you came.'

Daniel held up his hand in Lorenzo's direction, as if guzzling an imaginary pint, the universal sign for 'Do you want another?' Lorenzo held up his empty glass in response, the universal sign for 'Yes, I do!'

It was four or five drinks later when Daniel realized he'd somehow, at some point, draped his arm around a woman's bare shoulders, and that it had dropped to dusk outside. Gaby had never come back to introduce him to anyone – in fact, he hadn't seen her in ages. But it didn't matter. He'd had his second pint to steady his nerves, and his third because the second had tasted so good. Once the penny dropped that there wouldn't be a big introduction to a stranger to navigate, he supped at the pint Lorenzo handed him a bit later too. He was accidentally quite drunk by then, and hadn't really said much as he'd continued to watch Lorenzo's performance to his audience of admirers – but he hadn't needed to. He knew his role when it was the two of them out together: in the handful of times they'd gone to a bar Daniel often became the silent one, which, he'd been told by women more than once, made him seem brooding and mysterious.

That was laughable to him – not least because they'd all have no idea he was tipsy instead, not brooding – and his mum would soon set anyone who thought that of her son straight, but on occasion it had worked in his favour. The woman he'd made eye contact with earlier on had continued to catch his eye across the group of them, eventually leaning in as he headed to the bar again to say, 'Order me a large red, would you?' He'd looked at her and nodded. She was pretty. He was thinking about what the dating guide had said about having options, about not putting one person at the centre of your affections, about shopping around to take the pressure off. It was around that time he'd put his arm around her.

'Let's get out of here,' she said to him, not long after, hot and breathy in his ear. Daniel looked at her. Somehow, they had peeled off from the group and were pressed into a corner together. Her hand was suddenly on his chest, the flat of her palm cool against the cotton of his shirt. He knew if he looked down, she'd be looking up at him and it would be an invitation to kiss. She was offering to go home and have sex with him.

In another life, ten years ago – five years ago! Or, to be frank, even last year – he would have said yes. He would have taken her home and had sex and seen her for a few dates afterwards, both of them trying to make the pieces of themselves fit, even if they didn't. But after his dad, he knew life was too short to waste it on people he wasn't crazy about.

'Sorry. I . . .' he began, taking his arm off from around her.

The girl looked disappointed, but also undeterred. 'Do you have a girlfriend?'

'No,' Daniel said.

'Because I don't kiss and tell . . .' the girl continued, stepping closer to him again. Daniel put his hands on hers to lift them off his stomach, where she'd lightly rested them in a way that was, Daniel wasn't so drunk as not to notice, quite nice.

'I'm sorry,' he said, firmly, and to her credit the girl simply shrugged and walked off.

At home, in bed on his own with a pint of water on his bedside table, Daniel listened, against his will, to seven minutes of banging and moaning coming from Lorenzo's room, before it stopped and somebody left the bedroom to pee, leaving the bathroom door slightly open. He could tell by the way it echoed. He didn't sleep well that night, and when he did finally drift off he had weird dreams about being an octopus. He had something in every hand, and desperately wanted to pick up a book he'd found but he couldn't pick up the book without putting something else down. And he didn't want to. In his dream, as an octopus, he got so upset at the idea he'd have to let something go in order to look at the thing he so desperately wanted to look at that he woke up in a pool of sweat, panting and out of breath and feeling really, really sad.

He wished there was somebody else in bed beside him.

He wished he was in bed with his best friend, in a house they owned, maybe even with rings on their fingers.

Daniel wanted what his mum and dad had had. He wanted it so terribly badly. And not just with anyone.

He wanted it with the love of his life.

14

Nadia

Nadia had a feeling all day that something wasn't right. A sort of ominous heaviness in her tummy, and an anxiousness that made her snap in the lab more than once.

'I'm sorry,' she told her assistant, when she found herself losing her temper over the reconfiguration of a stubborn bit of code that wouldn't quite translate to what they were working on. 'In fact, you know what? I know we're on a deadline here but let's take a break. Twenty minutes. I'll come back with cake.'

Nadia grabbed her phone and left the office building, heading towards the market to her second-favourite bakery in the city. Her first-favourite bakery was the cupcake shop on Church Street in Stoke Newington, down the road from where she lived. If you got them at the right point in the day it was possible to get almost a whole quarter of a full-sized red velvet cake, with so much icing it needed two cups of tea to help wash it down. On a less frosting-based day, Nadia liked the cookies at her second-favourite bakery, which were inspired by New York's Levain bakery – the cookies there had been invented by an Olympic swimmer who needed a way to get in as many calories as possible in a short amount of time. They were dense and light, full of chocolate chips but so moreish it never seemed like enough. They cost almost six pounds each and so it wasn't so much the fat content as the price that put Nadia off going too often.

Typically, she treated herself right before her period which – ah. Nadia pulled up the period tracker app on her phone, knowing before it told her that she was definitely pre-menstrual. Yup. The flashing dot told her to expect a bleed tomorrow, and suddenly her dark mood and short temper and desire to both burn the world to the whole damned ground and eat innumerable calories as she did so made sense.

It was later, right as she got changed into a different top, putting on extra deodorant and wondering where her Tic Tacs were, that Nadia felt a twinge in her tummy that meant her period was a day early. She hated that feeling – the feeling of a period coming before she was ready – and instantly knew she'd have an awful night, wishing she was at home. She hated that she felt obliged to go because of this stupid set-up Gaby had arranged. She was in no mood to flirt and be coy and diminish her accomplishments until she got a read on the extent to which this guy might feel threatened. The set-up was all cute and lovely in theory, but she felt gross, and really was more determined to find out who the man on the train was than go tonight. Who knew what kind of guy was waiting to meet her at the Sky Garden? Although, to be fair, who knew what kind of guy was waiting to meet her on the train. Urgh. She looked at herself in the mirror.

Come on babe, she willed herself. *Show up to your own life.*

Meet you there, she texted Gaby. *Gonna walk off a bad day. My period came early.*

Gaby texted back, *Hurry! The poor guy is a bag of nerves! It's cute, but also get here and put him out of his misery!*

Nadia sent back the running girl emoji, signalling a pace she didn't feel. Her friend was only trying to be good to her, she knew.

She was about thirteen minutes into the twenty-minute walk when her mood lifted. The fresh air blew away her cobwebs and gave her back some perspective on her life. Nothing *bad* was about to happen: the feeling she'd had all day was the simple biology of her menstrual cycle. She was about to walk in to a beautiful venue with a summer view of the London skyline, her two closest friends in the world there with an open bar and a potentially handsome man. Even if nothing came of tonight, she'd read in *Get Your Guys!* that refusing to practise flirting with men you *didn't* fancy was like saying you'd learn your lines only once you got on stage. That book advocated flirting with everyone, always, everywhere, just to be polite and friendly and getting used to being a little nervous, so that when the true man of your life is finally in front of you, you don't blow it.

Yes, Nadia thought to herself. *I will go and practise my flirting.* She lined up some witty things to say, imagining herself smiling and charming and drinking and laughing. She would have as good a time as she had set her mind to, and in the half-mile walk in the sunshine, she'd decided she'd have a lovely time.

And then she saw him.

Awful Ben.

The night she broke up with him – an act that took more

courage than anything she had ever known, and a full three weeks to build up to – she sat and took it as he said horrible, hurtful things to her.

He told her she was worthless, that nobody would ever want her, that she was broken and didn't know how to love anyway.

She'd called him a cab and knew she would never hear from him again: that his proud Brazilian blood would mean she was dead to him, which suited her just fine. She needed to not see him. He worked just outside of London, meaning the chances of passing him on any day were minimal; but, of course, though London is big, the daily paths most people take are small, and just as the posh people knew Notting Hill like the back of their hands, and ad execs knew every twist and turn of Soho, single and hipster mid-thirties professionals knew by heart the streets of Spitalfields and Commercial Road. *Of course* if Awful Ben was to come into town for a date, this was the part he'd come to. And it looked like a date too – or even like he could be with a girlfriend.

While her thoughts were drifting ahead to the summer party, Nadia had glanced up from her feet only to experience the horrifying realization that her emotionally manipulative and downright disordered-personalitied ex-boyfriend was stood before her – she had literally walked into him.

She hadn't seen him since she'd live-tracked his Uber home on her app, making sure he got back to where he lived before she took the photo of them out of the frame on her bedside table and cut it into tiny little pieces.

She could see him saying something, but she couldn't hear the words. Her body was ice cold and it felt like not enough air was reaching her lungs. Awful Ben was still moving his mouth. It was like time had frozen and sped up, both at the same time. She blinked several times in quick succession and felt sick and suddenly her tummy hurt.

'You are in a world of your own,' he said.

It was weird how he said it. It was an accusation, but also said totally neutrally. It felt aggressive to Nadia, but the woman on his arm – a beautiful, radiant woman, with full cheeks and kind eyes – smiled, as if that must be a private joke between them. What had he said about her? Did this woman on his arm know what he was capable of yet?

'I . . . I don't want to talk to you. Excuse me.'

Nadia pushed past the two of them, stepping out into the road to do so and only narrowly missing a cyclist who screamed at her, 'Fucking hell! Watch it!'

She heard Awful Ben say something about *the ex I told you about, poor thing,* and she remembered, in that moment, how he'd said that to Nadia the night they first met, about the girlfriend before her. *She was never well.*

Nadia kept walking, her head spinning, with a dogged refusal to look back at him. She knew he was watching. Knew he was furious she'd caused even the tiniest bit of a scene.

Crazy, that was the word he had used, all that time ago. He said his ex was crazy. And now Nadia felt crazy too. And it was awful, horrible – she'd bet her whole life that the woman who was now hearing about his crazy ex would one day herself be crying in the street near a work party being called crazy by him too, when the only thing crazy was how Awful Ben picked away at the women he said he loved and tortured them into thinking there was something wrong with them.

But the problem was *him.*

It made Nadia want to scream. She wanted to scream, *and* run back down the road to tell the woman to save herself and dump him now. But if she did that, she really would seem crazy. She wouldn't have listened to anyone, least of all an ex, if she'd been warned. She would have thought that whoever tried to tell her not to pursue a relationship with him was jealous. *That's what they teach us*, Nadia thought to herself, miserably. *They teach us that other women are the competition so we don't talk to each other honestly and figure out that they're all fucking fuckers.*

She reached the Sky Garden and looked up. There was no way she was going in. She was crying, she realized – and, as she fished her phone out of her pocket, trembling a little too. She called Emma.

'Babe, where are you?' answered Emma. 'I've seen this guy Gaby has for you. He's cute. He's your type. Like, fucking game on, babe!'

Nadia's voice wobbled as she said, 'I'm outside. I just saw Ben.' And then she sobbed hysterically.

'Fuck. Okay. I'm coming. Stay right there. I'm coming.'

'The table in the corner, please,' Emma said to the hostess of the chic hotel. Emma had a theory that if in doubt, go to a hotel bar because they're always emptier than pubs or stand-alone restaurants. She was right. Nadia felt safe here. It was half empty and they could sit at the back, out of the way, their own little world within a world.

Gaby was with them. The three settled into a corner booth and Emma ordered them the salted caramel chocolate brownie with two scoops of ice cream, the sweet and salty popcorn, and a large pot of peppermint tea with honey on the side. Everything was to share.

'There was so much I thought I would say to him if I ever saw him again,' Nadia said, playing with the label on the

124

bottle of water at the table. 'And I just froze. Urgh.' A tear rolled down her cheek. 'He looked so smug too – like he knew he'd caught me in a weak moment or something.'

'What did she look like?' Emma asked, intrigued.

'Question vetoed,' said Gaby, giving her daggers. 'It literally doesn't matter. He'll do the same to her.' Gaby had known something was off with Awful Ben almost immediately after Nadia had started going out with him; she and Nadia had had their only fight over it and after they'd made up Gaby knew she had to let her friend make her own mistakes. 'It happens to a lot of women at some point.'

The tea arrived, and the women fell silent as the waitress unloaded her tray and told them dessert would be right with them.

'You don't have to be okay, you know,' Gaby said, once she'd gone. 'I'd want to cry and scream too.'

Nadia nodded. 'I hate that you don't get over someone like, once. You have to do it again and again and again, every time you think of them.'

'You've been doing really well,' Emma offered. 'You've been lighter, happier. More positive. You've been in The New Routine to Change Your Life!'

'And now I'm taking a huge leap back,' Nadia said, miserably. 'I'm so mad that he can control me! Still!' She burst into tears again.

'It's not a leap back, not at all.' Emma soothed her. 'Babe – healing isn't linear. And look how far you've come. You were able to process all that craziness that happened, and then tell us and process it again, and seeing him – it's another way to process it. Because it was real. What he did to you, how awful he was – it was all real. I promise you: none of us is fucking up like we think we are.'

Nadia welled up again, and nodded. It was all she could do, nod, like an external manifestation of the internal realization that yup, he really had stolen not just the six months of her life that they'd dated, but the six months afterwards too, which she'd needed just to make sense of how she'd let it happen. How she'd become his victim. She was a strong, positive, go-getting woman and it shamed her deeply that she'd let a man put out her flame.

'Stop it,' said Emma. 'I can see you beating yourself up again. None of this is your fault. It's all him. You are a survivor, and he can't hurt you anymore, okay? You control this ship.'

The dessert arrived, with three forks, and the women picked the edges off the brownie.

'I'm going to order the cheesecake too,' said Nadia, sadly.

Emma winked at her. 'Good idea.' And then, 'Darling, you know what? Why don't the two of us go on an adventure this weekend? We could go to Soho Farmhouse. Sleep in a massive bed. See some celebs. Row a boat on that tiny pond. Let's get out of London, shall we?'

Nadia thought about it as she stirred in the honey to her tea. It sounded good to be anywhere but here. To be somebody else, somewhere else.

'Would I have to talk to anyone except you?'

'Nope.'

'Would I have to do things to be a fun friend or can I wallow and feel bruised and sad?'

'You can feel bruised and sad.'

'Okay. Yes. I'd like that.'

Emma put her arm around her friend. 'I'd like that too.'

Gaby held up her hands. 'Thanks for the invite, guys!'

Emma didn't miss a beat. 'You're at your mum's this weekend!'

'I know, but you could still have asked me.'

Nadia said, 'You're at Marie-Jean's this weekend? That's nice. Tell her I say hi.'

Gaby said, 'I will do. I'm jealous of your plans now, though.'

'The perks of survival,' said Nadia. 'When you cry, your friends whisk you away.'

'Only if you have good friends.'

'Yeah. God, can I date you instead?'

Emma laughed. 'Join the queue,' she said.

'Wouldn't it just be so much easier?' Nadia leaned in for the last part of the brownie. 'You guys don't get upset at who earns more money or feel emasculated if somebody else picks up the bill. You don't have to wait a beat too long to text back because it's not masculine to be too eager, and god, can you imagine fucking a woman? Like, worshipping a vagina instead of thinking it is vaguely gross and something to be embarrassed about? That's the thing I envy about lesbians: everybody is invested in how great the pussy is. I've been with too many guys who sort of tolerate it, because it's the thing that they get to dip into. But they don't truly love it, or understand it. Imagine dating somebody who actually understands how periods work, instead of having a vague knowledge that it means mood swings and blood? I just think that would be beautiful.'

'I agree,' said Gaby, her attention turning to the waitress. 'Can we get the cheesecake too, please?' she smiled at her.

The waitress nodded.

Emma said: 'Me too. Like, I wonder what it would be like not to have to perform womanhood, as well.'

'Like being genderqueer?' Nadia said.

'Yeah!' said Emma. 'I guess. The boxes of "male" and "female" are so narrow: if you're a bloke, it's best to behave this way and if you're a chick, it's best to behave this other way. What if there was no such thing as man and woman?'

'I think I'd still love the dick,' Nadia laughed.

Gaby said, 'I don't know if you would, though. I'm not telling you how you feel, but do you love dick because mostly that's what you've assumed about yourself? What about a man with a vagina, or a woman with a penis?'

'A lesbian with a good dildo?' Emma added.

'My auntie Linda wouldn't know how to address the Christmas cards!' Nadia said, laughing.

'She could try simply using your names!'

'No Mr and Mrs, or whatever?'

'Exactly. That's some antiquated patriarchal bullshit anyway.'

'I agree,' said Nadia, as the waitress delivered the cheesecake.

'Thank you, darling,' Emma said to her.

Nadia liked this. Sitting with her friends and talking and being safe and not judged and everyone trying to understand themselves a little better. This was her happy place. She just wished she didn't only ever remember to take stock of it after she'd been sad. *You don't need a romance to have a romantic life*, she thought, watching her two friends smile and laugh together. She felt so lucky to have them.

15

Nadia

Soho Farmhouse in Oxfordshire was a green, leafy space populated with a lush restaurant and spa area in converted barns. Emma flashed her black membership card at the gates – a membership that was a few thousand pounds a year but guaranteed a table next to a handful of minor celebrities and bankers-turned-creative-investors who thought they were somehow bohemian because they'd put the cash injection into an actress's website, or a musician's charity event.

Nadia and Emma were in cabin thirty-four, and after unloading the car they took their 'house bikes' down the smooth tarmac lanes, enjoying the quiet as they zoomed up and down, simply to zoom up and down. Nadia knew the room should have been at least five hundred pounds a night (though Emma insisted she'd got a deal of some sort and so Nadia only owed her two hundred for the weekend, which seemed suspicious to Nadia, like Emma was being nonchalant about the difference because she earned more), so it was ironic that from the outside each cabin had been modelled to look like a tin hut on a Siberian roadside. Still. The sheets were thick cotton and there was a real fire and the balcony hovered over a small river, making it easy to whittle away a solid thirty minutes or more just staring at water. And it was peaceful. Really, really peaceful.

'Babe, how do you feel about a facial?' Emma said, when they sat outside with steaming cups of Earl Grey. 'You know how your skin gets when you've been crying.'

It was true – Nadia got even more acne along her jaw when she was stressed or upset and since giving up milk she'd been doing so well. Her skin had been clear for two weeks now, and she'd be damned if Awful Ben would be the reason it didn't stay that way. To anyone listening, what Emma said could've sounded catty, like she was some kind of frenemy, but Nadia knew she meant well. She supposed Emma couldn't control her running into Awful Ben, but she could control sixty minutes of pure indulgence by a woman who knew how to extract blackheads.

'Do I have to talk to anyone?'

'No. Well. Just the facialist. To tell her you're sad and you want a boost.'

'Okay. Maybe a pedicure too. I feel more in control of my life when my toes are nice.'

'Done and done. I just have to make a phone call to the office, and then I'll let the concierge know.'

Emma opened the sliding glass doors to retrieve her phone from charging inside, and Nadia sat with her feet curled up behind her. Looking out over the stream, Nadia idly wondered what kind of man would make a gesture like writing in to a newspaper. When Emma had picked her up that morning she'd tossed the paper across to her and said, 'He's written to you again,' in a sing-song voice, and as they'd driven out of the city and into the countryside Nadia had replayed his new advert to her again and again in her mind. *You're funny. Do you get told that a lot? Funny and cute. How lucky am I?!*

She was enjoying the slow burn of it. Things had gone way too fast with Awful Ben – she knew now that it was called 'Love Bombing'. Men like Ben seduced hard and fast and quickly, so that the love was disorientating and you lost yourself in it. Once upon a time Nadia had thought that was how love was supposed to be, but she'd learnt the hard way that what was so much better was taking steps slowly, deliberately. Checking in with each other along the way. That's what Train Guy felt like to her: like a chance to grow something beautiful, over time. There was a reassurance to it. And it was the bit about luck that made her smile. *How lucky am I?!* Train Guy had said. She felt lucky too. Lucky to still believe she had a chance at love. Even if Train Guy came to nothing, writing back and forth with him was fun. She resolved not to think about Awful Ben anymore. He was the past. She could decide her own future.

Nadia snapped out of her reverie to a low murmured voice around the back of the cabin.

'Emma?' she said, craning her neck around the side of their place to see her stood with her back to her. Emma spun around, a funny look on her face.

'Coming!' she said, whispering something into her mobile.

She disappeared from sight and Nadia heard the front door open, before her friend appeared by the screen door to the balcony.

'Facials in twenty minutes!' Emma said, opening the door. 'And I was thinking, how do you feel about the pub down the road for dinner? The Ox and Cart?'

She seemed a little wired to Nadia, but Nadia didn't say anything. Instead, she settled on, 'Facials: excellent. Pub? Less keen on going out if I'll have no make-up on. Shall we get room service instead?'

'Great,' said Emma, her brightness almost a bit forced.

'Are you okay?'

'Me? Yes. Of course. Are you?'

Nadia stared at her friend. Something wasn't right.

'Yeah, I'm feeling better,' she said.

16

Daniel

'Well, what about the time you stole that bouncer's waistcoat, and he chased you all the way down to Walkabout and then broke your nose?' Jonny laughed, as Dean delivered another round of beers to the table.

'Oh my god – he should have gone to jail for that!' Daniel was hysterical at the memory. They'd been ribbing Jeremy for a good ten minutes about how out of control he was in third year. Daniel looked around the table in the front room of The Ox and Cart, where his mismatched collection of friends sat. There was the love monster Jeremy, now happily settled down with Sabrina and father to two kids – his second had just been born. Jonny lived with his wife Tilly, not far from Terrence, whose Cotswold estate they were all staying at as his pregnant wife was away for the weekend. Terrence had become a professional poker player at eighteen and used the money to put himself through an undergraduate degree and then an MBA, turning ten thousand pounds into three million by the time he was twenty-eight and adopting twins a few years ago, almost out of a need to keep occupied. And now he'd be a dad to a third! Sam was there, and Taz, Dean too; and although Daniel wished all the uni lads were there, being together with this group was enough. He was having a brilliant time.

'Yeah, but Jimmy was shagging his girlfriend, and she asked us not to press any charges, remember? She was scared he'd find out?' Jeremy had had several girlfriends that year, not so much because he was a cad, but more because he really did have that much love to give. He could charm a lamppost and believe everything he said, as he said it.

They'd all piled into the house after a delayed train to Charlbury from Paddington after work, starving and tearing into the pizza in the oven that had gone both soggy and crusty at the same time after being reheated, because Terrence still didn't understand how the Aga worked.

'I'm from a backstreet terrace in Manchester!' he said, as way of apology. 'I only learned what heated floors were two years ago!'

They'd made their way down the road to the pub, and easy banter and memories were stirred up in record time, juxtaposed with the new lives they all lived, all married or fathers and in Terrence's case, millionaires too. In the years Daniel had known his 'group', he'd always felt at home. There was a shorthand between them that had only got shorter since doing shots as freshers and competing over who could list the most obscure band. They could have drifted apart in their late twenties, when life got busy and more complicated than they were used to. But it hadn't. They'd gone the distance together. They were as tight as ever, even if they all lived in different places now. They didn't see each other enough, but when they did get together it was like being in university halls all over again.

'How you doing, you know – after your dad?' Dean had said on the train, not long after they'd boarded. Daniel had vague recollections of them being at the funeral, but he'd been in no state to string sentences together.

Daniel told them all the truth.

'I was a mess,' he'd said, 'but I'm doing all the right things to get through it and feel pretty okay now. The doc gave me some pills and I go and talk to someone about my head and see my mum a bit more in case she's lonely.'

'Fucking hell, yeah,' Jonny had said. 'I've only been married eighteen months but fuck me, if anything happened to Tilly I don't know how I'd get up in the morning.'

'We're here for you, pal,' Dean said, raising his beer can towards him so that all of them saluted the memory of Mr Weissman, silently saying a prayer that it hadn't been them to lose their father. It was a strange rite of passage to pass through first: Terrence had been the first to get married, and Jeremy the first to become a dad, but Daniel was the first to have lost a parent.

He felt better just for being with the people who made him feel safe. The ones who'd seen him pull an all-nighter because he left essays until the last minute and the ones whose sisters he'd snogged when they'd come to visit and the ones who'd got so drunk with him the night of their graduation ceremony that they'd all ended up in the hospital while Taz got his stomach pumped, eating McDonald's and sobering up as they talked about what they wanted for their lives. For all of them, the answer was the same: to lead better lives than their parents had. They'd all managed it.

Daniel got up to go to the loo, and Dean said, 'Your round

on the way back, mate!' Daniel flipped up his middle finger at him good-naturedly as he walked to the Gents. He peed and noted in the mirror as he washed his hands how bright-eyed he looked. He was still buzzing about his latest advert getting published so fast. He was able to enjoy being where he was, in the moment, with his mates, because he knew that right now she could be reading his reply and that at half seven on Monday morning something brilliant could happen. Would happen – he could feel it. Life was good. He could honestly say, for the first time in ages, that he felt positive about what was coming next. About the future.

He stood beside a couple at the bar of the country pub as he waited to put in an order for the next round. It was hard not to eavesdrop, really, and it sounded like their first mini-break. The first mini-break is, as Daniel and his friends had long concluded, a relationship rite of passage, especially for young professionals from a city where house-shares were the norm. The first mini-break was normally the first time you'd get totally uninterrupted time together, with sex that didn't have to be quiet in case the person in the room next door heard, or saw you nip to the loo in the buff in the middle of the night. Daniel thought about his first weekend away with his ex, Sarah. He'd planned a whole schedule around what he thought would be romantic – a country hotel, afternoons in a rowing boat on the lake, champagne in the room on arrival. As it turned out they'd had a horrible fight on the train ride there and then erroneously assumed there'd be a line of cabs waiting at the station to take them to where they were staying, but there weren't. They'd stood in the drizzle that would later make rowing on the lake a write-off for forty-five minutes until a car they'd ordered from the number stuck to the information board arrived.

They'd made the best of it, each trying to put on a brave face. But they'd both been a little crestfallen that it hadn't all rolled out as perfectly as they'd imagined. Was it strange to imagine going away with Nadia? They could even come here, to this exact pub, and after sharing a bottle of red wine by the fire he could tell her, a little tipsily, that he'd come here right after he'd written to her again and he'd promised himself there and then that he'd come back, and with her. He looked over his shoulder at his buddies. He wanted what they all had – happy marriages that meant they had somebody to share the highs with, and hold the hand of when things were less good. He loved all of their wives – even Rashida, who could be a bit bossy, a bit strident – and he was so excited to one day introduce his person to them all too.

'So she wrote back,' Daniel heard a man's voice say, 'and it was this cocky and funny and kind of provocative answer, and they've gone back and forth a bit, and now everyone is waiting to see if they go out. I don't know –' he paused to take a sip of his wine '– I think it's one of those things where everyone is like, "She wrote back! They have to get married now!" Or whatever. Because it's like a movie or something, you know?'

Daniel cocked his head and tried to listen to what the woman said in response. He was so sure they were talking about him, and about Nadia. About her note to him. Was that egotistical of him? But surely there weren't a string of people writing letters to each other in the newspaper. Maybe he was imagining things because he was excited by the day. That must be it.

'What can I get for you, mate?' the barman asked, and Daniel held up one hand and two fingers to signal seven pints, and said, 'Seven of the Abbot's, please, mate.'

Daniel craned his neck to continue to listen to the couple.

'Well, if it were me,' the woman was saying, 'I'd want a big romantic gesture like that. Like, if you meet somebody that way . . .' And then Daniel couldn't hear what she said after that. *Well,* he thought. *Even if they're not talking about us, that's still worth remembering. Big romantic gesture. That's like Romeo said. Got it.* A shudder went down his spine. He'd thought of him and Nadia as an *us.*

He delivered the booze to the table and Jeremy was in the middle of a story about his new kid, his second, and how his penis was like a tiny sprinkle system and they'd had to buy a Penis teepee.

'I'm not kidding,' he was saying. 'It's a tiny teepee that you put over the kid's dick, so when he pisses himself as you change him it doesn't go all over you!' It was the kind of Dad Talk Daniel couldn't contribute to, not being one himself, but it was nice to be a part of. He was just happy. Happy to be here and be alive and have the whole promise of a future in front of him. Nadia's face drifted into his mind and the lads continued to play 'dad one-upmanship' with their various anecdotes.

And then he chastised himself: *Fucking hell mate, try having a date first.*

He finished off his pint and tuned back in to the rest of the group, telling himself that was enough fantasizing for now. Somebody asked if they should hop in a cab and go down to Soho Farmhouse for a nightcap because Terrence and Dean had membership so could get everybody in, but the idea was sunk by the rest of the group who decided to head back to the house.

'Okay, fine,' Terrence said. 'But I swear to god, she'll kill me if you smoke in the house so just . . . well, fucking don't, okay?'

138

Rowdily, they stumbled out of the pub and into the last scraps of country summer light. Jonny and Dean both pulled packets of cigarettes from their jean pockets and promptly sparked up.

17

Nadia

'I'm just saying,' said Nadia, 'that you seem a bit distant, is all. Like, whatever it is, you can tell me.'

They were sat at breakfast in the courtyard of the club, handsome waiters buzzing around them and the promise of poached eggs with hollandaise sauce on the way.

'I. Am. Not. Hiding. Anything,' she said, enunciating every syllable. 'Don't crowd me, okay? If I want to talk, I'll talk!'

She said it shiftily – not mad, or angry – she was like a teenager who didn't have the words for her feelings yet. But the feelings were most definitely there.

Nadia couldn't figure it out. She'd waited all weekend to say something, thinking every time she caught Emma's mind wandering off halfway through the conversation, or noting how she obsessively checked her phone, that surely it would be the last time. Nadia gave Emma imaginary chance after imaginary chance, but she kept using them up. Nadia had gone from being slightly irked to totally outraged to now genuinely concerned about Emma's behaviour. It was like she'd had bad news she didn't want to share, or was waiting for bad news to come. Nadia's own funk had lifted enough to be aware of the company she was in, and the company she was in was undoubtedly in pain.

'It's only because I'm worried,' Nadia said. 'I thought I was the broken one this weekend. But I feel like you need some TLC too.'

Emma softened.

'Oh, I'm sorry,' she said, acknowledging the waiter with a smile and muttering thank you as her orange juice was delivered. 'I don't mean to snap. I'm obsessed with my phone because of work and I promise I'm not doing anything other than listening to you 100 per cent. I'm enjoying myself! I am!'

Nadia reached out to touch her friend's hand.

'Me too,' she said, not buying what Emma was saying at all. 'But also I'm here, okay?'

'Okay,' Emma nodded, smiling.

Their eggs came, and they ate, observing with a nudge when an Australian pop star from the noughties walked past their table, and smiling broadly when Brooklyn Beckham walked past with Madonna's son. It was a clear and bright morning, and the place bustled with Sunday morning energy: lots of cashmere sweatpants and Sunday supplements and cappuccinos. Camera phones were against the rules, but Emma still took a photograph of their food.

'What time is the class?' said Nadia, eventually.

'Oh, bugger, yes: we should think about going down there actually. We've got about twenty minutes.'

'Awesome.'

They'd both laughed in serendipitous glee as the Sunday's

social schedule had been slipped under their cabin door the night before while they'd been eating ribs and sweet potato skins. In amongst an organic skincare workshop and a core workout class, there'd been the details for a fascial release session with a world-renowned expert.

'I can't believe it!' said Emma. 'This is what I was telling you about – the thing Denise at work did! After her divorce!'

Nadia peered over at where she was pointing. The leaflet said,

> *Myofascial Release is a safe and effective hands-on technique that involves applying gentle sustained pressure into the Myofascial connective tissue restrictions to eliminate both physical and emotional pain and restore motion. Taught by Ivanka Nilsson.*

'I'm still not sure about this . . .' Nadia said. 'But. Okay. Fine. Let's do it.'

The pair signalled for Emma's membership card back and she signed for the food, allowing it to be charged to their room, and in their Lycra leggings and Nike trainers – the uniform of any exercise class – headed to the gym.

For the first twenty-five minutes of the hour-long class, Nadia was almost hysterical in her laughter. What they were doing was ridiculous to her. Ivanka Nilsson turned out to be a six-foot-something blonde Swede who had the air of a shot-putter about her, and there were only five people in the class. Her English was flawless, but retained an authoritarian air to it – Nadia often found that about native Nordic speakers: their directness came across in the way they intoned their English. She was slightly afraid to be caught laughing, like she'd be told off. It was made worse by the fact that Emma was totally into it and was mostly listening to the instructions with her eyes closed ('Intuitive release,' Ivanka called it), so Nadia felt even more adrift and silly. Basically, the whole point was to find where it hurt to roll your body on a tennis ball, and then gently move back and forth so that whilst yes, it was painful, ultimately (or so said Ivanka), it would eventually cease to hurt.

Well yes, thought Nadia, *because I've gone bloody numb.*

'There are two ways to treat malaise,' Ivanka said, walking between the five mats in bare feet, heel-toe, heel-toe, heel-toe. 'Our emotional trauma is stored in the fibres of our body, in between our muscles. Our bodies hold on to sadness, and grief, and it causes physical pain. Sometimes, we bury these emotions so deeply that symptoms do not demonstrate themselves for many, many years. But they are there. And so, by rubbing deeply into this fascia using a simple tennis ball, we access these hidden emotions, and we release them.'

Nadia looked over at Emma again, hoping to roll her eyes in united sympathy. Emma was lying on her back with the tennis ball just above her right bum cheek, making small circular movements so that her body rotated over the ball. Her eyes were closed, and to Nadia, at this angle, it looked like . . . she was crying?

'I repeat,' Ivanka said, most likely in response to Nadia's insistence at peeking at everyone else. 'This is more beneficial to you with your eyes closed, so that you may enter communion with your body. Listen to what it is telling you. Listen to the stories it has buried. It wants you to know them. To find them. Seeking out the dark parts of your story allows you to shed light on them, and in shedding light you will cease to be afraid.' *Heel-toe, heel-toe, heel-toe.*

Nadia tried the tennis ball under her bum like Emma had

it. Nothing. She moved it to the left and tried it there. Nothing there, really, either. A sort of weird digging sensation, maybe, where the surface of the ball dug into her skin, but it didn't feel like a *release*.

She moved the ball up a bit so it was in the middle of her back. Nadia moved her feet up so her soles were flat on the floor, knees bent, and used the leverage to move her body up and down on the yoga mat. The ball slipped further up, to near her shoulder blade and behind her heart. There. There Nadia felt a hot, pulsating sort of pain, that if she had to identify out loud she'd only be able to locate as right in the middle of her body. She kept her eyes clamped tightly shut as the ball moved back and forth, back and forth, digging deeper and deeper and deeper. She altered the motion so that instead of up and down she went around and around, the heat rising and rising, and Nadia saw in her mind an amalgamation of every time a man had dented her heart.

She thought about Awful Ben, and her school sweetheart, and the guy in her uni halls who had slept with her and then ignored her. She thought of all the nights – endless nights, it seemed – that she had stayed home alone, her phone by her side, waiting for a text message from a member of the opposite sex to validate her, to validate her existence. She thought about her grandfather's affair and how he'd left her grandmother for their neighbour, and she thought about how much she wanted to love and be loved in return. That her appetite for it might consume her whole, because for all the pep talks she gave herself there was something, buried very, very deep, that told her that maybe she wasn't worthy of it.

'Good,' said Ivanka now, kneeling down beside Nadia. She

felt the woman's hand on her shoulder. Nadia's face was wet through with tears. 'This is fascial release.'

Winding through the tight back lanes that would eventually give out to an A road and then the motorway, the women drove home in companionable silence. Nadia reflected on the lightness she felt after the fascia class – like her shoulders were no longer bunched up in stress around her ears and her breath shallow, like she couldn't quite steady herself. Her whole body had been tense since Thursday night – maybe longer. Nadia hadn't realized how she'd carried anxiety in her jaw, tension in her arms. How had a tennis ball relieved her of all that? It was a miracle. She came out knowing that she had to take her life in her own hands, that she had to take charge of her own romantic destiny. Emma absentmindedly sang along to a Spotify playlist she'd made of all her favourite love songs, and Nadia noted that she seemed happier now too.

Nadia typed in the URL for *Missed Connections* on her phone and stared at the submissions box. She took a breath. *Take charge of yourself*, she repeated in her mind. She typed:

Train Guy: You, me, coffee on the platform at 7.30 a.m., Thursday? Love, Coffee Spill Girl (though I promise not to spill any on you)

She read it, and reread it, wondering if it was too to-the-point, and if they were supposed to write back to each other a little bit more first. But, surely not. Surely the whole point of *Missed Connections* was to get a date in the diary and not miss what otherwise wouldn't have happened. They'd established a rapport and she'd enjoyed that, and maybe before this morning she would have gone back-and-forth a little more. But now she'd decided: she desperately wanted to meet him, because she understood how she was a woman worth meeting.

Yes, Nadia decided. *I am going to be a modern, go-getting woman and get this off the page and into real life. I am ready for my future.*

And with that, she hit 'send'.

'Did you get that feeling too?' Emma asked her, a little time later. 'That you were having some big amazing release?'

'Yeah, it was so strange. Like, she was right! There was something hidden in there, and I got it!'

'Me too,' said Emma.

'Mine was in my heart, if you can believe that,' said Nadia.

Emma smiled. 'I can.'

Nadia smiled too. She could as well. 'Where was yours?'

'A bit all over, actually,' said Emma. 'Mostly around my pelvis though.'

'Ooooh, how telling!' said Nadia, about to make a joke about her sex life that was rudely interrupted by the ringing of a phone. It wasn't Nadia's ringtone. It was Emma's. Emma's hand jutted out, off the wheel to where it sat below the radio, just as Nadia's did.

'I'll get it!' Nadia trilled, since Emma was driving, and she went to pick it up just as Emma said, 'No!'

Emma clawed at Nadia's hand so that Nadia ended up holding one end of the phone and Emma the other. Startled, Nadia looked at her friend, and Emma turned her head away from the road and looked at Nadia, and Nadia didn't understand. In shock, she dropped the phone, registering the panic on Emma's face, who suddenly let go too, just as something happened outside of the car, beyond the windscreen.

Nadia followed Emma's gaze, and it all happened so fast, so quickly, but so slowly at the same time. No reactions were fast enough. There were people in the road – men. A group of men in the road. The car brakes screeched and the car jerkily slowed down.

No, no, no, no, no, no, no, Nadia silently prayed. Or did she say it out loud?

Both women screamed as the group in the road turned their heads and registered the car, dividing themselves by either propelling forward or pulling back. The car came in at a halt, stopping inches from where the crowd had just been. There was silence. Shock. Nadia turned to Emma, who still had both hands on the steering wheel, her arms fixed straight in front of her, panting.

'Ohmygod,' she said.

'You're okay,' Nadia said, unclipping her seatbelt. 'Emma – you're okay! Fuck.' She went into organization mode. Rolling down the window, she said to the group to her left, 'Are you okay? We're so sorry!'

'Fucking sorry?' said one, in a Barbour jacket and wellies. 'You almost bloody killed us! Jesus.'

Nadia turned to Emma. Her face was deathly white. 'They're okay, babe. Can you hear me? They're okay.' She lifted the handbrake and put on the emergency hazards. 'Emma?'

Emma turned to her. 'That was . . . horrible!' she said, promptly bursting into tears.

'Oh babe, get out. Come on. Let me drive. We need to get out of the road. Go on.'

The women clambered out of the car, where thankfully the group they'd nearly hit had already headed off into a nearby field. They were mad. Really, really mad – but at least that was better than being hurt. One of them turned around and shook

148

his head, but Nadia was relieved that they all kept walking. She climbed into the driver's seat and drove them to a nearby pub car park.

'Bugger me, that was close,' she said, closing her eyes to finally catch a breath.

'Yeah,' said Emma. 'That was . . . yeah.'

Nadia switched off the engine and pressed her forehead to the wheel. It was no good thinking about what *could* have happened, but it was hard not to.

'What happened?' Nadia said, eventually.

'I just took my eyes off the road for like, a second,' said Emma. 'That's it. I just panicked.'

Nadia shook her head and then turned so she could see her friend. 'But why? I went to answer your phone and you freaked out. Why would that freak you out?'

'I didn't know who it was,' said Emma, as if that explained it.

'I really need you to talk to me,' Nadia implored. 'I need you to tell me what's going on. Emma!'

Emma stared blankly ahead and shook her head. 'No,' she said. 'Just drive.'

They didn't speak another word until they'd got back to London.

'I'll text you later this week,' Emma said, as a goodbye.

'Okay,' Nadia nodded, sadly. 'I'm here, you know. When you're ready.' She didn't know what else to say. She'd never seen her like this before.

18

Daniel

'Fuck me!' one of the lads said. 'Watch out!' Daniel was vaguely aware of a giant shove into the middle of his back, forcing him to stumble up the grassy verge at the other side of the road. Before he could turn around and see who it was, he heard an almighty screech – the sound of car brakes – and whipped his head around just in time to see Sam fling an arm out in front of Terrence, who had been about to cross the road behind him.

A cream Mini skidded, swerving slightly, and stopped exactly where Terrence had been about to walk. Dean and Jonny, who had already climbed over the fence to the field that would loop them back around to the pub, shouted out, 'What happened?'

Daniel motioned for them to come over without turning around. He couldn't take his eyes off what had just happened.

'. . . Nearly bloody killed us!' he heard Terrence say, foaming at the mouth in anger. Nobody was hurt, thankfully, but he could see the driver still gripping the steering wheel, knuckles white and deathly pale. She looked like she might throw up.

'Are you all right?' Daniel called, meaning both Terrence and the driver.

Terrence dragged his attention away from yelling at the passenger of the car through the car window and looked at him.

'Yes, mate,' he said. And then, directing his fury back at the car, 'No thanks to this BLOODY LUNATIC!' He hit the bonnet with the flat of his palm and he crossed in front of it, startling the driver, who seemed to burst into tears.

Daniel looked back to where the car had come from – to be fair, they had all crossed over just after a blind bend. Daniel didn't think it wise to bait Terrence in any way, though, so didn't mention it. It was just lucky everyone was okay. He tried to catch the eye of the driver to share a sympathetic smile, ducking at the knees slightly to get a better look. *She needs to get out of the way*, he thought, and watched as the hazard lights came on, blinking in the early afternoon light. It looked like whoever was with her knew what to do. *They'll be okay*, he thought. He turned around to climb over the fence where the rest of the guys were.

'I'm bloody shaking!' Terrence was saying, and Daniel saw Sam turn around and give the car the finger as its engine roared into life again. It drove slowly away. For a second Daniel thought it was Nadia driving. He shook himself out of the thought. *You're obsessed*, he told himself.

'Talk about earning that beer,' Daniel said, forcing himself to get the energy of the group back. He grabbed Sam's shoulder and steered him in the direction of the pub. 'Jesus.'

'First round is on you, mate,' Sam said. 'That was nearly the end of us!'

'You know what?' Daniel replied. 'I'm feeling generous. First round is absolutely on me.'

19

Nadia

On Monday, Nadia started again with The New Routine to Change Her Life. She spent Sunday evening doing what she thought of as a 'Big Shower'. A small shower is like what her mother would ashamedly call a sailor's clean – a quick splash of warm water upstairs and down, and on occasion a hair wash. A Big Shower is dry body brushing and a teeth-whitening sheet, a deep cleanse and exfoliation and double shampoo and hair mask. A Big Shower is shaved legs and armpits, a body oil on damp skin, followed by separate face masks for the T-zone and chin area, collagen under-eye mask, and actually using a hairdryer to keep the frizz at bay for the morning. By the time Nadia had soaked off the masks, used a midnight oil, hyaluronic cream, moisturizer, exfoliated her lips and dabbed under-eye cream on with the third finger of her right hand, like she'd seen on YouTube (apparently that finger has the most nerve endings, so applies the least amount of pressure), she was so exhausted that it wasn't a problem to be asleep by

10 p.m. She woke up before her alarm, the summer sun bright through the gap in the curtains, and was up, dressed, and out of the flat by 6.45 a.m.

She sat on the 73 bus to Angel, firing off a text to check on Emma, and it occurred to her that she'd be earlier than her normal 7.30 train, and it was the 7.30 train she needed to be on if she wanted to see Train Guy. She had twenty minutes to kill.

Coffee, she decided. *I'll go get coffee.*

By the station there was a small cart – a sort of van that doubled up as a coffee station once the back doors were opened and revealed an espresso machine and milk frother. The owner, a squat man with no hair who had a friendly smile and called everybody 'love', had a few short stools and tables out, so Nadia took a seat and put on her sunglasses and enjoyed feeling, if only briefly, like she was in the piazza of a European capital instead of a roadside overlooking what was technically the A1.

She had a sudden pang for her mother in that moment – the last time she'd seen her was on a girls' trip to Rome they'd had over Easter weekend. Nadia plugged her headphones into her iPhone and hit the icon to call her.

'Well, look who it is!' her mother laughed down the line, after only two rings.

'I know, I know,' Nadia said. 'I'm a disappointment of a daughter who doesn't call enough.'

'You are darling, yes. But as long as you're busy having fun instead of calling, your old mum doesn't mind.'

Nadia smiled. She loved how kind and forgiving her mother was, and how she accepted others exactly as they were. 'I am, Mum. I just got back from a weekend at Soho Farmhouse with Emma, and I've got a good feeling about this week. How are you?'

Nadia and her mum chatted about the dog, and Nadia's work, and, bizarrely, considering it was not even August, what their Christmas plans might be, when suddenly Nadia realized the time. She hit the screen of her phone. It was exactly 7.30. She'd missed her train.

'Darling?' her mother said. 'Are you still there?'

'Yes, Mum,' Nadia said, 'I'm still here. I . . . I didn't realize the time.' She hung up not long after and slowly made her way to the station.

Dammit! She chastised herself. *Goddammit!*

Tomorrow, she promised herself. *I'm going to bloody well make that train tomorrow. Train Guy will just have to wait.*

She idly picked up a discarded newspaper on the platform and checked the paper to see if her advert had run, and to her surprise – wasn't it only twenty-four hours ago she'd sent her submission in? – it had. It calmed her nerves. She didn't have to be on time tomorrow, or even the day after – as long as she made it to the platform for 7.30 on Thursday, she'd be fine.

If he turned up, of course.

It was Gaby who texted her a photo of *Missed Connections* the next day, where Train Guy had written back. Nadia didn't understand – her adverts before were taking at least a few days to get published. She wondered if there was somebody on the news desk of the paper giving them a helping hand to write to each other faster. The notes were becoming daily, now.

His letter said:

Morning coffee? How about evening drinks? I once over-heard you talking about your work, with a colleague, and

*you, Devastatingly Cute Blonde, are really smart. And
your messages back to me make you smart, and a flirt.
We could have some fun together, not to mention good
chat. What do you think? If I say 7 p.m. on Thursday, at
the bar opposite where you got your charity investment,
will you say yes? I think this is our stop.*

Yes! thought Nadia. *Yes, Yes, Yes!* She bobbed up and down
on the spot, her whole body shaking with excitement. *I'm
going to meet him!* she thought, *I am actually going to bloody
well bloody meet him!* She knew it. She'd known all along this
is where it was heading, even when she hadn't wanted to
admit it. She was about to meet a funny, charming, romantic
man who had already done all the right things and in the
space that she had only just cleared in her heart she felt it:
it was going to be brilliant. She pulled up the submission
box for *Missed Connections* as soon as she had Wi-Fi signal
on her phone, and sent back:

*Train Guy: You're on. 7 p.m., Thursday. I think I know
where you mean. And, for what it's worth, I'm excited.
See you then, Train Girl.*

20

Nadia

'The only thing I can think,' Nadia said, pouring the bottle of Albariño into the three glasses evenly, 'is that he means The Old Barn Cat. The day I convinced Jared to believe in my non-profit idea, we went to the courtyard there. I just . . . I don't understand how this guy knows about it?'

'Unless the guy . . . is Jared!' said Gaby, holding up a glass to signal that they should cheers.

Nadia was horrified. 'Don't say that! No!' Gaby knew Jared because she often worked closely with the board of directors at work. Even joking about a man like him was a step too far. 'Jared genuinely had tickets to Fyre Festival. Absolutely not.'

Gaby snorted. 'I can believe that,' she said, sadly.

'Gang! Hello? We're celebrating?' Emma lifted her glass to knock it lightly against Gaby's. 'Here's to love, lust and romance,' she said.

'To love, lust and romance,' said Gaby, coyly.

Nadia scowled. 'You two are laughing at me! Don't laugh at me.' She took a huge gulp from her glass, refusing to join them in a cheers. Was it just her, or were they mocking her slightly?

Gaby looked away and directly to Nadia. 'Oh no, sweetie. No, no, no. No we're not. We're—'

No. They weren't mocking her.

Nadia sighed. 'Oh stop it,' she cut Gaby off. 'I'd be laughing too. It's all so ridiculous.' She was actually in a playful mood tonight, daring to get excited about her forthcoming date. She couldn't help but think that everything she'd been through, everything she'd endured and every doubt she'd ever tortured herself with, it was all in service of this. *Of course* it had never worked out with anybody else, because she was always supposed to meet *this guy*. Right? That was how it worked, wasn't it? That's what all the couples she knew said – that in the end, the path was always leading to the one they ended up with. Katherine had once said, 'You only have to get it right once, Nadia,' and Nadia understood that now. There was no such thing as a past relationship failing when relationship success was still to play for. When the right man came along, nothing about her past could be a failure. It was all working towards the one big success that would matter. Nadia didn't believe in soulmates so much as she believed that some people were simply worth making the effort for, and it was about finding the one willing to work as hard as she would to have something special. That one (or one in fifty, if Emma's maths was to be believed) who truly wanted an equal – that's what excited Nadia. From everything Train Guy had said – that she was clever and funny and that they'd have good chat together – Nadia could just *tell* that he had his head screwed on. That he was clever and funny too. And most of all, kind.

Emma took big gulps of her wine, almost polishing the glass off in one inhale. 'It's lovely,' she said, setting down her glass and already looking for their waiter to order more. 'All totally lovely.'

'And just a bit scary,' supplied Gaby. This was the version of Gaby that Nadia knew best: the slightly cynical, romantically careful one.

'Well, if I meet him at seven, I'll expect your phone call at . . . seven fifteen?'

'When there will be a horrible emergency.'

'And I'll have to come right away.'

'You'll be *terribly* sorry.'

'Devastated!'

'And scarper so quick that you'll forget to leave a number.'

The three of them laughed, articulating a blind date plan they'd all had for years now. In theory, it was easy enough to realize it wasn't going to work with somebody almost right away, but amongst them only Emma would really announce, fifteen minutes into a date, that it wasn't going to work and so they had better call it a night already. As a dating columnist she'd had a lot of practice, Nadia supposed, and when she dated like it was her job – because for a while it had actually *been* her job – it was easier to be businesslike about the whole thing. Meanwhile, Nadia had spent evening upon evening trying not to hurt the man across from her's feelings, willing herself to find the thing they were compatible on, or in agreement about. That was the downside to being a romantic: by being so committed to seeing the best in her dates she'd had several that should never have happened at all.

Emma widened her eyes. 'Oh my gosh – are you going to tell him your real name?'

'Why . . . wouldn't I?'

'I don't know. Safety? You don't want him knowing who you really are, do you?'

Nadia thought about it. 'That doesn't seem like the best start to a relationship,' she said. 'I don't think there's any harm in telling him my name is Nadia. Right?' She looked to Gaby for reassurance.

'No,' Gaby said. 'But also, listen: I still resolutely believe that you should meet Sky Garden Guy. I promise you – he is your man. I know Train Guy is witty and fun and whatever, but Sky Garden Guy is all of those things too.'

'Well, if Train Guy is a dud, yes, I accept your offer. That's even if he'd still like to meet after I stood him up.'

'I'm sure he would,' Gaby said.

'What are you going to wear?' Emma asked.

Nadia thought about it. 'I know this sounds weird,' she said, 'but I feel like I want to look as close as I do for work as possible. Like, that's how he knows me. If I turned up in platforms and sequins with a full face of make-up, I'd be mortified if he didn't recognize me!'

'Oh my god,' Emma said, 'I didn't think of that – he knows what you look like, but you have no idea what he looks like . . .'

Nadia nodded. 'I know. Every morning I get on that train and I think, "Is it you? Is it you? Or you?" And honestly, he could be any of them. But that's part of the excitement. And, you know. How bad could he end up being?'

Gaby shuddered. 'That would give me the creeps, knowing that I'm being watched.'

Emma hit her shoulder. 'She isn't being *watched*! Don't say that! Some commuter has noticed her a few times and thought she was cute. That's all.'

'Devastatingly cute,' interjected Nadia.

'Devastatingly cute. Fine. It's not like he's following her to work or back home and spying at her from the bushes.'

Nadia's eyes widened. 'Oh my god – do we think that could happen?'

Gaby gave a pointed silence.

'Absolutely not,' said Emma, shooting her daggers. 'And look. You are so smart, and so aware. You can get a read on people's energy like that.' She clicked her fingers as she said 'that'. 'And we'll call you so you have an out if you need it, which you won't, but if you do, then . . . well. You can leave and then move house and jobs and start wearing a wig and you'll never have to see him again!'

Gaby laughed in spite of herself, and the waiter came over with more wine. He asked if he could get them anything else.

'Yes,' Nadia said. 'Some new best friends, please.'

The waiter smiled and walked away.

'You're going to be fine,' Emma said. 'Isn't she, Gaby?'

Gaby smiled, not quite enthusiastically. 'Sure you are,' she said. 'And if you're not, I'm at the MoD on Friday. I can arrange to have him killed.'

Emma poured more wine into their glasses, even though she was the only one who had emptied hers. The three of them cheersed again.

At home, Nadia sat down with a blank piece of paper, a pen, and another glass of wine. At the top of the paper she wrote 'Pros and Cons'. On the left side, she wrote, 'Everything That Could Go Wrong If I Meet The Guy From Missed

Connections'. Under it, she put:

- Potentially all a big catfish.

- Potentially he thinks he is writing to somebody who Is Not Me, and will be totally devastated and insulted when I turn up, and won't be able to hide the look of disappointment on his face. Will be like when food comes out of the kitchen at a restaurant and you're starving and you think the waiter is coming over to you and so you sit up straighter and bite your bottom lip in anticipation, but then it goes to the table next to you and you look like an arse.

- I will think we are getting on, and when I go to the bathroom he will pull out his phone and play on Tinder and I will see over his shoulder when I come back and be too polite to say anything. (Thus wasting a further two and a half hours of my life when I could be at boxercise, or with Emma – who says she is much better, but I am still worried about her.)

- My picture will end up in the paper, because I will go missing on the way home from the date, and he will be the prime suspect. Picture will be from my twenty-eighth birthday when I tried to save money beforehand by waxing my own eyebrows and had to draw them back on, and everyone will think any woman who looks as mad as I do probably brought it all on herself.

- I will find him dizzyingly charming and the chemistry will be undeniable and I will go home with him and

164

won't realize he's put Rohypnol in my drink and I wake up to see he has covered the whole bedroom in cling film and has a very sharp knife and I only just manage to escape before he starts carving me up into pieces to fry up and eat for breakfast each morning.

- I actually won't wake up from the Rohypnol and so will get carved up and nobody will ever find me and my mum will be really upset and won't know I'm dead – she'll just think I'm being selfish and have skipped the country for a laugh.

- He won't show up after all, and I'll have write to the newspaper to shout at him. (NB if I do that, I will do it very calmly and sensibly, in the manner of that nineteen-year-old on *The Lust Villa* who got dumped and gave a very rousing speech about loyalty, and not like when Sharon Osbourne stormed off *The X Factor* that time, ripping off her fake eyelashes and screaming at everyone uncontrollably.)

In the other column, she wrote: 'Things That Could Go Right If I Meet The Guy From Missed Connections'. Underneath it she wrote:

- I could meet the love of my life.

21

Daniel

Daniel paced up and down outside the bar, mentally talking himself through what was about to happen. *Come on*, he told himself. *This is no big deal. It's just a date.*

He forced himself to breathe in and out through his nose, doing the 'victorious breath' his mum had learnt at the one yoga class she'd ever done, twenty-five years ago. It was a loud and deliberate noise, like trying to steam up a mirror but with the mouth closed. The one and only thing she'd learned that day was that if you can control your breath, you can control anything. It had been the soundtrack to his teenage years, that saying, even though a nasty flatulence incident had meant she'd never done yoga again. ('It was your dad's braised bloody cabbage that did it – I made the loudest chuffing noise as I went into a forward fold! I can control my breath, Daniel – but I dare anybody to retain full sphincter control after his buttered bok choy!') For every knee scrape and heartache and exam stress, it always came back to: *If you can control your breath, you can control anything. Breathe, Daniel.*

Daniel laughed to himself at the thought that he could control any of what was about to happen, causing two men walking by to look up in alarm and scurry past him with their eyebrows raised, as if extreme romantic nervousness was catching.

I mean, potentially this is the last first date you'll go on in your whole life, he thought to himself, *and the last first kiss you'll ever have. Not that a first kiss is a given, but, you know, if everything goes well. Which it will, as long as you're not too over-eager. Like you are now, being fifteen minutes early, and giving yourself a pep talk instead of going in, getting a seat at the bar, and ordering a drink so she finds you already doing something instead of waiting to pounce like the title character in* Crouching Tiger, Hidden Dragon.

Daniel remembered his breathing. His dad would tell him to get a drink in him to calm down. He tried to reason with himself.

Go in. You'll be fine. Eat a Tic Tac and breathe deep. If you can control your breath – your breathing and being minty fresh – you can control anything. Go on.

Daniel took two big gulps of the summer air, July now giving way to August, London thick with syrupy heat, and pushed through the door of the bar. It was already half full with office workers out with their colleagues, what with Thursday being the new Friday. He caught sight of himself in the mirror as he grabbed a seat, and had his first kind thought about himself all afternoon. *You look all right,* he told himself, with his undone dress shirt rolled up to his sleeves, the way the fabric fell across his shoulders. He'd lost weight since his dad had died – probably he wasn't eating enough. It was hard to keep track of food when the world was ending. But Daniel's jaw looked sharp in his reflection and he thought for a minute how he seemed a bit rock 'n' roll. Grief and hope looked good on him. It was a small, silly comfort.

The barman made eye contact to let Daniel know he'd be next, and Daniel panicked about what to order. Did a pint make him seem too predictably blokey? A glass of white wine a bit too Stanley Tucci? If he ordered a bottle he worried he might as well say, 'I'm trying to get you drunk so I can shag you,' which was absolutely not the case.

Oh god – they weren't going to shag, were they? He hoped not.

Well. He wanted to, eventually, of course, not only because it had been a while since he'd dipped his brush in somebody else's paint pot, so to speak, but also because Nadia was beauty and grace personified so who wouldn't want to shag her – or, make love to, maybe. Was that too Mr Darcy, too inhibited? Oh god, why were dating and sex and love and romance so full of booby traps? Women got all the airtime when it came to hang-ups about sex, but Daniel knew it wasn't just him who got a bit out of sorts at the thought of doing it with somebody you liked. Insecurity wasn't the reserve of females. It was the reserve of humans, full stop.

The drink, Daniel, just pick a drink.

He knew a lot of his mates' wives went in for rosé or something bubbly when it was warm out, and he'd read in the Sunday supplements that cava was the new prosecco, since it was drier and naturally carbonated and actually a lot closer to champagne, but if she didn't know that and he was drinking cava he'd seem cheap, because historically everyone thought cava was cheap. The barman finished serving the guy at the other end and made his way over and Daniel could see him coming and oh god – what should he get? Fuck. He would have . . .

'A small glass of white, please. Anything. You choose.' He reached for his wallet and located his bank card. Handing it over, the tiniest visible shake to his hand, he added, 'And a shot of tequila too. I'll start a tab.'

22

Nadia

She floated through the corridor and down in the lift. This was it. The Date. Nadia hadn't been so convinced that her life was about to change since, well . . . since the morning she had declared The New Routine to Change Her Life, which was the morning she'd first seen his *Missed Connection*. If she really reached for it, Nadia could almost believe she had pulled this man into her life by sheer force of will.

She felt like anything was possible. After all of those stories she'd fed Emma for the column, and all the coffee breaks she'd had with Gaby the morning after the night before, wondering if it was she who was the problem, not the men she was dating, Nadia relished the double-time beat of her heart and the somersaults going on in her tummy. *This* was what life was about: getting excited and being deliberate with her fate and seizing chances when they presented themselves. *Put yourself in the way of beauty*, she'd read in a Cheryl Strayed book. That's exactly what she was doing. Daring to hope for her romantic future made her Superwoman, she thought. Turning up for a date with genuine excitement after everything – after Awful Ben – made her a bona fide hero. The hero of her own life.

'Look at you!' Gaby yelled, from across the lobby.

Nadia grinned, doing a little spin as she approached.

'What do you think?' she said. She was wearing a loose navy-blue Cos dress with flat navy sandals, and carried a navy-blue leather bag. With her blonde hair and a touch of red lipstick, not to mention the slight bronze the summer had given her, she looked like her most radiant self.

'You're beautiful, Nadia. Truly beautiful.'

Nadia took a big breath. 'Thank you,' she said. 'That was the exact right thing to say.' She pulled out her phone and looked at the time. 'Okay. I can't stay and chat. Destiny awaits! But – call me fifteen minutes in?'

'Yes ma'am. I've got you.'

'Okay. And, could you, like, wish me luck?'

Gaby smiled warmly. 'Nadia: go get 'em.' She winked.

Nadia headed for the bar with the confidence of Blue Ivy. She had a feeling she wouldn't be needing Gaby's call.

23

Daniel

Daniel had only just unlocked the screen to his phone when his mother's face flashed up, alerting him to the fact that she was ringing. It was the photo he'd taken of her at her sixtieth birthday that he'd set as her avatar in his phone, a gin in one hand and a half-smoked Marlboro Light in the other. Daniel had never known his mother had smoked until that night. She had told him sixty was the year she 'stopped giving so many shits, like Helen Mirren said', and that included hiding her four-a-day habit from her grown son. 'Life's too short!' she'd hooted, before they both knew just how short. Daniel had thought it was hilarious. 'All power to you, Mum!' he'd said, laughing, his dad simply shrugging as if to say, 'What can you do?'

Daniel stared. He wouldn't normally cancel her call but this was about to be the first moment of the rest of his life. He couldn't talk to her now. He didn't want to be on the phone as his future began. He deliberated for half a second before hitting the red cross, watching her face disappear. He waited for his drinks and, staring anxiously at the open door, waited for his date too. She'd be here any minute now. Any minute.

24

Nadia

Nadia took the back way to the courtyard, so she wouldn't have to battle with an army of commuters heading home, or walk past the massive pub on the corner that would no doubt be heaving at this time, the weather being what it was – London came alive in the summer that way, at the first hint of sunshine it was after-work drinks and walks along the South Bank – and if she crossed the road before the corner and took the first right, she'd be able to loop through the cobbled passage that would bring her out right opposite The Old Barn Cat without having to use her elbows to fight through throngs of half-drunk people. Not that she'd mind that. Everything looked beautiful to her. The sun was low and warm and she hummed lightly to herself as she ducked out of the crowds and through to the alleyway. She stopped just before the corner to pull out her compact and check her lipstick. *Perfect enough*, she thought to herself happily, *but I'll just add a little more.*

25

Daniel

'Hiya Mum, what's up? I'm a bit tied up at the moment.' She'd called Daniel again, not seconds after he'd rejected her first call. Daniel couldn't evade her twice. It wasn't like her not to take the hint. His instinct told him to pick up.

'Danny boy, darling – it's me, it's Mum.'

Daniel crumpled his brow. Obviously he knew it was his mum. 'Yes, Mum, I know. Of course I know it's you.' She sounded upset. 'Are you crying, Mum? Mum, what happened?' He presumed she'd got stuck trying to reverse the car out of the driveway again, or didn't know how to get the Apple TV on. There was a lot she'd had to learn about living alone, and much of it frustrated her.

The barman put a glass down in front of him – not one of those small wine glasses the French use, or worse, a tumbler like in some of the hipster places in Hackney. It was a tall, elegant, white wine glass, with thick globs of condensation already forming around the base. Beside it, a small shot glass of yellow tequila. Daniel reached for it, throwing it down his neck before he could question himself, letting the thick liquid burn at the back of his throat and warm his chest as it went down. That was better. It took the edge off almost immediately.

'Daniel,' his mother said. 'I . . . I don't know what's wrong. I can't stop.'

Daniel took the wine glass between his fingers and held it.

'Can't stop what, Mum?' He didn't understand, yet, just how badly she needed him. He still thought her call was an inconvenience. His tone was sharp, frustrated. He really didn't want to be on the phone when Nadia arrived. *I should never have picked up*, he thought. *Surely she's fine. She's always fine.*

'Cr-cr—,' the line broke quiet for a minute. In a very measured voice that sounded as if his mother was using every ounce of willpower in her body, she continued. 'Crying. Daniel, I cannot stop . . . crying. I don't think I am okay.'

She said it so matter-of-fact, and suddenly so stoically, that the irony of what she was saying and how she said it broke Daniel's heart clean in two. He understood, implicitly, that the façade of being strong had finally cracked. His therapist had said it would. In a way, he was relieved.

'It's okay, Mum. You can cry. I'm here for you. I love you.'

On the other end of the line his mother broke down into big, guttural sobs, and for a horrible minute Daniel couldn't do anything but listen. He was impotent. She cried, and she cried, and she cried, barely forming words, let alone coherent sentences. He stared at the cold glass of wine in his hand. He looked up to the door. He listened to his mother cry. Slowly he pinched the bridge of his nose, his brain whirring, his shoulders tensing. He didn't want to leave. He at least wanted to wait for Nadia to arrive, to tell her he had to go.

'I can't . . .' his mum said down the phone. 'What's the point without him, darling? I miss him. I miss him so, so much.'

It struck Daniel that it hadn't been easy for his mother to ask for help. She had cried in the days after his father's death, and on the day of the funeral, and then just . . . stopped. Held herself together. And for months Daniel had waited for her to crack – god knows, he had. That's why he was in therapy. But his mother never had. She had been almost dogged in her determination to push forward with her life, and Daniel knew that if her crash down to earth was anything like his had been, there was no way she could be alone tonight. She had been strong for him, when he had needed it. He knew that now it was his turn to be strong for her.

Daniel found himself saying, 'I'm coming, Mum, okay? I'll be half an hour. I'm coming. You are not alone. Do you hear me?'

'Okay. Yes.' And then, bursting into tears once more, 'Thank you.' Her words were barely audible.

Daniel leaped off the bar stool and looked around, willing – hoping – that Nadia would appear at the door before he had to go. It shattered his soul to think he'd have to leave before she got there, but it broke his heart even more to leave his mother for even one second longer than he had to. She'd never told him she needed him, but she was telling him now. And if he had to choose between Nadia and his mother. Well. He just had to trust that Nadia would understand. That she wouldn't have it any differently.

'You all right, mate?' the barman asked.

Daniel turned and looked at him.

'No. No, I'm really not.' He had to think fast. 'Listen. Can you do me a favour? I'm about to meet a girl. A woman.'

Daniel didn't know where it came from, this sudden burst of verbose passion, but he continued: 'The most exquisite, beautiful, devastatingly charming and kind and . . . fit woman. God, she's fit. And clever. But I've got to go. She's got blonde hair, to here –' Daniel held up a hand to his shoulder, his words tumbling out over each other to this man, this stranger, who admirably took Daniel's eruption of lust in his stride '– and she sort of pouts, like she's just discovered a new thought. And, and . . . she'll come in, and she'll be on her own, and can you ask her if her name is Nadia and if she says yes, tell her I'm sorry to miss her tonight, but I'll find her. I'll find her on the train tomorrow and I'll explain. Can you tell her that?'

The barman nodded. 'Sure thing,' he said, coolly. 'Nadia. Got it.'

'Thank you. Thank you!'

And with that, Daniel left, not knowing that if he'd waited even just ninety seconds more, he could have told her himself.

26

Nadia

Nadia took a seat at the bar, pushing a full glass of white wine to one side – it didn't look like it belonged to anybody, weirdly – and put down her bag. She caught her own eye in the mirror behind the bottles. She'd had a blow-dry at lunch-time so her somewhat frizzy blonde bob was a smoother, wavier blonde bob, and the Ruby MAC lipstick she'd chosen lifted her face. She looked like the best version of herself. She didn't want to toot her own horn but the possibility of unfolding romance made her face look brighter, somehow. She pulled her phone from her bag, hooked the bag under the bar so it was out of the way but constantly pressed against her knees so it couldn't get nicked, and surveyed the place.

There were people spilling out onto the pavement, people having drinks with colleagues after work, and one or two couples spread around inside, quite obviously on dates. Nadia couldn't see any men alone, lingering outside or sat off in a corner. She didn't know what Daniel looked like, so she had no choice but to sit and wait for him to approach. Nobody was behind the bar, and so she picked up her phone – it was only supposed to be on hand for an absolute emergency – and unlocked it whilst she waited. It was weird how sure she could be that this was it, this was the moment love would envelop her, whilst also needing to know that there was a Plan B. It was a push-pull of both believing and self-preservation. She'd read a quote on Pinterest that said, YOU ARE NOT ALLOWED TO BE A COWARD AND IN LOVE; YOU MUST CHOOSE ONE. The writer of that must have never been on a blind date, Nadia thought, knowing that the best part of having a Plan B was assuring yourself you'd never need it.

She opened up Twitter, half thinking she'd read the news so that if conversation lulled she'd have something to say about Syria or *The Lust Villa*, and waited for the barman to come and take her order. Every time she sensed somebody walk through the door she looked up. Not him. That wasn't him either. Humph.

She had a text from Emma that said, *Have you seen this?!* It was a link to Twitter. Nadia looked up again, just in case he'd come in, and then pressed the URL. It was a link to a hashtag, #OurStop

i'm so invested in the #OurStop couple. what a romantic way to meet somebody! said @EmmaEmma

and

anyone else think it's creepy that this guy has been eyeing her up and she's got no idea who he is? #OurStop from @girlstolevintage

and

I can't even get a man to text me back, and here are the #OurStop couple leaving love notes in the newspaper for each

other like an Austen romance, if Jane had Twitter said
@notyourgirl

Nadia scrolled, marvelling at what she was seeing. People
were following her story. Their story! And had opinions! And
a hashtag! #OURSTOP!

That was so bizarre to her – although, she thought, if she
herself wasn't the subject of the exchange she'd definitely be
texting Emma about it. This was London at its best: the
London where everyone was in on the same thing, the same
joke or movement or idea. She supposed that's why *Missed
Connections* worked in the first place: it wasn't just about
two people seeking each other out. It was about how we all
search for love, whether we admit it or not, and are voyeurs
for the love lives of other people. She couldn't wait to show
Train Guy. They were trending! It was the most auspicious
of starts. It felt like good luck. Oh, this was all so perfect!

'Nadia?'

Nadia looked up from her phone, where the barman was
staring at her.

'Yes?' she said.

Nadia was confused. Her guy worked here? And she was
meeting him . . . as he worked? The man was tall and about
her age, with dark stubble and good teeth and –

'I've got a message for you, from your . . . There was a
man here who said to ask for Nadia.'

Nadia didn't understand what the barman was saying. She
looked around, as if somebody was about to jump out and
say, 'Just kidding!'

'He said he had to go, and he was really sorry, and . . . oh
god, I'm going to get this all wrong now. You're clever?
Basically that he fancies you. He had to go and he fancies
you.'

183

Nadia blinked, blood rushing to her cheeks. Her body registered the news before her mind processed it. 'What?'

'The guy you were supposed to meet? Your date, I guess? He got a phone call, and then said he had to go, and he wanted me to tell you.'

Nadia looked from one end of the bar to the other, as if this really was a joke, perhaps a way for Train Guy to test if she was truly interested. There wasn't anybody else around.

'He left?' Nadia could feel tears pricking at her eyes. *Do not cry*, she willed herself. *Don't you dare bloody cry.* She was mortified.

'He left.' The barman seemed to suddenly sense how upset she was. 'He said loads of really nice things before, though. He . . . he came in, and he was looking at himself in the mirror like he was self-conscious and nervous.' The barman assessed Nadia's reaction, to see if this was helping. 'He ordered a glass of wine, and then his phone rang and, well, it's not like I was eavesdropping or anything, but to be honest I think it was his mum? He was trying to calm her down. And then he waited for a minute and then told me to tell you—' The barman stopped polishing his glass and set it down. 'Hold on, let me get this right. He basically gave you a load of compliments. He told me to look out for a beautiful blonde on her own, called Nadia, who was kind and clever and really hot and I think maybe he said charming?'

Nadia didn't know what to think.

'Oh,' was all she could manage, her brain already on a downward spiral of reasons why he'd *really* left.

You're ugly, she told herself.

No man would ever truly want to seduce you, a voice in her head said.

He must have had a better offer.

184

Nobody likes you anyway.

You're unloveable.

Disgusting.

Sad.

Pathetic.

'Let me get you a drink,' the barman said, trying to sound upbeat. 'On the house.' He could sense her dejection, and seemed to feel desperately sorry for her.

'Thank you,' said Nadia, emotionless, feeling rooted to the spot. The words stuck in her throat. How could she have been so stupid? Of course there was no guy, no date. Of course she was sat there alone. Of course! Did she truly think that she was so irresistible that a handsome man would worship her from afar and write her letters and be everything she had ever dared hope for? Who was she kidding? Life wasn't a fairytale. Life was barely even a coherent story. Shit happened and people sometimes fell in love, but a whole lot more people didn't, and obviously she was one of the ones who wasn't going to. It wasn't going to happen for her and she'd had her hair done and worn a new dress and shown off to Emma and Gaby, all for nothing. A rogue tear escaped from her left eye, and she blinked hurriedly after wiping it away, determined that she wasn't going to show herself up.

It crossed her mind that he could still be watching, that maybe it was a test, and she wanted to conduct herself with decorum and class. She was half tempted to call her mother, but didn't think she had it in her to explain everything that had happened. Her phone buzzed in her hand – she hadn't realized she'd still been holding it. It was Gaby – the pre-arranged emergency call.

If Nadia answered it, she could get her to come to the bar, to hug her and drink with her and tell her it was all going to be okay. But as Nadia let the list of options run through her mind, the call rang out, and all that flashed on her screen was 'Missed Call (1) GABY WORK'.

She'd have her glass of free wine and decide what to do. That would be it. She didn't know how to talk about it or who to tell, but she didn't have to make any choices just now. She could just sit, and let the icy smoothness of a cold white wine run down her throat, and she could breathe deep, and then go home.

'What can I get you?' the barman said. 'Anything you like.'

Nadia looked at him. His eyes were kind. This was a kind man, bearing witness to her humiliation. 'Do you have anything minerally? Like a—'

'Albariño? That's what your friend had.'

Nadia nodded. Her 'friend'. Huh. 'That would be great, thank you.'

The barman pulled down a glass and got the bottle from the fridge. As he poured it, he said, 'You can finish off the bottle,' and slid over the half-full glass and the dribble leftover. Then he slinked off to serve somebody else, leaving her to lick her wounds.

Nadia didn't know what to think. It occurred to her that Train Guy knew her name, because he'd told the barman to ask for a Nadia. How? She wondered if he'd ever had any intention to meet her – did he plan to string her along? That made no sense, though. There would be no reason why a stranger would do that. Unless it wasn't a stranger – what if it was somebody who knew her, and that's why they knew her name and which train she got on and about the investor? She wondered if it was Awful Ben. *God*, she thought, *surely not. Surely not Awful Ben?* That would be too cruel, even for him – plus, he had that new girlfriend now. Nadia locked eyes with herself in the mirror again and watched herself drink. She finished the glass of wine in two big gulps. Her ego was bruised and her heart dented. She felt so stupid for hoping. She'd really thought this was it.

As the alcohol coursed through her veins she let herself feel it. She was devastated.

She poured the last of the bottle into the glass.

Will I ever be loved? she wondered. *I didn't know it would ever be this hard.*

27

Daniel

'Henry's gone,' she said, opening the door to him, tears streaming down her face, leaving dark tracks of mascara that faded as they reached her chin.

'Mum,' said Daniel, 'who is Henry? What's happened? Come on. I'm here now.'

Daniel wiped his shoes on the mat and slipped them off. With his hand on the small of his mother's back he steered her through the hallway, with its flowered wallpaper and everything with either a polka dot or a love heart on it. He'd never understood how his father could bear it. It was like Dunelm had had sickness and diarrhoea, and his parents' semi was the result. He sat beside her on the sofa that sagged a little in 'her' part, worn from a nightly place in front of the TV, next to the armchair that had been, until recently, his dad's. *Maybe it always will be dad's*, he thought, realizing how he hadn't wanted to sit there because it 'belonged' to somebody else.

He put his hand on his mum's arm. 'Who is Henry?'

'Henry! The hoover!' his mum said, shaking her head as if he was stupid for not understanding right away. How could he have not immediately understood that his mother was crying over the vacuum cleaner? Is that why he'd left his date – the thing that he had wanted more than almost anything else in the world? For a missing hoover? 'He's gone!'

Daniel searched her eyes as a way to try and understand what she was getting at. She'd been doing really well: hadn't endlessly cried to him weeks now. She'd been a pillar of strength, which was good, because whilst Daniel knew his mother's emotions weren't his responsibility (his therapist told him that at every session), it was a lot easier to keep his own head above water when she was doing well. Maybe now, though, it was his turn to be strong for her.

His mother sighed, frustrated.

'Henry. The hoover. We've had him almost as long as you've been alive. And he's been good – you know – he's lasted a long time. Things did last a long time back then. It's not like now, where they build stuff to automatically break down in two years so you have to replace it. You know. What do they call it? When they make things break after two years?'

'Planned obsolescence.'

'Yes. Planned adolescence.'

'Planned *obsolescence*. Or built-in obsolescence – the policy of planning or designing a product with an artificially limited useful—'

'Oh shut up,' she snapped lightheartedly, through tears. 'You sound just like your father. Knowing everything.' She sounded as if she wasn't sorry that her son sounded like his dad at all. Daniel noticed that her mascara had run to the inner corner of her eyes, so each one had a little black dot in the corner.

'Well. That. Your father wouldn't let me replace Henry because even though he's started to smell a bit, and isn't sucking up as well as he used to, he's still in good shape. And you know, it can be hundreds of pounds for a new one! That's a holiday!'

Daniel really didn't understand where this was going.

'And you're upset about . . .?' he said, while thinking to himself, *I'll bet she's there, now. I'll bet she waited and I never came and she thinks I don't care. That I'm an asshole.*

'He's gone!' She was talking quite calmly, now. 'I put him outside, under the car port, thinking how I must clean the car out. It's a mess, and I took Tracey from darts home the other night and was suddenly so embarrassed by the state of it. I bet she thought I was a right pig – there were wrappers and it was dusty, and I suppose after your father . . . well. I spring-cleaned the house today too, because I realized I'd not really been looking after the place.'

Maybe she doesn't care anyway. Maybe she never showed. Maybe she's there, and already being chatted up by the barman, or one of the guys from the corner table out with his fancy City-boy friends.

Daniel looked around and nodded. 'It looks great, Mum.' And it did. His mother had always prided herself on a pristine home. A pristine, very floral and chintzy home.

I shouldn't have left.

'No! No, it doesn't!' she insisted. 'Because Henry is gone! I never got around to doing the car. I left Henry out by the bin and I thought I'd do it tomorrow, and then that became the day after and the day after, and the truth is, I couldn't really be arsed, so he sat out there for maybe a week, and today I needed to vacuum the house, and I went to get him and he's gone.'

Daniel stood up and went towards the front door. He felt his frustration at having had to leave his date leaking into how he was talking to his mother. He hated that version of himself: even as a teenager he'd talked to both of his parents with respect. That was how he was raised.

'I'm sure he's not, Mum. Where would he have gone?'

'Stolen! I bet he's been stolen!'

Daniel put his shoes back on and went outside to look by the bins, and when he couldn't see the hoover there, he looked *in* the bin.

'You're not looking anywhere I haven't already!' His mother sank down to sit on the doorstep. 'Oh, Danny,' she said, her bottom lip wobbling again. 'Right before he met you at the pub, on the day he . . . on that day, we had such a big fight. He said no way was I to buy a new hoover, and I thought he was being a tight bastard, and got mad. And he'll think . . . well, I'll bet he thinks I've done it on purpose!'

Daniel wandered back over to his mum. 'He doesn't think that, Mum. He doesn't think anything. He's . . .'

'Oh, I know he's dead. But he's here. Watching over us all. And he'll be all crossed arms and big angry scowl thinking I "lost" –' his mother made air quotes in front of her face '– Henry, and with him gone I thought I'd get away with it.'

'Mum, your husband has died and your hoover smelled bad. I think you're allowed a new one.'

'So you don't believe me either!'

'Either?'

'First your father, and now you!' She pulled a tissue from the pocket of her dress and blew her nose. She was back to talking hysterically, her words all tumbling over each other. 'Well, I'm telling you, Henry was out here by the bins, and now he isn't. He's been stolen and it wasn't my fault.'

Daniel dropped down on the outdoor step beside his mother. He didn't say anything, but knocked his knee against hers as a sign of solidarity. She was officially nuts, but he didn't mind. He was half in love with a woman he'd never met and wrote to via the newspaper because he thought his dad would like it. He could understand his mother feeling strongly about the vacuum cleaner on his dead dad's behalf too.

He hoped he hadn't upset Nadia. He hoped that maybe she hadn't even turned up at all, and so had no idea he'd stood her up. It would have sucked if he'd stayed there, though, and been the one to have been stood up. But he'd rather that than her, waiting, alone, thinking he didn't care.

After a while, his mother said, 'I miss the miserable bugger.'

Daniel smiled. 'I know, Mum. Me too.'

'I wake up in the middle of the night and think he's gone for a wee, and I wait for him to come back to bed. And then I remember.'

'I know.'

'And I feel . . . angry. I'm so mad at him for dying.'

'I know,' Daniel said sadly.

'I want to scream and shout at somebody. But at who? The bloody scrap man who probably nicked the hoover?'

'Ahhhh,' said Daniel. 'The scrap man. Yes. If Henry was out here for a week that would make sense.'

'Yeah,' his mum said.

Daniel reached out his arm to give her a squeeze.

'I know it's awful. You don't deserve this. You don't deserve to be without him.'

He didn't realize until his voice cracked that he was crying too. Big tears rolled down his face, matching his mother's. She'd stopped crying until she looked up at her son, and the

193

pair of them sat in the late evening sun, partly laughing at their big display of emotion, and partly continuing to sob, mother and son united in the grief of missing the man of their lives, wondering how they might carry on without him.

Daniel was glad he'd come after all. It was just the two of them now. They were a team. They needed each other.

28

Nadia

'Anyone sitting here?'

Nadia looked up to see a tall, red-headed man with a crooked smile. He was gesturing at the seat beside her. Nadia's second wine glass was empty and the bar had filled up around her. The spot beside her was the only empty seat. How long had she been sitting there? Long enough to drink two large glasses of white wine, she realized.

'Yes, yes, of course,' said Nadia, remembering her manners. 'Yes, somebody is sitting there?'

'No. Nobody is sitting there. Yes. Yes, *you* can sit there.'

The man was insistent with his eye contact and held Nadia's gaze. She swallowed, hard. She was a little bit drunk – she'd been so excited about the date that she hadn't eaten properly since breakfast, so the booze had gone straight to her head. Something in the air shifted. The man stood in front of her, looking, for a beat too long. It snapped Nadia out of her daydream and into the present.

'Are you waiting for somebody?' he asked, settling in next to her.

'I was,' she said. She cleared her throat, aware that she sounded a little croaky. 'But they can't make it,' she added, louder.

'And now the lady drinks alone?'

'And now the lady drinks alone,' Nadia repeated. Wow. She had slurred that sentence a little – her speech was definitely impaired. She should go home. Or at least eat something.

'That's such a shame,' he said, and Nadia smiled weakly. She could feel his eyes on her, but she wasn't in the mood. She didn't want to play cat-and-mouse games with a stranger at a bar – she wanted to mope and feel sorry for herself and lament how terrible all men were because they got your hopes up and then trashed them in the gutter.

'This might seem very forward of me, but – do you want another drink? I have half an hour before my buddy gets here.'

Nadia looked at him – this man sat beside her, where her date should have been.

'You're asking me for a drink?' she said. 'Just like that?'

'Just like what?'

'You're gonna sit down next to a woman you don't know and offer to buy her a drink, like a Nora Ephron movie?' Nadia wasn't flirting, but there was a definite recklessness to her. Two drinks and one missed connection was enough to make her feel like she didn't have to be polite, or coy, or nice. She didn't have to contort to make herself likeable. She was mad as hell. After two drinks she'd gone from devastated to distraught to angry and now, she realized, she had zero fucks to give. All men were the same, she thought: destined to screw her over. What did she have to lose by entering into battle with this one?

'I don't know who that is, but yes. Call it a radical social experiment where one lone man tries to see if it's possible to meet a woman without the aid of a dating app. Apparently in the olden days that's how it used to happen, you know. Men and woman would just have a conversation, out, in public, and if they liked that conversation they'd keep having a conversation, until they decided they'd like another conversation on another day, and maybe another one after that. Experimental times.'

'How do you not know who Nora Ephron is?' Nadia replied. 'She defined an era. Our whole generation grew up on her.'

'I'll have to educate myself,' he said.

'Start with *You've Got Mail*, and once you understand her genius, read *Heartburn*.'

'*You've Got Mail*! I've heard of that!'

'*I would send you a bouquet of newly sharpened pencils if I knew your name and address . . .*'

'Pencils? You say that like it's romantic.'

'Oh, but it is,' Nadia said. Was she being charming? She thought she was being acerbic, but the man's eyes sparkled at her.

'I'm Eddie,' he said, reaching out a hand to shake hers.

'Hello,' she said.

Eddie smiled. 'It would be typical for you to tell me your name now,' he said.

'Nadia.'

'And what do you do, Nadia?'

'I work in artificial intelligence.'

'Beautiful and clever, I see.'

Nadia raised an eyebrow. 'My robots have more original pick-up lines than that.'

'I told you, we're going old school tonight.'

'The oldies are the goodies?'

'The goodies are the goodies,' he repeated, which didn't quite make sense, but the way he said it made Nadia nervous. 'So, same again?' he pressed, nodding his head towards her empty glass. Nadia shrugged.

'Sure,' she said. She surprised herself with her answer.

When the barman delivered two more glasses of wine, he said: 'Your buddy opened a tab on his card. Do you want me to put these on there? Or do you want to take his card for him and give me a new one, or . . .?'

Nadia could feel Eddie's eyes on her. 'No, no,' she said, tempting as it was to order a bottle of whatever was most expensive and charge it to the man who had stood her up. She didn't even know his name! 'Ah,' she added. 'Actually, maybe I could take it for him?'

The barman shrugged. 'Sure,' he said. He reached back and got the card. Nadia figured at least she could see what name was embossed on it. She took it off the barman. It said D E WEISSMAN – not a name that meant anything to her.

Eddie whipped out his bank card in the time it took Nadia to reach under the bench for her bag. 'Allow me,' he said. 'We'll start a tab on this one,' he said to the barman.

Nadia slipped D E Weissman's card into her bag.

'Thank you,' Nadia said, knowing full well she shouldn't have another drink without eating something – but doing it anyway. She was here, she looked good, and a funny man was interested in her. Surely it wouldn't hurt to wait with him until his friend came? A little flirting was making her feel good – like she wasn't wholly repulsive to all of mankind. Yes. She'd stay for half an hour, just for one more, if only to remind herself that she was fine.

Okay, she was tricking herself into thinking she was fine, but genuine okayness was sure to follow, wasn't it?

'Cheers,' said Eddie, motioning at her with his glass, and Nadia raised hers in the air to meet it.

'Here's to doing it the old-fashioned way,' she said, sounding a lot more confident than she felt.

She really wasn't going to stay long.

29

Nadia

Nadia's alarm went off at 6 a.m. She'd set her phone to go off automatically every day, since she kept getting drunk the night before and forgetting, but she hadn't remembered to turn it off as she went to bed last night, distracted as she was by Eddie kissing behind her ear, down her neck, gently and slowly making his way to her front, to her breasts, her stomach, to her—

'Shit.'

She hit the alarm off. Her head hurt. Eddie didn't move. He slept on his front with his head turned away from her, lightly snoring with every inhale. Nadia sat up and blinked slowly, rubbing at her eyes. It was light outside, but not as light as it had been. *The days are getting shorter*, she thought, her hangover evidently making her grumpy and partial to depressing sayings her grandmother used to utter. It was hardly the bleak midwinter. It just felt that way, in her head.

She looked over at the man beside her. How the hell had

that happened? And then it came back to her. A dare. A bet. A challenge that she'd lost, and drank a shot for. Tequila, she thought, bile rising in her throat at the memory of it. She couldn't remember how long she had stayed for, or why Eddie's friend hadn't arrived. She picked up her phone to a text from Gaby: *Glad you're having fun!* it said. The only message Nadia had sent before that was, *GETTING VERY DRUNK QUITE HANDSOME.* Gaby wouldn't have known that she didn't mean Train Guy. She meant . . . oh god. This guy.

She padded to the bathroom and ran the shower. Memories continued to come back to her in pieces: her hand on Eddie's arm as she laughed, Eddie's hand on her upper thigh as he whispered something, another round being ordered, and then another. She hadn't meant to sleep with him. Hadn't meant to let it all go that far.

Oh god, she thought, filled with regret. *Oh god, oh god, oh god.*

She peed – a radioactive pee, as dark as her head felt – and turned to run a shower. She could smell the alcohol evaporating as she stood under water so hot it was almost scalding, slowly waking up.

'Morning, beautiful.'

Eddie pulled back the shower curtain, letting in the cold air. Nadia instinctively covered her boobs and crossed her legs, which was weird considering some of the things Eddie had seen last night.

'I'll take a piss and then climb in,' he said, leaning across with puckered lips. Nadia didn't know what to do. She leaned to meet him and their lips pecked. He smiled in response and disappeared again.

Nadia listened to him pee and – wait. Could she smell

it too? Could she smell his piss? Eddie was whistling to himself, almost cheerfully, and Nadia wondered how he could function. Maybe her headache was as much of an emotional one as a drink-enforced one – she remembered, now, that Train Guy had stood her up, and her tummy sank all over again. That bastard.

Her water ran cold as Eddie flushed the toilet. Nadia turned around to wash her face, thinking maybe the cold water would close her pores (wasn't that a good thing? Helpful for clear skin?) and then there was another shot of air behind her and Eddie hugged her from behind. She could smell his morning breath.

'Last night was amazing,' he said.

Nadia didn't know what to say. She wanted to say, *Excuse me, do you mind? Can I shower alone? You're being horribly presumptuous.*

But instead she smiled weakly and said, 'I'll get you a toothbrush.'

Barely rinsing off – she'd wonder all day why her head felt itchy, and then remember that she hadn't washed out the conditioner properly – she inched past Eddie's wet body.

'Hey,' he said, grabbing her in a moist embrace. 'Come here.'

He was acting like her boyfriend. Like they'd been together weeks or months, not like they'd just met last night – literally, not even twelve hours ago. Nadia didn't know the polite way to tell him not to be so clingy, not least when, to his credit, he'd done a superb job of being a gentleman and making sure she came again and again the night before, her pleasure as much centre-stage as his own. That was a low barrier for a lover, and yet true nonetheless. Nadia had slept with many a man who didn't seem to care less if she came or not – and most certainly performed with the idea that sex was over once he had come. Eddie had been generous and thoughtful, at least. On reflection, he couldn't possibly have been as drunk as she was.

'Hmmmm,' she said, barely grazing his cheek with her lips and ducking out.

As she got dressed in her bedroom he appeared in the doorway, naked and dripping.

'I think you took the only towel,' he said. Nadia's jaw dropped. He was hard, and it was obviously an invitation. He reached for the damp towel she'd discarded on the bed.

'I'll just use this,' he said, leaning over provocatively. He held her eye and Nadia looked at his crotch and he loved that she was looking but she hated that she was. She pulled her eyes away and busied herself in the mirror. She picked up and put down several pots: moisturizer and eye cream and primer, everything designed to make her look more human than she felt. Eddie dried himself off behind her, and then executed his most shocking, perverted act of the morning: he began politely making the bed.

Oh god, thought Nadia. *I've managed to have a one-night stand with the nicest man in the world.* It was lovely that Eddie was being so thoughtful and kind but in absolutely no way did she want anything to do with him. Train Guy had been the last straw. Nope. That was it. She was taking a break from men, and focusing all the energy she could otherwise have given her love life on work. She'd resume romantic hopefulness after Christmas, or maybe after her next birthday. She didn't have the stamina for it right now. She was done. Finished. No more sexy romance love-time for Nadia.

She just had to politely extract herself from the topless man in her bedroom first.

'Which direction are you heading in?'

'Huh?' she said. 'Me?'

Eddie smiled. 'No, the other woman I made scream my name last night. Yes, you.'

'Oh. Erm.' Nadia was stalling. She couldn't bear to think they'd ride into work together. That wasn't what this was. She'd made a mistake. Unforgivable, really. If this was the other way around and she had slept with a man who was being arcticly cold, she'd pitch a fit and blame the patriarchy. This was an embarrassing double standard. It wasn't like she'd deliberately used Eddie as a confidence boost last night, it was just things that things had got out of hand. And they were both adults. Casual sex could happen. That was okay, right?

'Northern line to London Bridge,' she said, weakly.

'Great,' Eddie replied. 'That's the direction I'm headed too.'

Nadia winced and forced a smile in response. 'Great,' she said, meaning exactly the opposite.

30

Daniel

Daniel didn't know what else to do aside from making sure he was on the 7.30 through Angel. He needed her to be on that train. When she was, he'd promised himself that he would march right up to her and say, 'I'm sorry. My dad died a few months ago and my mother was very upset and I didn't want to leave. But I had to. I'm all she's got. My name is Daniel and it is me who has been writing to you. You don't have to forgive me for standing you up, but please: all I ask is that you give me a second chance at a first impression.' That's what he was going to say.

He had, in fact, a whole speech planned out in his head, and he was nervous and excited and determined to deliver it. He'd got back from his mum's house late last night. Holding her as she cried was hard – holding her as she held him, because they both cried, was hard – and the late night and worry showed on his face. But he had showered and put on a crisp, clean shirt, shaved and used mouthwash and moisturizer, and as the train passed through King's Cross he took a breath, knowing her stop was next.

Please, please, please, please, please, please, he willed silently. *Please be here.*

As the train pulled up he eagerly looked out of the window, and there she stood, right in her usual place. Radiant and perfect and Daniel's tummy leapt and he clenched his fists in victory. She was here! The train lined up so that the doors he stood beside were the ones that would open for her.

Okay pal, he coached himself. *This is it. This is your moment. Do yourself proud.*

The doors opened, one or two people stepped off the train, and space was made for her to get on. Daniel straightened himself up and arranged his features into an encouraging smile, ready to say her name.

'Nadia?'

The tall ginger man who stood slightly behind her beat him to it. He was wearing a leather jacket and had stubble and cocked his head towards the left, saying, 'This way, babe.'

The train was unusually quiet, and the pair got seats together right at the end of the carriage, the guy reaching an arm proprietorially over her shoulder and pulling her in towards him. Daniel adjusted himself to get a better look. Nadia had her legs crossed and the man had his other hand on her knee. Daniel edged closer to where they were, straining to hear what the man was saying. It was something about plans for the weekend – did she want to go to Columbia Road Flower Market? They could start at the end with the cafés and get coffee and pastries, and then walk up and look in the shops and end up at the pub at the other end, maybe think about lunch. He had a whole weekend itinerary for them, spilling out from the tip of his tongue and Daniel knew, right in the space between his belly button and his gut, just from that small snippet he'd heard, that they had a life together. He didn't know how he'd missed the signs – although, admittedly, this was the first time he'd seen them together. Maybe all those other days, the ones when she wasn't on the 7.30, she was actually commuting in from his house, from somewhere else in London. He looked like the kind of guy who lived south of the river. Peckham, maybe, in one of the new developments that everyone had said wouldn't sell and now went at half a million for a one-bed. That would make sense: that's why he didn't see her every day.

He followed that trail of thought. If Nadia had a boyfriend, it occurred to him, then surely it couldn't have been her who had been writing back to the adverts. He'd presumed without question that it was, but now he felt stupid: it could have been anybody wanting a bit of excitement responding to those notes. Maybe it was like horoscopes: all the details applied, if only you searched hard enough.

Somebody else had obviously misunderstood, and he was inadvertently impressed by what somebody else had written. There must be a woman out there, somewhere, convinced Daniel was courting her and maybe that was the woman he would have met last night, because Nadia would have been none the wiser. He felt really bloody stupid. He looked up and around the carriage to see if there was a blonde woman holding a coffee in the vicinity – a woman who had convinced herself Daniel had meant her. There was a sixty-something woman with strawberry-blonde hair and a briefcase not far away, peering at her phone screen over her glasses. And a twenty-something blonde with her hair in a French braid that reached her waist, sat in jogging bottoms and trainers and with a sports bag at her feet, listening to music and seemingly checking out the woman opposite her. Was it either of them?

Daniel looked at Nadia and her boyfriend again. He briefly wondered if, and half hoped, they were polyamorous. That was increasingly common in London now, he'd heard. He'd seen it on some of the apps too. 'Ethically non-monogamous', some of the bios said. But from the way her boyfriend sat close to her, breathing her air, whispering in her ear – no way. Daniel couldn't see it. He didn't put judgement on anyone with enough love for more than one person, but no. Nadia's boyfriend wasn't one of those people. Daniel just didn't get that vibe.

She didn't look the least bit upset or put out, Nadia. There was no air to her that suggested she'd waited for a stranger last night, and been stood up. Not one bit.

Colour filled Daniel's cheeks and the back of his neck. He suddenly felt nauseous and hot and light-headed and ridiculous. He'd spent all this time planning and imagining and it turned out he'd been having an imaginary relationship with a woman who had no idea he even existed. He seriously considered the fact that he might be going mad. This was mortifying. How would he explain it all to Romeo, or Lorenzo? Even himself? He wanted the ground to open a Daniel-shaped hole that he could step into, so that he'd never have to ride this train and be reminded of his delusions of amour ever, ever again. What a sad, pathetic fool he'd been.

Of course he hadn't been writing to Nadia!

Of course she wasn't interested in him!

None of this was real!

He'd been a damned fool, and played himself. As the train pulled into the station he lingered as Nadia and her boyfriend walked ahead, and he watched them go.

You need help, he told himself. *You batshit crazy bastard. You've imagined this whole thing!*

Daniel walked slowly to work, his brain doing the mental arithmetic of just how bonkers he was. He felt like he wanted to get hold of old copies of the papers, the ones where he thought he'd read her response. Was he so deluded that he'd made it up, in his head? It suddenly felt entirely possible. His shirt collar felt tighter at the thought, his neck clammy. He hated her boyfriend. Hated him. There were no specifics to this hate, but it was there. Daniel couldn't get what he thought was a smug and self-serving demeanour out of his mind. Who did he think he was, making romantic plans and checking in to make sure it was cool with her? Who the hell was he to let her walk ahead, and kiss her cheek in affection, and generally exist as a gentleman?

Fuck you, Daniel thought.

'My brother, my man! How did it go!' Romeo said, watching Daniel approach through the lobby. 'You okay?' he said, sensing his mood immediately. 'You don't look great.'

Daniel felt like he was struggling to focus.

'I'm a fucking idiot,' he said, his voice hardly above a whisper. 'I made it all up. All of it.' He laughed, hysterically. 'I don't even know if you're real!' he said, reaching out to pat Romeo's arms, his face. 'Are you real?'

Romeo took his friend's hands and put them at the side of his own body.

'Last night either went super amazing, or super terrible,' he said, wide-eyed. 'And I've got my suspicions on which one.'

'I was so stupid,' Daniel was saying. 'So stupid!'

'Ah,' said Romeo. 'And therein lies the answer. Super terrible?'

'You won't believe this,' Daniel said, his eyes unable to

focus. 'I had to go. My mother called, it was an emergency, and now this morning I just saw her with her boyfriend! She has a boyfriend! And if she has a boyfriend, no way was she there last night, because women with boyfriends don't show up at bars to meet people who are not their boyfriends but who they met through an anonymous column in the paper, so!' Daniel's words were all crashing into each other, like he couldn't get them out of his mouth as fast as they entered his head. 'AND SO. Either I have been writing to a totally different woman, or – and this is what scares me, really fucking scares me – maybe I just imagined the whole thing. Maybe I am ACTUALLY INSANE. I'm so stupid!'

Romeo shook his head. 'No, man. I don't believe that. You've got to be confused or something. I saw those adverts. She's real, all right.'

'I really don't even think she showed up last night. She couldn't have done! She was out with her boyfriend! Fuck. I would have sat there all night waiting for her. I don't know what's worse: that a totally different woman could have shown up, or this was all some joke to her – or somebody – and I would have waited for ever for nobody.'

Romeo was his typical, level-headed self, listening to Daniel rant and rave and still saying good morning to anybody else who passed through the lobby.

'Okay. You. Me. Pub after work, okay?'

Daniel's eyes found his. 'Pub after work,' he repeated, like he was in a trance.

'Okay? Meet me down here at 6 p.m.?'

'Okay,' Daniel said.

Romeo was talking slowly, making sure Daniel got calmer right in front of him. 'Go upstairs and get a coffee and read your emails and . . . Well, to be honest I'm not entirely sure what your job actually is, but go upstairs and do it. At lunch-time go for a walk and eat a sandwich, and just . . . keep your head down today, okay? If I didn't know any better I'd think you were on drugs.'

'I'm not on drugs,' said Daniel.

'I know, mate. But keep a low profile anyway, okay?'

'Okay.'

'And Daniel? All is not lost. I promise you that.'

Daniel didn't believe him.

'You just can't argue with a Wetherspoons, you know?' Romeo was saying, as he and Daniel weaved through the Friday-night throngs of workers on the pavements, all hurriedly walking towards the beginning of their weekends. 'Those prices, man. It's not to be sniffed at.'

They settled into a table in the corner, Romeo insisting on getting in the first round, which Daniel objected to strongly but Romeo was adamant about. He tootled off to the bar and Daniel sat and waited. He'd calmed down considerably since this morning. He had done next to no work and had had Percy hold all of his calls. Percy had done exactly as he was told, not even putting through Lorenzo's attempts to find out what had happened on the date. Percy could tell something was up, but didn't pry. He simply followed Daniel's instruc-tions, and also brought him back a cookie at lunch, silently leaving it on his desk, smiling, and returning to his work.

Daniel had had a series of texts from Lorenzo over the course of the day, none of which he had replied to:

Well, it can't have gone that well because I heard you come home alone last night, the first said.

The second: *Although it was about midnight, so you obvi-ously had *something* to say to each other.*

He sent a third, not long after: *Are you ignoring me because you're gutted she wasn't interested?*

The fourth: *Well, fuck her, mate, you know? I never thought she was a big fucking deal in the first place.*

Later, he'd sent another: *What time you home tonight, mate?*

Waiting for Romeo, Daniel picked up his phone with vague ideas of finally texting Lorenzo back, but he didn't know where to start. He hoped Lorenzo would be out when he got home, and maybe after a chat with Romeo and a good night's sleep he could think about what he was going to tell him. He was pretty sure Lorenzo would find the whole thing hilarious and pathetic, and be horribly unsupportive. Daniel didn't know if he could take being laughed at. Not over this.

When Romeo came over with their drinks – two ciders – Daniel said, 'I just feel really stupid.'

Romeo took a sip. 'Well, let me tell you, straight up, that you are not actually stupid. Feel it, sure. But know that you are not actually an idiot.'

'Aren't I?' Daniel said.

'No.'

The pair worked at their drinks.

'I'm gonna need you to hear me out on this,' Romeo said eventually. 'But I'm pretty convinced you've got to talk to her. To Nadia. Directly. I don't believe for a second you want to walk away from this without knowing exactly what the truth is.'

'I'm terrified of the truth,' Daniel said. 'I feel crazy. I feel like I just need to forget this whole thing. I need to start getting an earlier train, and dating the old-fashioned way – using an app.'

'Is that really what you want?'

'No. Yes. No.'

Romeo digested his response. He was an interesting listener, Daniel thought. He actually listened to what Daniel was saying instead of simply being quiet until it was his turn to talk. Lorenzo often spoke over the top of Daniel, dominating the conversation. Romeo was a lot more like his uni mates.

'Listen,' he said. 'Is this the first time you've seen this other guy?'

'Yes.'

'So really – who knows who he is. I've said it before and I'll say it again: if there's no ring on her finger and she really is the one who has been writing to you, she's either with him and not happy, or not with him and you've got the wrong end of the stick.'

'But she might not have been the one writing to me – that's where I'm at now. I don't think she is.'

'Well. The next time you see her, man, you gotta talk to the woman face to face. Pick your moment. Make a little eye contact and see if you get a smile, but fucking talk to her, man.'

'And say what?'

'I find hello is a good opener.'

Daniel raised his eyebrows at him.

'Doesn't necessarily need a response, could just be you being polite, but if she likes the look of you you'll know it. She'll say something back. There'll be signals, man. Trust me.'

'Do you think I should send another letter in to the paper?'

'I think you're past that now, don't you? This crossed-wires shit is some Greek tragedy shit, man. Messages through other people, all smoke and mirrors. Talk to the woman face to face, like a grown man. Don't miss your chance like I did, with Juliet. You've got this! It's just a chat! But it's a chat that will set you straight again, you know? Maybe she has terrible breath or is rude to strangers, in which case your crush will be cured. I know I don't know you too well, mate, but what I do know is that you need to feel like you've done your best. You don't wanna keep on wondering what happened.'

Daniel swilled the last of his cider around in the bottom of his glass. 'What if I wrote and just said, sorry – I came, but I had to leave?

'That's an option.'

'Yeah,' said Daniel.

'Gimme your phone.'

Daniel handed over his phone. Romeo typed for a few seconds before passing it back to Daniel, who stared at the screen. In the notes app he'd written:

> *I screwed up, Coffee Spill Girl. I left, and I shouldn't have, and now I'm worried I blew it. I know you don't get a second chance at a first impression, but how's about a first meeting on the second try?*

'That's good,' said Daniel, sadly. He stared at his phone. He really did want to apologize to her. 'I might actually send that, you know. If she'd been alone today I would have said almost exactly that.'

'Go for it then, if that feels right. But I have a feeling you might see her sooner than you think.'

'Maybe,' said Daniel. 'I might send it just in case. It will make me feel better.'

The pair talked about their weekend plans for a little bit, both agreeing that another pint was too much but they'd go in for a half and then part ways. Daniel was exhausted, his shoulders tight and eyes aching. He could feel his breathing getting deeper for having had a drink, and told himself he'd

216

go for a really long run in the morning to truly shake off his week. He'd download *Guardian* Soulmates, thinking that maybe he was too old for apps and needed something with a monthly payment plan, so he knew the women on there were serious. He needed to get out there and connect with a woman who was actually real, and genuinely wanted to meet him, before he spooked himself into thinking it would never happen for him. Jesus. Is that what it had come to? Genuinely considering *Guardian* bloody Soulmates?

'Hey, you know what you should do?' Romeo said, when Daniel got back to the table. 'You should text that woman who was doing the set-up for you. When you went to the Sky Garden.'

Daniel groaned. 'Are you kidding me? Technically, I was stood up that night too! I turned up expecting to meet a woman who never bloody came! And the woman supposed to be doing the introductions disappeared as well!'

Romeo laughed. 'Okay, okay, mea culpa – bad idea. Hinge it is then.'

'Hey, how's your love life going? Aren't you seeing some-body?'

Romeo smiled. 'Yes boss, I am. Date number four on Sunday.'

'Date number four,' Daniel said, raising his glass to him. 'Imagine that.'

Romeo caught his eye. 'There's plenty to go around,' he said. 'You'll get a fourth date with somebody too.'

Daniel sighed deeply. 'I believe you,' he said.

'Want me to see if Erika has got any friends? We could double-date!'

Daniel considered it. 'I mean, fucking maybe, man. I'll let you know.'

31

Nadia

Nadia got home that night exhausted, battling a hangover, and to a bundle of HB pencils on her front step. *What the hell . . .* she thought, crouching to pick them up, and then admonishing how difficult her headache made even that. All day she'd been fantasizing about getting home, taking off her bra, opening all the windows (but closing all the blinds), and ordering in truffled Mac 'n' Cheese and New York cheesecake from her favourite restaurant on Newington Green. She was nearly there. Freedom was almost hers.

The pencils really were arranged like a bouquet, and on a more energetic day she'd have whipped out her phone to Instagram them immediately. As it happened, the note caught her eye and any notion of photography was instantly forgotten.

You've Got Mail, and it's a bouquet of newly sharpened pencils, it said. (*I look forward to finding out what that means*). *Last night was lovely. See you soon, I hope, Eddie.*

Nadia rubbed her temples. This was a lot to process. Eddie, as in last night Eddie. Eddie, as in had kissed her goodbye in front of her work with an open mouth Eddie. Eddie, as in . . . must have come back to where she lived during the day or at the very least taken note of her address to get somebody to deliver this gift Eddie.

She'd mentioned that scene from *You've Got Mail* only in passing, right before he'd even asked her name. And he'd remembered? Intellectually, Nadia knew this made him what Emma and Gaby would call A Good Guy. He'd made her bed after making her come, and sent a variation of flowers the next day to boot.

So why didn't that make her instantly swoon?

Nadia thought of her second favourite part of that movie, after the pencil line, when Meg Ryan is asked by the man who just broke up with her if she has anyone else. They'd both known the relationship was over, and he has already moved on.

'*No, no . . .*' Meg Ryan tells him, dreamily '*. . . but there's the dream of someone else.*'

Nadia hadn't thought about Train Guy all day, really – aside from being furious at him, and cursing him with a lifetime of singledom for having dared to stand her up. But standing on her doorstep with a gesture of kindness from one man, it was the other one who flooded her mind.

'Absolutely not,' said Emma down the phone five minutes later. 'No way. Train Guy bolted! He's done! He's finished. He blew it!'

Nadia was lying on her bed, on her stomach, the right side of her face pressed against the bedsheets. She'd found an old pack of Milk Tray in the drawer of her desk she kept emergency cards and stuff for re-gifting in: Sanctuary Spa body lotions and candles not made of soy wax. She'd been thrilled to find a selection box in there that was only a month out of date. She hadn't even ordered her Mac 'n' Cheese yet. The Milk Tray was her starter.

'Listen to me very carefully, friend,' Emma pressed on. 'The one good thing to come out of him not showing up is that it put you in the path of the man you actually needed to meet. He's ginger and proud! He made you come! He gave a romantic gesture which I don't totally understand but proves he'd paid attention to you! If you don't let yourself be open to this man, you're stupid.'

'I'm hungover,' complained Nadia. 'Be nice to me.' She slid in a Salted Caramel Charm, chewing noisily.

'Oh, this is me being nice to you. Trust me.'

'How much weight can we give to the fact that, now I think about it, the barman said it was his mother who called?' Nadia eyed up a Hazelnut Whirl. 'And that's why he left so suddenly?'

'Zero. Less than zero,' Emma said.

'Less than zero?'

'Less than zero! It could have been the Queen of Sheba on the line, and he still could have waited for you to walk through that door so he could explain why he was leaving face to face.'

Nadia pouted down the phone.

'Don't pout at me.'

'How did you know I was pouting!'

'I can read you like a book, even when I can't see you,' Emma said. 'And stop bloody chewing so loudly. It's like being on the phone to a washing machine.'

Nadia laughed.

'There could have been a family emergency . . .' Nadia said. 'A terrible accident that meant he couldn't wait.'

'Doubtful,' said Emma. 'Question though – and bear in mind the answer to this doesn't get him out of this *at all* – but just to sate my own curiosity: were you on time?'

'I am proud to say that I was literally a minute past the hour. That's as on time as it gets for me.'

'It is. I'm impressed.'

'I was really excited! If I hadn't stopped to talk to Gaby in the lobby I'd have been a minute early!'

'Well. He might still have already gone by then. We'll never know, will we?'

'I could write to him in the paper and ask him . . .' Nadia said. She was down to the Strawberry Temptations in her chocolate selection. She decided no hangover was worth that, and pushed the box away from her, causing a lone crumb of Perfect Praline to smear across her bedsheets, leaving a brown mark. *I should change these anyway*, she thought. *I'll bet they're covered in—*

'Guess what I'm going to say to that?' Emma replied.

'Absolutely no way?'

'Absolutely no way! Correct!'

'Stop. Shouting.'

Emma took a breath. 'Listen. Train Guy is over. Ov-er. But Eddie is not! See him again, just once. In daylight. Over coffee, so your judgement isn't impaired. Give him a chance to win you over. You deserve that.'

Nadia couldn't articulate why she didn't feel able to do that, so settled on: 'Fine. I hereby suspend judgement. I'm going to have a bath and watch *Sleepless in Seattle* now. You're too bossy for my headache.'

'Okay, good. I love you. I say all this because I love you.'

'Are you around this weekend? Sunday brunch?'

Emma faltered. 'Um, I'm not sure. Can I text you?'

'Sure,' said Nadia. 'But also, before you go: are you okay? How are you feeling?'

'I'm good. I'm okay.'

'That's it? Just tell me what happened last weekend.'

'Nads, I love you. I promise I'm fine.'

'I don't believe you. But. You know. I'll be here when you're ready.'

As she hung up and pulled up Deliveroo on her phone to finally order some proper food, she reasoned that Emma was, indeed, correct. Surely it would be self-sabotage to block Eddie's number in the hope that he took the hint (and also forgot her address). That's what she had thought about doing. She was better than that, though: if she blocked the number of a man she'd slept with with no explanation – a man who had sent her a bouquet of newly sharpened pencils! – that would make her a total cow. And the romantic karma would surely come back around to hurt her. No. She had to act according to her value system despite how awkward that felt, because that's how she'd been raised. That's the treatment she'd want. Kindness first.

As she ate her dinner on the couch later, she surprised herself at how, even as she mopped up cheese sauce with half a focaccia, she continued to pine for the imaginary man on the train. Anyone could have been sending those notes. She kept thinking about a man who she had never met, who she had never seen or heard speak, when an actual real-life man had been in her bed last night. She *should* at least be polite and text Eddie a thank you, she reasoned. It was a cute gesture, and he hadn't done anything wrong except emphatically not being Train Guy. He couldn't help that.

Thank you, Nadia sent to him. It bothered her that she had to use iMessage because he didn't have WhatsApp. What an inconsequential thing to be bothered about, and true all the same, she thought. Before she could type anything else he replied, *I'm doing it. I am undertaking my homework.*

??? she typed back.

The movie! The Nora Ephron back catalogue! That's a very important fact about me: I follow instruction very well. He followed it with a photo of a beer held up to a TV that was, indeed, playing her favourite film. There was a familiarity to sending a photo, an intimacy. Nadia figured that having sex was about as intimate as it got, but she didn't actually believe that. Sex was one thing, but this guy was making himself emotionally available to her. She could see a few framed photographs at the side of the TV, and using two fingers to zoom in assumed them to be of his mum and dad, and maybe a dog.

Nadia smiled to herself and sent back: *I rather gathered that last night, Eddie.* She was being sexually provocative to hold him at emotional arm's length, a tried-and-tested tactic she'd used many times before.

Eddie sent back the purple devil emoji and then, frustratingly refusing to be led down the provocative path typed: *This is actually really well written. Like, you think the characters are these stock characters performing to type, but just when you think the rich bookstore guy doesn't have a heart, you realize how kind he is in spite of his family. And you think she's all romantic and hopeful and then she says something spikey and cutting but true. Everyone surprises me, in every scene.*

Nadia wrote back: *Firstly, don't be that guy.*

It was Eddie's turn to type back a string of question marks.

The guy who is surprised by a woman's recommendation and uses the word 'actually' as if it is remarkable that a female recommendation of a female-led movie would be right.

Noted, Eddie typed back. *I only meant I didn't think I'd be into a romcom, but I accept your point.*

It's so much more than a romcom! Nadia wrote back.

THAT IS WHAT I AM SAYING WITH CHARACTER DEVELOPMENT!!!!! Eddie replied. *WE ARE SAYING THE SAME THING!!!!*

Okay!!!!!!!! said Nadia in reply.

Jesus!!!

Nadia sat up straight from her vegetative state on the sofa. Eddie was . . . smart. And saying insightful things, and also not letting her be an asshole to him. Like, he was sticking up for himself whilst also telling her that he heard her. In spite of herself, Nadia was impressed.

She changed tactic. *I'm glad you're enjoying it.*

I am, he said. *She reminds me of you.*

Who does?

Kathleen.

Meg Ryan reminds you of me?!

Yes, Eddie typed back. *Maybe it's the hair.*

Maybe, Nadia replied, trying on the character of Kathleen for size. She liked the comparison.

Or maybe it's the defensive attitude masking deep romanticism, he typed, adding in a winky emoji.

Touché, said Nadia. And then, in spite of herself, because she had Emma's voice ringing in her head and he was being sweet and she didn't, actually, have anything to lose: *So, this weekend, right?*

Are you asking me out? said Eddie, ignoring the fact he'd suggested to her this morning that his whole weekend was free. She deserved that. She deserved being made to put herself out there a little when she was riding him so hard. She admired that – that he was making her declare her interest as clearly as he had declared his. It felt full of self-respect.

I am, she said. *Sunday. Let's do something nice on Sunday.* She had a twinge in her heart that betrayed her excitement. *Enjoy the movie! x*

32

Daniel

'Mate,' Daniel said, swilling the last dregs of his beer at the bottom of the glass. 'I don't have words for the extent to which I am not interested in tonight. Really and truly – I'm pretty sure you don't need me.'

Lorenzo raised his eyebrows and shook his head. 'I need you, dude.' He finished his drink and signalled to the barman for two more.

'No,' Daniel said, firmly. 'I've got to pace myself.' He waved Lorenzo's hand away and held up one finger to the barman. The barman nodded, message received.

'It's not as if I'm asking you to set your hair on fire and put it out with the back of a shovel just for a laugh. This is a group of hot girls! You could even get laid if you wanted!'

'But that's the point, isn't it?' said Daniel. 'I don't want to.'

Lorenzo, as predicted, hadn't been hugely sympathetic about Daniel's failed date and lost romance as he'd relayed it all as they'd eaten toast and jam in the kitchen together that morning.

'Bollocks to her, mate,' was how he'd summarized it. 'Come out with me tonight. You could get any of the girls from the RAINFOREST party on their knees for you, and they'll all be there. Becky said so.' Becky was the girl Lorenzo had brought home after the work event the other week.

In lieu of any sort of emotional intelligence, Lorenzo got weirdly sexual, but Daniel knew he meant well. It was just, well . . . Lorenzo's version of 'meaning well' was exhausting.

The barman put down another pint in front of Lorenzo, and he picked it up, emptying half of it in two huge gulps.

'It's Saturday night! Come on! We're young, we're single, we're a pair of good-looking dudes. What's wrong with letting our hair down?'

Daniel raised his eyebrows at him, and regretted ever being dragged out in the first place. He'd had a rush of understanding that he couldn't just stay in front of the TV all Saturday night, and that a few drinks with Lorenzo wouldn't be the end of the world, but now he was out and the bar was busy and Lorenzo was being particularly loud and louty, he regretted it. He wasn't in the mood to manage Lorenzo's outgoingness.

'For fuck's sake,' Lorenzo continued, noting Daniel's sour expression. 'Just . . . at least pretend to have a good time? Becky wanted to go out with her mates, and I wanted to see Becky – I mean, she's super fit, so *duh* – and I can't be some weird guy in a group of girls waiting for them to stop talking so he can get his dick sucked, so . . . this is you doing me a favour. Although how *my* invitation for peeling *you* away from the sofa is somehow *you* helping me out I'll never know. Anyway,' he paused as he finished off his pint in another two long gulps, 'I said eight and it's eight, so let's go.'

The guys walked quickly under the arches of Hoxton station and rounded the corner to see four women standing in a tight circle, all on their phones. Daniel recognized the woman who'd tried to kiss him, as well as Becky, whose face lit up at Lorenzo's. Daniel thought the other two women must have been at the party too, but he didn't recognize them. They kind of all looked the same, with honey-coloured hair just below their shoulders, all of them in high-waisted jeans and leather sandals, with lots of gold jewellery layered around their necks and wrists.

'Ladies,' said Lorenzo, shouting as they approached. 'What a sight for sore eyes!'

Becky said something Daniel couldn't hear to the group as they all looked up, making everyone giggle. He felt self-conscious, but he didn't know why. The girl who had hit on him at the party made eye contact and smiled sweetly.

'We meet again,' she said, as the two men made their way around the group, kissing the cheeks of each woman.

'We do,' said Daniel. 'You look nice. I like your –' he struggled to identify something that stood out from the rest of the group '– nail varnish.'

The girl laughed. 'Thank you,' she said. 'I just got a manicure this morning. Self-care Saturday and all that.'

Daniel smiled and nodded politely, not knowing what self-care Saturday was, but not feeling invested enough in polite conversation to follow up. At least he was out, breathing fresh air and wearing cologne. He'd moped enough last night, ordering in truffle Mac 'n' Cheese from halfway across London, and throwing in a cheesecake to boot. When he'd woken up this morning he'd put a wash on and changed his sheets, gone for a run, had breakfast with Lorenzo and then headed out to the Wellcome Collection for a bit of culture.

It was a slow, quiet day, but void of much human interaction, and so here he was, engaging with people.

'Shall we go then?' Lorenzo asked the group, rounding everyone up. 'I saved us a table at Lilo and Brookes. No big deal, but yeah, I know a guy.'

Daniel turned to the nameless girl beside him.

'What have you been up to today?' he said, forcing himself to be friendly and sociable, and struggling to listen to her answer.

At the bar, the group assembled and in a fit of generosity Daniel said, 'Right then – what's everyone having? First round is on me.'

He handed over his credit card to pay, having realized at Wetherspoons the night before that he'd left his debit card at the bar when he was supposed to meet Nadia. He couldn't face going back for it, so he'd cancelled it and ordered another to be delivered in the post. In the meantime, the £115 total for six drinks – six drinks! Over one hundred pounds! – went on his Amex. Daniel delivered the tray to the table and thought about what Romeo would say about the cost. They should have all gone to Wetherspoons.

A few hours into the evening, Daniel suddenly stepped out of himself to acknowledge that actually, it was almost as if he was having fun. The woman who'd hit on him at the party last time had made friends with a guy from another group, and so that guy's friends had joined their table and they'd held court, telling stories and laughing with the other girls and him. It took the pressure off the 'performance' – he just got to chat and not worry about flirting or being flirted with. Daniel ended up talking about Arsenal with one of the guys, passionately defending their starting line-up in the Premier

League final match – still a sore point for many a fan. The guy had said some clever and funny things, and then, out of nowhere, said, 'I'm going to the bathroom, mate. Do you want any?' He put a finger against one nostril and snorted up through the other. Daniel looked around the group. Ah. They were all high.

'Nah mate, I'm all right for a minute,' Daniel said, hating knowing he was the only one not disappearing to the loo for cocaine. It wouldn't be long before everyone got shouty and self-obsessed and sweaty and horny too. Lorenzo and Becky had made out occasionally all night, but Daniel noticed now that the spaces between their kisses had lessened and lessened, and just like that Daniel stopped having fun and made his excuses to leave.

'Daniel!' he heard from behind, as he checked his phone to see that his Uber was only two minutes away. 'Daniel!'

It was Lorenzo, with a very out-of-it Becky on his arm. She staggered and swayed, and had the fixed, airless smile of a woman who had no idea where she was. She didn't look high – she looked very, very drunk.

'Give us a ride, buddy,' Lorenzo said cheerily.

'Two minutes,' said Daniel, glancing at his phone. 'Oh. One.'

Becky could hardly support her own head. She mumbled something and pushed her hair from her face. 'You okay, Becky?' Daniel asked.

'Nkdhrhf-drunk, isall,' she said, which Daniel took to mean 'I'm drunk'.

'Can I get you something? Where are the others?'

Lorenzo looked annoyed at the question. 'Chill out. She's with me. She's okay.'

Daniel stepped towards him and lowered his voice. 'I don't think she really knows where she is, mate,' he said. 'You shouldn't take her home like this. Let's get her back to the girls.'

Lorenzo looked up, meeting Daniel's eye, puffing out his chest. 'Mind your own business, mate.' He said 'mate' as if it meant exactly the opposite, aggressive and mean.

'No, dude, I didn't mean . . . just. Look at her! She should go home.'

A black Prius pulled up alongside the kerb.

'Daniel?' the driver said through the open window.

'All right mate, just a minute,' Daniel said. Turning back to Lorenzo he continued, 'Come on, she's in no fit state. Let me cancel the cab and we'll find the others and they can make sure she gets back okay. I think she lives with one of them.'

'Mate,' Lorenzo said, almost in air quotes. 'She's fine. The cab's here now. Let's just go.'

Daniel hesitated. He thought he was going home alone and now Lorenzo was there with a woman who should not, on any terms, be going anywhere except her own bed. But what was the worst that could happen? Surely Lorenzo would pass out as soon as she did anyway. And it's not like he thought Lorenzo would do anything stupid, but . . . well . . . Daniel resented having to bear witness to it. He stepped aside and let his friend open the car door. This wasn't his call to make, he reasoned.

'She's not gonna be sick, is she?' the cabbie asked, and Lorenzo told him she was fine.

Daniel climbed into the front seat.

'Evening,' he said to the driver.

'Evening.'

The four of them drove in silence, with Daniel vaguely aware of slurpy kissing noises coming from the back seat. He

232

didn't want to turn around, or worse, get caught staring in the rear-view mirror or the dark glass of the car, but he was increasingly uncomfortable. It didn't seem right to him that Becky was so drunk she could barely speak, and Lorenzo was obviously taking her home to have sex with her. Did she even know where she was? He regretted having let Lorenzo get her in the car. If that was his sister, or one of his girl mates . . .

'Hey, Becky – you okay back there?' he said eventually, to which he got a mumbled reply that, in his book, meant she couldn't be far away from either passing out, or throwing up. He stole a glance in the rear-view. Lorenzo was looking out of the far window, sleepily, but his hand was far up Becky's leg, his long fingers stretched out so that his thumb reached into the crevice between her legs.

They pulled up at home, and the two men had to practically give Becky a fireman's lift up the stairs to their flat. It was weird. It felt like being a caveman who had clubbed a cavewoman over the head and dragged her back.

'She can have my room,' Daniel said, as they opened the front door. 'And I'll take the sofa.'

Lorenzo laughed. 'She'll come in with me, stupid.' Becky slumped into the armchair Daniel normally reserved for watching TV.

Daniel looked at her. 'Listen, Lorenzo.'

'Don't "listen, Lorenzo" me.'

'You can't . . . you know. Get consent.'

'Woah! Who said I was going to fuck her?'

'Nobody. I didn't mean—'

'Fuck you, man. What are you fucking saying?'

Daniel held up his hands, in surrender. 'I'm saying I'll get my duvet and sleep in here, and she should go in my room with a pint of water and fully clothed. That's all.'

Lorenzo's face flashed purple with rage. 'I'm not some fucking creep. What do you think I'm going to do?

'Nothing . . .' Daniel tried to sound calm. Emotionless. Non-judgmental. He kept his voice level. 'Lorenzo, you're drunk. Just go to bed.'

Lorenzo pushed Daniel's shoulder. 'You're drunk!' He pushed Daniel's shoulder again. 'Fuck you!'

Daniel pushed him back, instinctively. 'Don't push me.'

Lorenzo pushed him again. 'Don't push me!'

Daniel wasn't sure how it happened, but one of them lunged at the other – he'd say tomorrow morning that it was Lorenzo who'd forced his hand, but he couldn't be sure, they were both drunk and angry – and Daniel could only remember a feeling of almighty pain, the sensation of liquid running down his cheek. There was screaming. Oh god, there was screaming.

'Stop! Ohmygod! Stop!' It was Becky. She was crying – sobbing. Really, really, sobbing. Daniel adjusted his focus and saw Lorenzo lying on his side, groaning. He touched his hand to his face and then looked at his fingers. Blood. They'd beaten the living daylights out of each other.

Becky continued to cry – a weird, confused cry, but a cry that indicated she'd sobered up. The cushions were pulled off the sofa, the coffee table had dragged the rug underneath it into a ball, and Daniel wasn't just breathing deeply but panting.

'Becky,' he said, sounding as authoritative as he could under the circumstances. 'I'm going to call you an Uber, okay?'

Becky made eye contact with him and nodded through tears that were now stunned and silent.

'Come on.'

It hurt Daniel to stand, and looking in the living-room mirror he understood why: there was a bruise shining brightly at the top of his right arm, which he could see because his shirt had popped open and been pulled down, and there was another shiner below his right eye too. He looked sweaty and dirty and bloodied and a mess. 'Where's my phone?' he asked, and Lorenzo silently handed it to him from the floor, his eyes fixed firmly on the ground. He looked almost as bad as Daniel did.

'Get your bag, Becky. We'll wait outside.'

Daniel and Becky waited outside, neither of them knowing what to say. The Uber pulled up, and Daniel opened the door for her.

'Get home safe.'

She nodded.

Inside, Lorenzo had tidied up the mess they'd made. The cushions were back in place and he'd sorted out the rug and coffee table. There was just a single lamp on, and his bedroom door was closed. Daniel thought about knocking on it, but didn't know what he'd say. He wasn't sure what had just happened, really. He just knew he was relieved the girl wasn't behind that closed door with his flatmate. He just . . . Lorenzo shouldn't have brought her home, and that was the end of it.

He leaned in close to the mirror, and even in the dim light he could see the bruise, already deeper and brighter. It hurt to touch.

'Fuck,' he said quietly, a sentiment he'd continue for the next four days, when the bruising looked worse before it looked better.

33

Nadia

Nadia had ended up seeing Eddie earlier than planned, on the Saturday instead of the Sunday. They'd texted all of Friday night, with Eddie giving Nadia a blow-by-blow account of what he thought about first *You've Got Mail*, and then when Nadia said she was going to watch *Sleepless in Seattle* because she loved Meg Ryan, he timed it so that he played the same movie in sync with her from his house. They messaged back and forth, unpacking the plot in real time, talking about their lives and cracking jokes in between talking about the movie. It was 2 a.m. by the time Eddie had said: *This is nice. You. Me. Us.*

And it had been. Eddie was good company, even via a phone screen, and in the end Nadia took a breath and typed, *Hey – I don't suppose you're free tomorrow, are you?*

For you I might be . . . he'd said back, and so at 11 a.m. the next day they'd met for coffee at Granger & Co. in King's Cross, and coffee turned into brunch, and brunch turned into a slow meander down to the Wellcome Collection, which neither of them were particularly bothered about, but it was an excuse to be together, to keep talking. After the exhibition they walked some more, and Nadia hadn't realized she was guiding them towards the direction of her flat, until it was 4 p.m. and Eddie had said, 'What now?'

'We could stop at Tesco,' Nadia said, 'and then go cook at mine?'

Eddie pulled her in for a kiss, then – the first time he'd done so all day, to the point where Nadia had found herself wanting it to happen and convincing herself that she'd misunderstood and they were only spending time together as friends. Or strangers who'd slept together once. Their hands had brushed as they'd walked, and it hadn't gone unnoticed when Eddie had found the exact spot of the curve of her hip to guide her around the corners of the gallery. Knees had knocked as they ate and he'd put his arm around her neck, across her shoulders, a few times. But until then, no kiss. Body contact but no kiss, and when it finally happened Nadia found herself wanting more of it.

They'd got supplies for a simple pasta and pesto dish at the Tesco Extra on the corner, and a bottle of wine and some fizzy water, and kept kissing as they drank on her patio, and boiled water for the noodles, and once they'd eaten the kissing got deeper, and deeper, and then, come Sunday morning, Nadia woke up next to him again, convinced he was the guy for her. *You might have been right . . .* she texted Emma, to no reply. *He's pretty awesome . . .*

They'd spent all Sunday together, going out to read the papers over breakfast like they'd been a couple for years, and this was their normal, weekly routine, before taking the overground across the city to take a big walk up the heath and stopping for roast beef in the beer garden of a pub nearby. It was nice to belong to somebody for a whole block of time: not to be hurtling across London to do a workout with one friend and then lunch with another and head home alone after somebody's Saturday-night birthday dinner or drinks. Nadia felt rooted that weekend, spending time with one person – a person who seemed to like her an awful lot. The 'couple behavior' that had bugged her on Friday, by Sunday night felt comforting and welcome.

I like how this feels, she'd told him, snuggled into his neck on her sofa in front of a David Attenborough documentary.

And she did.

Train Guy who? she smiled to herself. In three days, her life had changed completely. Now that she'd let herself entertain the idea, Eddie was actually almost everything she wanted.

On Monday morning, when she saw Train Guy had written back to her in the paper, she decided to ignore it.

I screwed up, Coffee Spill Girl. I left, and I shouldn't have, and now I'm worried I blew it. I know you don't get a second chance at a first impression, but how about a first meeting on the second try?

No, she thought. *Not when there's a man right here who shows up when he says he will. Sorry, Train Guy.*

34

Daniel

On Monday, when Daniel got home from work, he hesitated at the door before he put his key in the lock. Lorenzo was home. Daniel didn't want to see him.

Pushing open the door, smells of garlic and salmon wafted through the hallway. Daniel's first thought was that if Lorenzo was hosting a date in their living room – a date with no warning, no less – he'd go straight back out again, probably to his mother's. His second reaction was to think, *How dare he impose on the house this way?* In theory Daniel didn't care who Lorenzo had over, but it was fucking poor form to have somebody over two nights after they'd thrown punches at each other over his treatment of another woman.

In so many ways Daniel had had no right to get involved with him and Becky, but . . . he just knew it wasn't right. He knew that Lorenzo would have taken Becky into his room if Daniel hadn't have stopped him, and that was just wrong. Daniel had saved Becky from doing something she probably wouldn't remember doing, but he'd saved Lorenzo from doing something he'd never be able to un-do too, no matter how blurred the line was. Daniel's conscience told him there were no shades of grey here, even if Lorenzo would've argued for them.

Lorenzo had been gone all day Sunday and come home after Daniel had locked himself away in his room, but in the forty-eight hours since it happened, Daniel had convinced himself that he was absolutely right to have stood up for Becky that way, whether she knew it or not. Whether Lorenzo knew it or not.

'Hello?' Lorenzo yelled, appearing at the kitchen door. 'Oh, hey man. I'm, erm . . . making pasta al salmone.'

Daniel nodded, and searched for clues as to who else was there.

'I got in a bottle of Malbec too.'

Daniel scrunched up his nose. For him? Was this for him?

'I'll open it,' Lorenzo said.

Daniel took off his jacket and threw it over the arm of the sofa as he heard the pop of a cork easing out of a bottle neck, and the sloshing of liquid against a glass. Lorenzo reappeared with two glasses and handed one over. Daniel took it.

'I'd have thought you'd be hungover,' Daniel said. 'Still.'

'I think you knocked my hangover out of me,' Lorenzo said. If that was a joke, neither of them laughed.

They sipped their wine. Eventually, Daniel moved to sit at the table. He wasn't sure what there was to talk about, really. There was nothing he really wanted to say.

'I know the other night was stupid,' Lorenzo said, awkwardly hovering by the table. 'I . . . I know that. I was a twat.' Daniel listened. He *had* been a twat, yes. It was good

242

that he understood that. 'And I texted Becky, and obviously she's . . .'

He kept letting his sentences trail off. Daniel almost felt sorry for him. Almost.

'She's told me not to text her again. Which, erm, you know.' And then his bottom lip wobbled and he burst into tears. A grown, thirty-something-year-old man with a bruise on his face and a glass of red wine in his hand let out a low guttural noise, like an animal in a trap.

'Oh mate, I don't know what happened,' he said, wiping at his eyes and trying to pull himself back together. 'We'd had sex before and I thought she was up for it. But she said . . .'

He trailed off.

Daniel's resolve to stay angry softened – but only slightly.

'I'm at a bit of a loss for words to be honest, mate,' Daniel said. He took a sip of his wine, measuring out what he wanted to say. 'I didn't think you were like that. Like – pervy.'

Lorenzo nodded, his face scrunched up. 'Are you gonna call the police?'

'The police?'

'To report me.' Daniel thought he meant about the fight, which obviously he wasn't going to do because he'd been just as much to blame. But then Lorenzo countered with, 'To report what I did to Becky.'

Daniel opened and closed his mouth, settling on saying: 'No. Of course not. Nothing technically happened, mate. But like – what if I wasn't there? You know? That's what's . . .' Now it was Daniel's turn to struggle to finish full thoughts. He wished he'd never gone on Saturday night. He wished he'd stayed home, like he'd wanted to. He didn't want to be having to explain the basics of consent to Lorenzo.

Lorenzo nodded. 'I know. I feel sick about it. Because if you hadn't – I mean, I didn't think I was doing anything wrong. But Becky says I should've known better. Her text was pretty brutal. She didn't pull any punches. And she's right. And I'm really fucking embarrassed.'

'Not to sound like your dad or anything, but I'm proper disappointed in you.'

'I know.'

Lorenzo sat down in the armchair across the room. Daniel drank. Lorenzo stared at the floor.

'It's just not that hard, you know? She doesn't have to say no for it to not be a yes.'

'I know,' said Lorenzo, shaking his head. 'I know that now.'

Daniel didn't know how to end the conversation. He was so, so mad that his flatmate could be so stupid.

Ah, that's interesting, he thought to himself. *You called him flatmate and not friend.*

And just like that, Daniel had inserted the emotional distance between him and Lorenzo.

'I'll go and plate up this food,' Daniel said, eventually. 'I appreciate you cooking.'

35

Nadia

Weeks passed. Nadia saw Eddie a few times a week and spent most weekends with him. He'd met both Gaby and Emma only once, since they both seemed increasingly hard to get hold of, but they'd liked him and said encouraging things, and yes, Gaby had texted afterwards to say: *Listen, he's wonderful, but before you get in too deep I really do think you should meet Sky Garden Guy! Like, really, really!!!!!*

Nadia had texted back a GIF of one of the Real Housewives of Atlanta shaking her head and saying, 'Nooooo, thank you!' and neither of them had brought it up again. Nadia just needed Gaby to understand that she was fine as she was. She'd said herself Eddie was a good guy. What was she supposed to do? Forever believe that good was not good enough, and that she had to strive for amazing or earth-shattering? No. Nadia was happy with Eddie, who was everything a boyfriend should be. Kind of. Probably. Okay, she was forcing it a tiny-weeny bit, but what choice did she have? This man was very into her, and she'd be crazy not to be into him too. And she did love his company. Her heart would catch up with her mind.

She *did* want to see her friends more, though. She wondered if it was her fault that it had been a few weeks since a brunch, or lunch, or drinks. That she'd been sucked in to the early throes of passion, of romance, and had maybe neglected her friendships a bit.

She'd started going into work later, choosing to have five more minutes with Eddie's lithe frame curled around her own, snuggled down under the duvet as the leaves on the trees outside of her window turned from bright green to golden around the edges, September pulling in. Arriving at the office later often meant working through lunch to make up the time, so she didn't get to walk to the market with Gaby for burritos. Not being home alone meant not being able to sit in front of the TV with her phone in her hand, texting Emma about their days, or what they were watching, or about the dates they'd just been on or had planned.

Nadia made the decision to book in a friend date – she didn't want to be that girl. The girl who let her whole life slip away from her because of a man. She didn't feel trapped or like she had to shrink her life in order to make room for Eddie. With him, it was more like he was fun to be with, and she liked being around him. She *loved* being part of a two. Finally, she was with a man who was caring and generous and sensible and knew his own mind. It would be weird if she didn't want to see a lot of him, wouldn't it? Plus, she liked who she was when she was with him: she laughed a lot, and said witty, funny things.

'Babe,' she said, one night at his place, down in Peckham. 'Do you mind if I bow out of movie-night Thursday?'

In less than a month they'd settled into a routine that meant they went down to the Rio in Dalston for the 8 p.m. showing of whatever was on and then walked to her flat. They'd made a silent pact that it didn't matter what it was – they'd go. Nadia got the tickets, and Eddie paid for the popcorn, gleefully pouring a bag of Maltesers into it so that halfway through a handful they'd get a surprise chocolate boost.

Eddie poked his head out from where he was cooking dinner in the kitchen. 'Mind?' he said, incredulous. 'Why would I mind?'

Nadia smiled. 'I suppose I thought you might miss me too much,' she said.

Eddie threw the tea towel over his shoulder and came over to her, leaning over the sofa to issue a kiss.

'Well, yes, of course I'll miss you,' he said. 'But I presume you're seeing the girls?'

'Exactly,' Nadia said. 'I'm going to see if Emma can come out to play.'

'Perfect,' said Eddie. 'Maybe I'll go out with the boys.'

Nadia reached for her phone and messaged Emma:

Nadia: *HELLO! Can you do a dinner this week?*

Emma texted back immediately – one of the things Nadia liked most about her, and had found so frustrating lately. She'd been taking 48 hours to get back to her.

Emma: *What are you thinking?*
Nadia: *Thursday?*
Emma: *Ah – I'm heading out of town Tuesday till Friday.*

247

Nadia: *For work?*

Emma: *Yeah! So . . . Friday? Saturday?*

Nadia: *Yup! I've got Mary's birthday on Saturday night, but other than that!*

Emma: *Noted. How's it going with The Ginge?*

Nadia: *Don't call him that! Also, would you hate me if I said how nice it is to have somebody to do stuff with?*

Emma: *Why would I hate you for that! It *is* nice to have somebody to do stuff with! . . . I mean, you like him too, though, yes?*

Eddie called through from the kitchen, 'Five-minute warning, babe! Fish Wellington with hollandaise sauce incoming!'

'I'll lay the table!' Nadia shouted back.

Nadia: *Of course I like him! Literally, he is plating up homemade fish Wellington as I type.*

Emma: *Okay, well – enjoy, and I'll let you know about the weekend later in the week if that's okay!*

Nadia: *Okay!!*

The next day at work, Nadia made a point of texting Gaby to connect too.

Nadia: *Coffee in the lobby in five?*

Gaby: *Oh babe! I'm on annual leave this week!*

Nadia: *What!!!!!!*

Gaby: *I had holiday to use up before the next big project starts and I'm not allowed to breathe without permission. I'm at home!*

Nadia: *Damn. I need a warning about these things!*

Gaby: Lol.

Nadia: Are you around for drinks? Dinner?

Gaby: Some of the time! I'm around at the weekend?

Nadia: Oh. Okay, cool. Yeah, the weekend works! Are you staying home the whole week?

Gaby: I'm going to leave town for a few days – get some fresh air, maybe by the sea. Do you wanna do Bellanger for brunch? Sunday?

Nadia: I do. I'll book a table so we can sit outside if it's still warm. I'm loving this ever-lasting summer.

Gaby: Perfect! Thank you!

Nadia: Enjoy your time off. I'm gonna miss you!

Gaby: ☺ ☺ ☺

The next morning, Nadia felt dejected. It truly was lovely to be seeing somebody, but she wanted to drink and wear lipstick and be fabulous with her tribe. She missed one drink turning into two bottles, and hungover brunches, and being a plus-one to whichever restaurant Emma had to review that week. Still, at least she had somebody else she could spend the time with. Eddie showed up on time, called when he said he would, and they had good sex.

They spent Sundays together, going to the market and getting ingredients that Eddie knew what to do with: he fed her poached cod in pistachio and parmesan crust, and made his own clotted-cream ice cream, and often cooked in double batches so that she could freeze the leftovers in a Tupperware and have it in the week.

She had a sated sex drive, a fridge full of food, and company as the nights drew in.

She was lucky.

She loved love, and what she had was surely going to

lead to it. She'd be greedy for wanting any more than what she had. But . . .

The lab was empty that morning, and with nobody around she pulled up Twitter on her screen, typing into the search bar at the top right: *#OurStop*

She didn't do it often, but sometimes, on occasion, she liked to remind herself that the whole letters-in-the-paper thing had happened, and other people had not only seen them, but felt so moved by them that they'd used a special hashtag to talk about them. Nobody had written anything since the last time she checked. It was @Your_London_Gal who had said: *I can't believe the #OurStop guy didn't turn up, and then asked for forgiveness from her! I wouldn't write back if I was her. No way. I really wanted a happy ending for them though!*

When she'd first read that, Nadia had felt grateful for the support – vindicated in her decision. But reading it now she felt a twinge of regret.

No, she thought. *He doesn't deserve that.* She forced herself to focus on the man she did have, chastising herself for being so weak as to search for the hashtag in the first place. Doubts were the ego's way of keeping us small, she told herself. She forced herself to believe she was allowed to let Eddie make her happy.

Your place or mine tonight? she texted him, knowing her diary was totally open that week and thankful to know Eddie would scoop her up from work and take her on an adventure. She never thought of Train Guy when they were together – not anymore. It was only when Eddie was out of sight that Train Guy sometimes crept into her mind.

Yours, Eddie texted back. *I'll come meet you after work?*

She sent back three love hearts and then pulled up the

notes app in her phone. She looked at what she had drafted a week ago:

Train Guy: Okay, I forgive you now I've made you think about what a fool you made of me, having me wait for you in a bar you'd apparently already left. Consider me furious, and very forgiving. I will allow you to make it up to me, in whatever way you see fit. Coffee Spill Girl x

She weighed up, for the millionth time, the pros and cons of sending it in.

Pros: She could actually get to meet Train Guy.

Cons: It was horribly deceptive to Eddie, who had been nothing but wonderful to her.

Pros: When Train Guy didn't reply, it would ultimately put that whole thing to bed for her, and she could properly commit to Eddie, and forget him once and for all.

Cons: If she did send it, and he replied, she'd be forced to act, and with her friends being so absent lately she wouldn't be able to guarantee that she'd make the right choice, because she had nobody to sound it all out with.

She let out a long, low sigh.

She didn't send the note.

36

Eddie

'I just get the feeling,' Eddie said across the table to his best friend, 'that she's holding something back. Like, she's there, sat next to me or walking beside me or opposite me at the dinner table, and we'll talk and laugh and make jokes and plans, but just occasionally, sometimes, it's like her mind wanders off and she's thinking of something – or, I dunno, I guess I worry some*one* – else.'

'Oh, that sucks,' said Callie sympathetically. The two had known each other since they were ten years old, growing up as neighbours, and losing their virginity to one another, but ultimately deciding that they were better off as friends. Callie had come to Eddie's university one weekend in his first year and met his course-mate, Matt, who just happened to be at the Student Union with them that night, and now the two were married, had two kids, had survived one bout of chlamydia and secured a mortgage on a beautiful corner apartment off Old Street. Matt was across the street with the kids at the park, playing on the swings. Eddie and Callie could see them from where they sat by the window, and waved occasionally.

'Do I sound crazy?' Eddie continued. 'I can't tell you anything specific, really. It's just a feeling.'

Callie shrugged. 'You get a pretty good read on people, Ed. If your gut is telling you something . . .' She trailed off. She didn't want to actively encourage him to doubt his relationship. He'd been so happy when he'd FaceTimed, the weekend after he'd met her. Callie knew he looked at the life she had with Matt and wanted it for himself – he'd always been unabashedly romantic. It had just never worked out with any of his girlfriends, for some reason. The six months she and Matt had had to double-date him and Melania were six months she'd had to block out of her mind – that woman was a frozen pea tester, for god's sake! How had Eddie managed to date a woman whose job was to assess the temperature of frozen peas on the production line! – and she'd understood when that had to end, but most of the other girls had all been nice enough. Callie really felt for him.

'But maybe you can give it time. If most of the time you have fun, enjoy it for what it is.'

'Do you think?' Eddie said. His phone buzzed. It was Nadia. 'Oh – sorry, Cal.'

'Hey babe,' he said down the phone to her.

'Hey babe,' Nadia replied. Eddie wasn't sure when they had started to use the term 'babe' with one another, but he liked it. He liked having a 'babe'. Sometimes he even said 'baby'. 'Can you pick up some Sellotape on your way over? I tried to wrap Mary's gift for tonight, but can't find the tape.'

Eddie liked being asked to run errands – he wanted to be the guy you could call to pick up bits on the way home.

'Absolutely,' he said. 'Text me if you need anything else?'

'I will,' Nadia replied. 'Are you having a nice time? Did you tell them I'm excited to meet them some time soon?'

Eddie looked across at his friend, watching her watch her kids and husband. He lowered the phone from his mouth and said to Callie, 'Nadia said she looks forward to meeting you.'

'Oh!' said Callie. 'Us too, Nadia! We've heard such great things!'

The unspoken truth between Callie and Eddie had been that the very reason Nadia hadn't met them yet was because Eddie was still unsure. Or rather, Eddie was unsure that Nadia was sure.

'I've gotta get back to my breakfast, babe, but I'll see you in about an hour, okay?'

'Okay! See you soon!'

She hung up.

Callie signalled across to the waitress for the bill, saying to Eddie, 'You know, it's only been, like, six weeks. Nobody has to be sure after just six weeks. I know you fell pretty hard at the beginning, but it can take time to grow a love. Maybe she is thinking of somebody else, but doesn't want to be.'

'That's true,' said Eddie. 'Like I told you, her ex was a mean sonofabitch. But I'm nothing like him.'

Callie handed the waitress her card and said to him, 'We've got this. Thank you for being such a wonderful godfather.'

Eddie smiled. 'Thank you, Callie.' He looked out across the park, seeing Matt and the girls headed back towards them. He wondered if he and Callie had a sort of telepathic married people's link, wherein Matt knew it was time to come back because Callie had settled up the bill, or Callie knew to settle up because Matt was about to leave the park and come back across with the girls.

'Uncle Eddie!' the youngest, Lily, squealed as he emerged with their mother from behind the glass door and onto the street. She ran towards him and Eddie scooped her up. Holding her out in front of him from under her armpits so that their eyes were level, Eddie said, 'Was that fun? Did you have fun at the park?'

'Yeah,' Lily said, kicking her feet with glee as she was suspended in the air.

'Shall I give you this pound I have in my pocket and take you to the shop?' Eddie said.

'Yes! Yes!' Lily squealed, at which her older sister tugged on the bottom of Eddie's t-shirt and said, 'Do I get a pound?'

Eddie put Lily back on the ground and knelt down to Bianca.

'You do,' he said, opening up his palm, flat, to reveal two one-pound coins. Bianca took both of them and handed one to her sister, and the pair led the way to the newsagent, discussing what they would buy.

'Typical Uncle Eddie,' Matt said. 'Loading the kids up on sugar and then handing them back.'

'Ahhh,' said Eddie. 'They might surprise you and buy an apple.'

'You gonna be this deluded when you're a dad?' Matt joked, and Eddie rolled his eyes. He didn't reply, but he thought to himself how much he'd like that – how much he'd like to be a dad. But the woman he was dating – he wasn't sure she was the one. He watched as Callie gave a wink over the top of his head to her husband, the two of them in their own little world, even if just for a second, their two kids trundling ahead. Their love looked like he wanted his love to feel, but he knew, even though it was inconvenient, that Nadia wouldn't be to him what Callie was to Matt. Maybe Callie had been right. It didn't matter that he couldn't explain it. It didn't make it *wrong*. It just meant that right now, it wasn't perfectly *right*.

37

Nadia

'Whatcha reading?' Eddie said, sneaking up behind Nadia and kissing her cheek as she sat at the bar of the Dean Street Townhouse, nursing an oatmilk latte. The weather had turned colder that late September week, forcing the population of London to switch from light jackets to lined macs, and open-toed sandals to ankle boots with socks. As Nadia had walked across Blackfriars Bridge and up past Somerset House and through Covent Garden, she'd gradually caught a chill on her bare legs that meant by the time she'd got to Soho she needed warming right through. As she'd supped at her coffee she already had a sneaking suspicion that it was too late, that she'd wake up sick tomorrow morning. She really hoped not. She was the grumpiest sick person in the world.

'Gah!' she said, flicking the newspaper closed guiltily.

Eddie slid into the spot next to her. 'I've never seen somebody so embarrassed to be caught reading the paper,' he said, good-naturedly. 'Were you reading the *Missed Connections* section again? You're obsessed!'

Nadia grimaced, trying to look playful. It was true, she did still check the *Missed Connections*, just in case. (*In case of what?* she thought. *In case some random guy wants to stand me up again?*)

'I just think it's romantic,' she said to him, sliding the paper away from her.

'I think having the courage to chat up a beautiful woman sat alone at a bar is romantic,' said Eddie, opening the drinks menu. He looked across to her and winked. He liked sitting side by side with her at a bar – it felt like 'their' thing, since that's how they'd met.

Eddie closed the drinks menu again, without ordering, and said, 'I want to say something. And I don't think you're going to like it.' He looked as though he was in pain – his face was screwed up funny. Nadia had never seen him like this before.

'Oh yeah?' replied Nadia.

'Yeah,' said Eddie.

She looked at him expectantly.

'I like you, Nadia. You know that, right? I liked you right from the moment you gave me a hard time when I sat down beside you that night.'

'I like you too,' Nadia said.

'Well. You see, that's the thing.'

Nadia creased her eyebrows together, struggling to follow.

'I'm not sure that you do,' Eddie said.

Nadia didn't understand. Of course she liked him! They'd spent most of their spare time together for almost two months now. They laughed and cooked and did all the things that couples do. She thought he was fun! A fun, nice guy!

'Why on earth would you think I don't like you?' Nadia said, bewildered.

Eddie stumbled over his words. 'Maybe I didn't say that properly. I mean, of course you like me. But I mean – sometimes it feels like you're . . . distant.'

'Distant?'

'Distant. Like you're with me, but your mind is somewhere else. I feel like we get on, and have a nice time, but I always thought . . . I supposed I always thought being with somebody would feel different, you know? Deeper, somehow. I feel like what we have here, it's fun, and it works, but it's not . . .'

'Deep?'

'. . . Yeah.'

Nadia didn't miss a beat. She knew what this meant. She knew by the way he hadn't actually taken off his coat, now she thought about it, that he was breaking up with her.

'So this is it?' she said.

Eddie shrugged. 'I didn't mean for it to be. But I've been thinking about it – I can't lie. I feel like I've kind of put it all out there, Nadia – given you all of me, and I don't get all of you back. It's a bit embarrassing.'

Nadia reached out to touch his arm. 'But babe,' she said. 'I told you. My ex, he was . . . I'm trying, okay? I'm really happy with you.'

Eddie narrowed his eyes at her, as if trying to read the spaces between her words. 'But could you be happier? With somebody else? Because . . .'

He wasn't finishing any of his sentences properly. 'Because you think that you could be?' Nadia supplied, and Eddie nodded.

Nadia didn't know what to think. There wasn't a huge

bodily reaction to what Eddie was saying – she didn't want to throw up, or cry. But her ego was bruised by it. Because what he was saying was that she wasn't enough. And all her old doubts and insecurities flooded back to her, about how she was never enough, about how no man ever truly wanted her, how she wasn't as easy to love as other women.

'I don't know what to say.'

Eddie half smiled. 'I guess what I wanted to know is: is there somebody else? Or, do you wish there was? Because I don't feel like enough for you.'

He didn't feel like he was enough for her? But wasn't he saying she was the one lacking? Before she spoke, her tummy did a little leap as she thought: *Train Guy.* Those notes back and forth that there had been, the anticipation she'd had – it had been exciting. But it was nothing – Eddie was an actual real person, whom she'd talked to directly and slept with and made plans with. She wanted more time to decide, was all. Needed more time to fall for him. She could, if she tried. She was sure she could.

'There's nobody else, of course there isn't!' Nadia said. 'Eddie, I'm having a really great time with you.'

Eddie nodded. 'Okay then,' he said. 'Well, I've told you how I feel.'

'So what now?'

'So, let's go home, and eat, and keep enjoying this.'

'Even though you think you'd be happier with somebody else?'

Eddie looked at her. 'I guess I just wanted some reassurance, is all,' he said. 'I'm falling for you, Nadia.'

Nadia took a breath. He was falling for her. She *was* enough. That felt good to hear. She needed him to fall for her. She needed to know for sure that she was enough. And she'd feel the same soon. Time. She just needed time.

'So . . . we're going to keep doing . . . this?' she said.

'If you want to,' Eddie replied, and Nadia did. She really, truly, desperately wanted to feel as deeply as Eddie did. She *wanted* to fall for this good, good man. She *wanted* to make him happy. She *wanted* to be happy herself.

'Let's pay and go,' she said, reaching for her bag. 'I just need to find my card.' She rooted around for her wallet, lost in the depths of her navy leather bag. She felt the edges of a plastic rectangle. 'Got it,' she said, triumphantly. She half wondered why her card wasn't in her wallet and when she fished it out she saw why. It wasn't her card. It was the card from that night – the one that said D E WEISSMAN. She'd forgotten she had that – his card from that night. She dropped it back into her bag like it was on fire, and Eddie said. 'I can get it, babe. *Ça va sans dire.*'

'Savva what?' Nadia said.

'*Ça va sans dire.* It's French. It means, "it goes without saying".'

'I have literally never heard that used in conversation in my life.'

'A lot of people haven't. But don't you think it sounds classy? *Ça va sans dire . . .*'

Nadia cocked her head at him. She thought it sounded pretentious, and suddenly, in that moment, everything about him bothered her. His stupid phrase and his stupid jacket and his stupid kindness and honesty.

'But like,' she said, pushing the issue, 'if a lot of people don't know what it means, why say it?'

'Because I like it,' he countered. The barman held out the card machine and Eddie tapped his card against it.

'But, wouldn't you rather be clear in your communication? It's like you're using it to be deliberately confusing. So that people ask you what it means and you get to tell them.'

Eddie laughed, nonplussed by her tone. 'What's wrong with that? I get to teach them something.'

'But it's showing off.'

'It's not.' That's all he said. *It's not.* And typically, that's why Nadia had respected him: Eddie knew who he was and what his values were, and wasn't swayed by what other people thought. And just like that Nadia went from desperate to hope and to try with this man beside her, to angry. Irrationally angry. She knew, frustratingly, that she was better than this. She knew, in the blood pumping through her pissed-off veins, that she had let herself down because she should have been honest with him. Should have told him that she *did* think of somebody else, *was* holding a part of herself back. She had continued to see this man because she had been lonely, and on some level thought this was all she was worth – an almost. She was so mad at herself! She knew, she fucking *knew*, that it was better to be alone than with the wrong guy. And she had tried with Eddie. Even if she hadn't explicitly known he was the wrong guy, in her gut she knew he wasn't the right one. Two months was enough to know. It was inconvenient to acknowledge that, but it was true.

Outside, Eddie said, 'What is wrong with you?' and Nadia turned to him and said, 'You're right, aren't you? This isn't working.'

Eddie's mouth opened and closed. 'Literally I tried to break up with you for your sake five minutes ago and you got me to give it another chance, and now you're breaking up with me?'

Nadia looked at him. She felt like a grade A bitch. She

hadn't meant to string him along. She hadn't meant any of this. She felt ashamed, then – ashamed to have acted less than her best self. It was at that moment that a familiar shape caught her eye, and even though Eddie was stood before her wanting a response, she was distracted. *It's Gaby!* she thought. She was so relieved to see her. She'd last seen her outside of work at their Bellanger brunch, weeks ago – and Gaby had only stayed an hour before having to dash off somewhere else. She'd been working across at MI6 on a project lately too, so hadn't even been around at the office. Even if Nadia couldn't communicate what was happening she'd feel stronger and braver just from a hug. Nadia hung back from calling her name, though. Something wasn't right.

Gaby was holding somebody's hand behind her, and Nadia saw Emma come into view. They were out without her. Why would they be out without her? Instinctively Nadia took a step back into the doorway of the bar.

'What are you doing?' said Eddie, to which her only reply was, 'Sssssshhhhhh!'

From under the awning of the restaurant, she watched her work best friend and in-real-life best friend, a heavy feeling settling in the pit of her stomach. *They've ditched me*, she thought. *They've ditched me to hang out without me.* Nadia felt humiliated – and also totally infantilized. She'd felt weird about them chatting with each other and how they knew things about each other more and more, as well as, well, not exactly ganging up on her, but definitely forming an allegiance together, acting like their own two-person army without her. Emma had outright lied to her earlier, saying she had a date. Nadia felt betrayed. And yet, she was mesmerized by watching what unfolded.

Gaby pulled Emma's hand behind her, and spun around

265

so that the two women were facing each other. Their noses pressed against one another. *Wow*, Nadia thought. *They're wasted.* But it was only 6 p.m. Were they really drunk? And then they kissed. Not politely, or like friends, but full-on hands-in-each-other's-hair open-mouthed snogged. Emma pulled away and laughed with her head tipped back, and Gaby put a hand on the back of her neck and sort of *ruffled* her, smiling.

'Fuck,' Nadia said, out loud. 'They're not drunk – they're in love.'

Eddie crouched down next to her. 'Isn't that—'

'Yeah,' Nadia said, watching them walk down the street until they disappeared, holding on to each other the whole time.

'Fuck me,' said Nadia, bewildered.

'You didn't know?' Eddie said.

Nadia stood back up, all the way, glancing one last time in the direction her two friends had gone. 'I didn't know,' she said.

Eddie nodded, concerned. 'Do you want a drink? One for the road?'

Nadia looked at him. This man, who even after she had picked a fight and been rude and mean, even after she had effectively wasted two months of his life, making out like she could love him when she'd known all along, if she was going to be really honest, that she wouldn't – even if she tried really hard! – was, as ever, upholding the very tenets of gentlemanly behaviour that would make him the perfect catch for somebody else.

'You're going to find the biggest, most brilliant love, you know,' she said to him.

'Thanks,' he said, sadly. 'I hope so.'

'You are. You're a wonderful man, and I'm sorry if I've left you worse than I found you.'

Eddie looked up at the darkening sky. 'I think I'm going to take a walk,' he said. 'Are you going to be okay?'

'About us? I will be.' She rolled her eyes. 'About my best friends secretly . . . what? Dating? Did it look like love to you? I don't even know. I guess this is why they've both fallen off the radar lately.'

'As long as they're happy, right?' Eddie said.

'Well, yes,' Nadia said. 'But it's easier to be happier for people when you know what's going on.'

Eddie smiled. 'Can I kiss you on the cheek?' he said.

Nadia offered up one side of her face, and Eddie said, 'All the best, Nadia. I hope you find what you're looking for.'

Nadia watched him turn away, in the opposite direction to the one Emma and Gaby had taken, and said in return, 'All the best, Eddie.'

She watched him amble down the road, his hands in his pockets and his overnight bag slung over his shoulder, and once he'd disappeared Nadia looked back towards where her friends had been. She'd been left in one direction, and left in the other, and as evening fell and the temperature dropped, she stood, all alone, not knowing where to head next.

38

Daniel

Daniel stood in the line that snaked around the field, wrapped up in his winter coat for the first time this season. The early days of November meant winter was officially on the way. He blew into his cupped hands and rubbed them together for warmth, and pulled his navy cashmere scarf a little higher up his neck.

'Bloody hell,' he said. 'I reckon there must be three hundred people in front of us, you know.'

Jeremy rolled his eyes, hitting him on the shoulder playfully. 'Ah mate, calm down – we'll be in there soon enough. Drink your juice.'

Daniel shook his empty can at him, signalling that he already had.

The group of them – Daniel and Jeremy and Sabrina, as well as Sam and Rashida, were queuing for a *Romeo + Juliet*-themed immersive cinema event at a covered parking lot near White City. Under their coats, which they'd stored in lockers inside, everyone was in costume according to a character they'd been assigned, and for four hours they'd roam through a set designed to look just like the film, interacting with actors who milled about in amongst guests, acting out scenes from the movie and making everyone feel like they too were part of the imagined world.

Eventually they'd settle down to watch the film surrounded by thousands of tea-lights, snuggled under blankets. Daniel had been to the *Blade Runner* immersive event last year, run by the same company, and it had blown his mind. He was beyond pumped to be back. He had high expectations for the night – despite the massive queue to get in.

'Here,' Jeremy's partner Sabrina said. 'Have another gin in a tin.' She handed him an M&S can, which he accepted gratefully.

'Gin in a tin,' Daniel said. 'Who knew?'

'We did!' chorused Rashida and Sabrina, clinking their cans against one another, laughing. It was nice how great they got on together, chatting away as much to each other as to the other men in the group. The uni WAGS had become friends in their own right.

'Pissheads,' admonished Sam, smiling.

Daniel had accepted his fate, lately – mostly hanging out with either Romeo after work or the couples from uni when he could. He didn't see much of Lorenzo, really, save for the odd five-minute toast-eating session before work, where their chat was full of the effort of keeping it light. He was mostly a permanent gooseberry, the forever third wheel. Every woman he knew had offered to introduce him to somebody (even his mother!), but Daniel had decided to take a break from dating after just three days on *Guardian* Soulmates, where he'd been confronted with women who specified the height of their preferred guy in their bios, or had a list of personality requirements so long that Daniel went cross-eyed even trying to get through them all.

Must have own house, own car, own friendship group and be able to deal with a confident woman who knows her place in the world, said one. *I wanna have kids, not date them!!!!* said another. He'd flicked through Michelle Obama's auto-biography when it came out, and seen the bits about how she'd met Barack, and how he arrived to her fully formed, knowing who he was. Daniel kind of understood what these women meant: they all wanted their Barack too. A man who wasn't looking for a woman to mother them, Daniel supposed, who wouldn't feel emasculated by a woman with her own money and life. He got that. Daniel appreciated a strong woman – his mother was one – and knew what it took in what was still a man's world to achieve great things and have a voice . . . but in a relationship he wanted a partner, some-body to build something with, not somebody who'd built her own thing and be mad that he didn't have his. From what he knew about a Barack and Michelle kind of love, it meant something soft and gentle behind closed doors.

But none of these bios specified that, in private, relation-ships were made up of everyday gestures of kindness and respect, and until Daniel had met somebody who felt like an exhale, who knew that it wasn't an assault on her feminism to make a cup of tea for them both, who would cheer for him like he pledged to cheer for her – well, he was good being part of his friends' relationships. He was finishing off his six-month contract at Converge, tying up the loose ends, and wasn't far off being able to exchange on a two-bed flat in Stamford Hill that he'd found, using the money from his dad's life insurance for the deposit. His mother had insisted he take it. She didn't need it, she said. Maybe he'd date again in the new year. Probably he would. He knew he had to show up for love, for love to find him. But right now he was tired. After his dad, and the confusion with Nadia and the paper, he needed time to regroup.

'Nearly there!' said Rashida, as they inched to the entrance after almost forty-five minutes.

'Are we ready?' said Sam, and the two couples and Daniel gathered by the final door through to where they'd spend their evening.

'Ready,' said Daniel, bringing up the rear.

They pushed through the door into the tented area of the park, so grand that it took their collective breaths away.

'This way, dear friends, and with but haste,' a woman in a black wig and tassel bra said. 'Let us but meet my uncle, who will tell you everything.'

Daniel loved it. At the *Blade Runner* event, they'd made it rain from the ceiling of an airport hangar and before the movie all the characters had hung from the ceiling upside down, doing a fight sequence. Stuff like this was why he loved London. Big-scale, massive, stupidly impressive events on a random weekday night. And yeah, it cost a hundred quid a ticket, but goddamn, there was a Ferris wheel – a Ferris wheel inside!! – and an old stage shaped just like the one in the film.

Now everyone had taken off their coats it was easier to see who was who: the Montagues all got shipped off to the other side of the space, dressed in blue, and Daniel and his mates were in florals of black and red, for Capulets – Daniel himself was in a black leather waistcoat with nothing underneath, and black jeans.

'Fuck me,' Jeremy said. 'All right, Iron Man?'

Daniel looked down at himself.

'No wonder you were cold!' said Sabrina. 'You're half-naked!'

Sam raised his eyebrows. 'To be honest, if I had guns like that, I'd have them on show too,' he said. 'You've been working out, bro!'

Daniel felt himself blush. Admittedly, it was a bit of an extrovert outfit, but he was embarrassed that all his friends were looking at him.

'I mean,' he said shyly, 'I've been at the gym a bit.' Rashida put an arm around him to save him from the others, saying, 'You look great, babe. Come on.'

They were led into another room, where everyone had to put on a mask they had brought along before being allowed inside a full-scale replica of the masked ball from the movie – right down to the aquarium where Leonardo DiCaprio met Claire Danes, peering at each other through ten inches of salted water and several slender yellow fish. Daniel loitered by it, wondering what it would be like to see the love of his life through the water, on the other side. He believed love would come. One day. Eventually.

The group spent a few hours meandering around the sites, bearing witness to a rap battle between houses, and a choreographed fight break out near the stage, where later a gospel choir would stand in a semicircle and sing 'Everybody's Free' and not even Jeremy would crack a joke, they'd all just stand in impressed awe.

'Shall we go and find a spot for the film?' one of them said, eventually, and the group agreed they'd better go and figure out where to sit, since the screening would start soon.

'Okay, you guys get set up here,' Daniel said, after they'd picked their spot, 'and I'll go get snacks? What does everyone want?'

'Look at those posh buggers,' Jeremy said, not registering Daniel had said anything, but instead nodding his head over to the VIP area. 'Posh bastards with their bean bags and blankets.'

Daniel turned to where he was looking and took in the atmosphere: he didn't mind that he wasn't VIP, over in the roped-off area. He knew those tickets were almost double what he'd paid. There was room for everybody, and there was a camaraderie in the air.

For a moment he watched a couple very obviously on a date smooth out their blanket and take off their shoes. The guy looked weirdly familiar to Daniel. He was tall, and very smiley, with bright red hair. Daniel watched as the man presented his date with a giant pair of woolly socks, and the girl tipped her head back, laughing. The man whispered something in her ear, putting his arm around her shoulder to do so, and the action took Daniel right back to the morning after he was supposed to have met with Nadia, when she was on the train with her boyfriend. The guy had the same ease with his body, the same comfortableness with intimacy and physical touch. And then the penny dropped: it *was* him! That was the boyfriend! The image of him listing off their weekend plans into Nadia's neck as he sat with a hand on her leg was seared in Daniel's mind. He was sure this was the same guy. Totally positive. The two of them arranged their snacks and drinks to the left and right of themselves and then snuggled down underneath a second blanket, wearing their socks, chatting together as if there was nobody else around.

'Couple of lovebirds over there, huh?' said Sabrina.

Daniel came to. 'Huh? Oh. Yeah. Actually, I think I know him.'

'Are you going to go say hello?' Sabrina asked.

Daniel shook his head. 'No. No, I don't know him that well,' he said. Daniel didn't actually know him at all. But. If he was right – and he was pretty convinced he was – if that was Nadia's boyfriend, then he certainly wasn't with Nadia. So, had they broken up? Daniel wasn't sure if that mattered. The only thing he had promised himself – and Romeo – was that if he saw her, he'd speak to her. But he hadn't seen her. She hadn't been on his train, or on the platform, or bustling through the crowds of other commuters. It was like she'd vanished. He hadn't thought about her for a few weeks, actually. He had even stopped reading the paper, because all he did was flick straight to the *Missed Connections* section, half hoping she'd written to him. She never had, of course, because why would she? His brain started to spiral, the way it had before: had it even been her writing back? What had he been thinking with all that nonsense? It was mortifying. He must have just been a bit brain-addled after his dad, clinging on to the weirdest things.

'Earth to Daniel?' Sam said. 'Hello?'

Daniel turned and looked at him.

'Huh?'

'Those snacks, dude. It's two popcorns, four pulled pork burgers and some beers.'

'And something sweet too!' added Rashida. 'If they've got Revels or Buttons or something.'

Jeremy stood up from where he'd been nestled into a spot on their picnic blanket. 'I'll come with you, mate. You can't carry all that.'

As they walked to the concession stands, Daniel threw a glance back over his shoulder. *I'm sure that's him*, he thought.

39

Nadia

Nadia wandered arm-in-arm with Naomi, her old colleague from a job years ago who had since left the world of STEM to become a professional Instagrammer with almost three hundred thousand followers. She was the one in the picture-perfect relationship with Callum, who was now officially her 'Instagram Husband', snapping her for uploads that she could command up to eight thousand pounds for. Nadia reflected on her hundred and thirty-three followers on her own account and wondered what she could charge. About thirty pence, maybe? She couldn't be too envious, though – it was Naomi's followers that meant she got offered free tickets to an event like tonight, something Nadia would have paid for anyway, but it was so much sweeter to be comp'd as a VIP.

All around them, people dressed as Montagues and Capulets meandered around, the actors placed amongst them reciting lines and having rap battles and generally adding to the atmosphere. It was like an immersive theatre event, with anything able to happen next. Nadia was thrilled to be there. She'd kept a low profile since breaking up with Eddie, heading to work and going to her classes at the gym and reading a lot at home on the sofa. She wasn't too saddened by the break-up – they'd been dating only a few weeks, after all. But it was the loneliness she was struggling with.

Not only did she no longer have Eddie, but after seeing Gaby and Emma together Nadia had made the decision to wait it out – to wait for them to come to her with her news. Except, so far, they hadn't. Nadia didn't reach out to them, and save for a cursory and distant text from Emma once a week, she didn't really hear from them. Gaby always seemed to be in a rush somewhere at work too, and that's why Nadia had forced herself to reach out to the old work friend she hadn't seen in a while. She figured Emma and Gaby had to hash out what was going on between them in their own time, and Nadia would just have to wait, patiently. On the sofa. At home. Alone.

Naomi and Nadia caught up on each other's lives as they walked: Naomi's brand deals and business and the difficulties of working with her husband.

'He drives me nuts!' she said. 'We're together almost all day, every day. But then, he takes the afternoon off to go to the health club or drives down to the coast to see his brother, and I miss him horribly.' She laughed at the predicament. 'I don't think it's healthy to spend so much time together, but I'm as obsessed with him as I ever was!'

Nadia smiled. She was envious, really, of how easily Naomi talked about her love for Callum. But also, it was more than that: there was a respect. A really deep respect for both him, and what they had.

'Are you seeing anyone?' Naomi said, following up with, 'I know that's the worst question in the world.'

Nadia smiled. 'It is, but also you're allowed to ask. And the answer is no. I was seeing somebody, a guy – we met in a bar, when I was actually stood up by another date, woe is me.' She rolled her eyes, pseudo-dramatically. 'And he was so great. But . . .'

'But not the one?' Naomi supposed.

'But not the one,' Nadia said. She sighed. 'Do you think I'm too picky?'

Naomi pointed in the direction of the VIP area and distractedly said, 'Let's go grab a spot over there.'

'Okay,' said Nadia.

'And do I think you're too picky? Oh, I don't know. Only you know that. I know that a lot of women – and, you know, probably a lot of men – fall in love even after they're married. For some people there's a lightning bolt that strikes when you meet, and for others it's more work.'

Nadia nodded along as they let a concierge hand them bean bags and blankets and gift bags.

'I don't think one is more right than the other,' Naomi said. 'It's just what works for you.'

They sat down and Nadia peered in the goodie bag: there was some coconut water and a handful of Lindt chocolate balls.

'Could you go in for a burger?' she asked.

Naomi smiled. 'I could always go in for a burger.'

They stood and looked across to the food area, where small lines had formed in front of each stand. 'That way, I guess,' Nadia said. And to close off the discussion of her love life: 'And I see what you're saying. I guess for now I am better alone, until I'm not. Self-contained, but ready for romance whenever the opportunity presents itself. Or something.'

'Or something,' smiled Naomi.

They meandered over to the burger stand, admiring people's outfits along the way, and almost being pulled into a battle of words in Shakespearean English, where a group had gathered around Romeo's mother and Juliet's nurse. The atmosphere was electric – it was a spectacular event.

The women joined the queue behind two dark-haired men – one in a Hawaiian print shirt and another in a black leather waistcoat with nothing underneath, and waited to order their food. Naomi clocked the men before Nadia did, using her eyebrows to make a funny face that inferred she thought they were appealing. A kind of *huh-huh-huh* in their direction. Nadia crinkled her face up, puzzled, and then once she understood what Naomi meant, leant forward to get a better look.

'And the thing is,' the guy in the waistcoat was saying, 'it's more of a comment on performative gender, I think – the way it's girls versus boys, even. That's so heteronormative! So the girls start preening more and the guys start peacocking more and, just to observe, it's fascinating.'

Nadia leaned her head forward a little more. Was he talking about *The Lust Villa*? And what's more, was he talking about *The Lust Villa* with high-brow gender analysis?

His friend, the one in the shirt, replied, 'I see what you mean, yeah. Like, well. You know. I don't wanna sound gay or anything but you've just got to let people be people, haven't you? Like, I'm really not or nothing – obviously I'm not.' The guy held up his hands, as if to prove he wasn't holding 'gay' in them. 'But it'd be pretty cool to watch two men hit it off. Like, if they were emotional and that, you know.'

'Exactly!' the guy in the waistcoat was saying. 'I mean like, I feel it, sometimes. When dad died in the summer and I felt like I had to be so brave because otherwise, you know, I was some massive poofter or weak or whatever. I like how it's becoming more okay for blokes to have feelings. My flatmate's a dick but I just made friends with this guy at my job, and he doesn't take the piss out of everything like Lorenzo does. He's just . . . nicer to be around.'

'Yeah man, that's rough,' his friend said. 'The Lorenzo thing. I never really liked him, and after what you told me . . .'

'Yeah,' the guy in the leather waistcoat said, craning his neck to see if the queue was going down at all.

Nadia was hooked. Who were these two men talking so eloquently and beautifully about their feelings? And about the best show on television? The guy in the waistcoat turned, slightly, and reached out to his friend's shoulder.

'How you doing anyway?' he said. 'I am so, so sorry about your granddad. I know how close you were.' The one in the shirt seemed caught off guard by that, suddenly welling up. Naomi was listening in intently too, and put a finger to each eye and ran them down her face, as if to say to Nadia, *He's crying.* Nadia could see all the hairs rising at the back of his neck. Bless him.

'It was his time,' the guy said. 'But fuck, I miss him, you know?'

'If you ever want to talk . . .' Waistcoat Guy said, and Nadia silently thought to herself, *Of course he wants to talk! He's asking to talk now! Do it now! He won't come to you again!*

The queue for pulled-pork burgers moved slowly in front of them. The guy in the waistcoat said, after assessing they'd be in line for at least another five minutes, 'What's your favourite memory of him?'

Nadia's heart exploded. What a man this guy was. Beautiful arms, able to talk about his feelings, smart too . . .

She realized Naomi was sort of nodding her head, as if to say, *Talk to him!* But Nadia couldn't interrupt this tender

281

moment. The guy had stopped crying and was saying something about how his granddad used to get really bad wind, but would always blame the dog, even after the dog had died. 'I'd give anything to have him here. He was a right sound bastard.'

The queue inched forward. Nadia pulled out her phone and typed into a blank note, *I am in love with these men in front!!!!! OMG!!!*

She passed the phone to Naomi, who read it and typed back, *More men like this please! Beautiful, open hearts. I've got a hard-on for it.*

Nadia burst out laughing as she read it, forcing the men in front to turn around, and the man in the waistcoat to hit his elbow on the corner of her iPhone, promptly knocking it to the floor. Without thinking, Nadia instinctively bent down to pick it up, but at the same moment the man in the waistcoat did too, muttering in a London twang, 'Fucking hell, I'm so sorry. I'm such a clumsy idiot!'

From where they both crouched down, him holding both her phone and the two food vouchers that had fluttered to the ground with it, their eyes met.

Nadia had the thunderbolt. The jolt. The course of electricity pulsed through every cell in her body.

'Hi,' she said to him.

'Hi,' he replied, smiling.

40

Daniel

Nadia broke out into a nervous giggle as they stood up.

'I don't know why I said hi,' she said. 'I felt for a minute that I knew you. Sorry.'

Her friend stood beside her, watching the interaction unfold, amused.

'Here,' Daniel said, holding out the phone back to Nadia. 'I hope I didn't break it.'

'It's got a case,' Nadia said, not even looking at it. 'I'm clumsy. I drop it all the time. Don't ever give me a baby to hold!' she added, giggling again. And then, straight-faced: 'That was a weird thing to say. Sorry. Again.'

Daniel saw Nadia's friend smile to the right of him, to where Jeremy was smiling back. It was as if they were agreeing to let the scene play out, content to both act as the audience.

Daniel and Nadia looked at each other.

Daniel repeated: 'So, this is yours.' He handed over the

phone. He couldn't help but notice it was open on notes. He wondered what she had been writing.

Nadia took the phone, and grinned.

Daniel's heart raced. His breathing got faster. This was it – this was his chance. His opportunity to say something smart and charming and clever that would make it okay to then say: *It's me. I stood you up after writing to you in the paper. Can we try again?*

Don't fuck this up, he told himself. *Come on!*

41

Nadia

Nadia's heart beat twice as fast as it had been. Had he read what they'd been typing? She took the phone off of him.

'Thank you,' she said.

'And this,' he said, giving her the meal vouchers she'd been holding too. She hadn't realized she'd dropped them as well.

'Ah. Cheers. It's my meal voucher.' What was wrong with her? Why was she being the most boring, ineloquent person on the planet? She needed to say something charming and disarming! This man was beautiful, with deep eyes that twinkled in mischief. He was just her type, physically, but more than that: from listening to him, even just for a minute, she knew he was emphatically A Good Man. A Good Man with good friends and a good moral compass and . . . oh god, he was so fucking sexy. Those arms!

'VIP perk?' he said, gesturing to the tickets.

Nadia nodded. Were they really going to make small talk

this way? She needed to pivot the conversation, to somehow open up the chit-chat to a little flirting. She was doing a god-awful job of giving him the right signals. And why wasn't Naomi helping, for god's sake? She was just stood there, watching, like somebody lost in a dogging spot.

'Well – it's Naomi's VIP perk. She's an Instagrammer.'

Waistcoat Man smiled at her. 'Nice,' he said.

Naomi was Nadia's most Conventionally Beautiful friend. Emma and Gaby, her friends from back home, all the women Nadia knew – they were all beautiful in their own way. But the reason Naomi's Instagram had taken off was because she was *conventionally* beautiful, with petite features arranged symmetrically and with straight, white teeth and skin that wasn't just clear, but glowed. That Waistcoat Guy didn't let his gaze rest on Naomi for longer than a millisecond – he'd barely noticed her at all in fact! – was unusual to Nadia, because as confident as she generally felt in her appearance – occasional acne issues aside – she was contentedly invisible when Naomi was around. Except – not to this man, she wasn't. This man seemed as transfixed by her as she was by him. It was like there was an invisible piece of cotton from his wrist to hers, a connection that was bone-deep. That tugged. They continued to look at each other, Nadia mentally berating herself for not being able to say something to start a proper conversation.

The man in front of her opened his mouth and took a big breath and seemed about to save them both from the lack of words between them. But then he closed his mouth again and simply broke out into a huge grin, that made Nadia grin, and there they were, two idiots, grinning.

Where do I know him from? thought Nadia, wondering if

feeling like you recognized somebody was all part of the feeling of unparalleled attraction.

'I'm pretty excited about this movie,' he said, eventually, and it made Nadia laugh. The simplicity of it. He used his thumb to gesticulate towards the big screen at the other end of the field. 'I remember the first time I saw it. I'd never understood why Shakespeare was good before Leonardo DiCaprio.'

'*Is love a tender thing?*' Nadia quoted, '*It is too rough, too rude, too boisterous, and it pricks like thorn.*'

The man nodded, impressed. He got the reference, and countered with a quote of his own: '*My bounty is as boundless as the sea.*'

'Oh. Shit. I don't remember any more,' Nadia laughed. This was it. They'd cracked it. This was the gateway she'd been grappling for. He was laughing too. Nadia could feel the rise and fall of her breath in her chest, and bit at her bottom lip anxiously.

'Nadia?'

It was a voice Nadia recognized. She turned around.

'Eddie!' she said, shocked but happy.

'How are you?' Eddie said, opening up his arms for a hug. He'd been like that from the night she'd met him: open, warm, loving, affectionate.

Nadia turned to Naomi, 'Naomi, this is the guy I was just telling you about. Eddie – this is my friend Naomi.' She paused for a second, to where the guys in front had been stood not ten seconds ago. She may as well introduce them too. But they were ahead now, at the booth, ordering their food. Nadia hadn't realized they'd made it to the front of the line.

'How've you been?' Eddie said. 'This is Alya, my girlfriend. Alya, baby, this is Nadia.'

Alya stuck out a hand. 'I've heard a lot about you,' she said, smiling.

'You have?' Nadia said.

Eddie laughed, 'All good, Nadia, don't worry.' He turned to Naomi. 'Your friend broke my heart a little,' he said. 'But then I met Alya, and realized why it had never worked out with anybody else.'

Eddie smiled at his girlfriend and put his arm around her again, pulling her in close. He was reassuring her. Marking his territory. Making his allegiances clear. Nadia was genuinely thrilled he seemed so happy, and told him so. It was easier to see him with somebody else than to think that in any way she'd hurt him and that he still hurt. It let her off the hook.

'Thanks, Nadia,' he said. And then: 'Anyway, we should probably get going. I think the movie is about to start.'

Nadia nodded.

'Nice to meet you,' Naomi said. As Eddie and Alya walked away, she asked, 'The not-quite-enough guy?'

Nadia nodded. 'Yup.'

She turned to locate Waistcoat Guy again, but when she searched for him by the food stand, where he'd been seconds ago, he wasn't there.

'Ah!' she said to Naomi. 'That guy! Where did he go?'

Naomi followed Nadia's line of sight and shrugged. 'Oh shit, I don't know!' she said. 'He was so into you!'

'I was so into him!'

'I could tell. It was like you were having sex with him with your eyes.'

Nadia hit her friend's arm.

'We'll find him. It's not that big here. Maybe he'll come back.'

Nadia looked around the area again.

'I hope so,' she said, and Naomi pulled on her arm so that she'd step forward to the food counter. 'He was . . . wow.'

42

Daniel

'Well,' Romeo was saying. 'You've got absolutely no choice. You've got to write to her again. You've used up your nine lives, man – if you were to see her by chance ever again, I'd be shocked. Like, seeing her last night was your last chance. You've got to write to her again! It's not like *another* chance meeting will ever, ever happen.'

Romeo had come upstairs to Daniel's desk on his break, after Daniel had sent him a series of texts telling him what happened at the screening the night before.

'You can't send me a text like that and not have me stage an intervention, friend,' he'd said, appearing by his side. 'What do you mean you lost her? How many opportunities are you willing to blow?!'

'You weren't in the lobby when I needed you!' Daniel said, by way of response.

'I had to go pee! Even security men get bathroom breaks!' Romeo had said, exasperated. Then: 'I can't believe you wandered off because her ex-boyfriend was there. You coward! You're better than that, man! You said yourself he was with somebody else.'

'Nah man, she didn't need an audience for that, did she?' Daniel said, still trying to unravel why he'd bolted that way. Romeo was right, though: how many chances did he want to blow? Maybe it was panic. He'd once heard that the only thing worse than harbouring a dream was having that dream come true, because then, what was left to want?

He simply couldn't explain why he hadn't loitered and waited for the guy to leave. Nadia was interested. He could tell. They hadn't been able to look away from each other – at least not until they were interrupted. His heart had quickened, his brain had gone blank, he'd not done much other than grin like an idiot at her, but she had grinned back, letting whatever energy between them exist to do just that. Exist. He hadn't held his breath in front of her, he'd exhaled. It was what he had been looking for. Inexplicably, he'd willingly walked away.

Daniel's face was serious. 'I agree. I think you're right. I think I should write to her. I just – I needed you to tell me it was a good idea, that's all. And you're telling me it is, so. That's decided then. I will write, and this time won't leave her waiting for me. We just have to hope she understands it's meant for her, is all.'

Romeo offered him a hand to shake.

'My man. Tell her straight up: *We spoke at Secret Cinema the other night, me in a waistcoat and you looking beautiful. I knocked your phone out of your hand, and I'm an idiot for not putting my phone number in it first. You get my train – the 7.30, at Angel. I think we might have written to each other before . . .*'

Daniel nodded along with every word Romeo said.

'Great,' he said, still nodding, amazed at how right Romeo seemed to get everything. 'Yes! Perfect.'

He moved the mouse to his computer and typed in the URL for *Missed Connections* submissions.

'Now,' Daniel said, fingers poised over the keys, 'repeat what you just said?'

Romeo pulled up a chair and cracked his knuckles. 'Okay, boss,' he said. 'Start with this: *We spoke at Secret Cinema . . .*'

43

Nadia

Nadia held her phone in her hand as the bus trundled down to Angel, where she would hop off and get the tube, like she did every day. Her instinct was to text Emma, but Emma was so absent that she didn't think she could stomach the three-day wait that had eased itself into all communication with her. Instead, she pulled up Instagram to look at the photo Naomi had posted from the night before, 'liking' it and leaving three flame emojis underneath as a comment. Nadia screen-shotted it, thinking she might post it too. It was right after she'd talked with that gorgeous guy in the waistcoat, and she had the look of trouble in her eye. Good trouble. She looked bright and fresh-faced and fun.

Nadia scrolled through the other photos that had loaded: a friend from school was on vacation with her husband in Sri Lanka. Her cousin's baby had crawled for the first time. Several Instagrammers had new skirts and shirts and boots and were reminding her that it would soon be Black Friday, *so click the link in bio for the full collection and don't forget to use the discount code!!!* She scrolled past them all.

Nadia stopped as she saw Gaby's latest picture, a close-up of her at Soho House, which was interesting to Nadia because she knew that Gaby didn't have Soho House membership. Of course, Emma did, and it was Soho House she'd seen them stumble out of that night they'd kissed. If Nadia looked close enough at the photo, a selfie taken in what looked like the bathroom, she could see what had been cropped out: beside where Gaby's own hair fell was shoulder-length honey-coloured hair – Emma's.

A million unkind thoughts crept into Nadia's mind. Logically, rationally, she knew her friends had a secret that of course they'd eventually tell her. But right now she was locked out of the world they were creating, whatever world that was, and mostly Nadia didn't give two hoots if they were dating or sleeping together or in love – she just wanted her buddies back. She wanted to be part of the gang again. She wanted to be happy for them, but being iced out was costing her her happiness, so it made it really hard to be excited for them. Nadia was angry, and resentful, at being put in this position. They didn't need her permission to do whatever it was they were doing, that isn't what she meant. But damn if her two best friends hadn't come together to form something that meant now *she* felt left out. And it really wasn't her place to sit them both down and say what she'd seen. She believed that implicitly. It was no big deal and a total game-changer both at the same time, and not just because they were both women. Her friends were gay – at least for each other. So what! But two friends becoming more meant the dynamics shifted, and it meant that Nadia sat on the 73 bus looking at Instagram and making the very conscious decision to keep on scrolling, without hitting like or commenting, like she would normally have done, eventually uploading the photo of her and Naomi from last night, captioning it, *My ride or die and I, as a pair of Capulets last night*, adding in three love hearts afterwards and hashtagging it #girlsnightout

Reviewing her work, and with the bus sitting in traffic, Nadia clicked on the geo-tag she'd put on the event – the marker that said what her location had been. It pulled up all the other photos that people had uploaded at the same location, and because she was bored, and mad, and above all else, nosey, she scrolled through a bunch of strangers' photos, stopping only when she recognized a set of arms.

Waistcoat Guy! she thought. *Gah!*

He was handsome, the only one in a bunch of friends not looking directly to the camera, but looking off, just slightly, to something out of frame. Everyone he was with was attractive, and Nadia recognized the friend he'd been talking with too.

The photo had been uploaded by a girl called @SabrinasLife, and from following through on her handle and scrolling down on her profile, Nadia could ascertain that she was in a relationship – married to, it looked like – one of the other guys. Waistcoat Guy was peppered in the odd group photo on her grid, mostly at what looked like kids' birthday parties in the suburbs, and holidays to places where the sea was so blue it was turquoise.

Nadia scrolled back up to the top of @SabrinasLife's page and looked at the photo from the night before again. She tapped on it, and up came everyone's tagged usernames. She clicked on that. Suddenly, she had a full window into @DannyBoy101's life.

He didn't post often, and he never used captions or hashtags.

There was a photo of him in a navy suit, stood next to what Nadia presumed was his mum, and a photo of him in the downstairs of Sager + Wilde, drinking a pint with his face half obscured by the glass. He'd photographed his feet by some train tracks, wearing trainers and coloured socks, and in the summer he'd been with a handful of mates in Oxfordshire, walking in the country fields and drinking pints in a pub garden.

He'd recently read Michelle Obama's memoir and had also photographed something at the Wellcome Collection. There was an old record of Frank Sinatra's and a photo of the TV with *The Lust Villa* on. Inexplicably, there was a photo of the paper on a coffee table too, one day back in the summer.

This is my kinda guy, Nadia thought. *I like how he sees the world.*

Nadia continued to think about him all day. She wondered how to go about it all – how to somehow bump into him again. She *could* just DM him on Instagram, but was that a bit desperate? What if that was a total turn-off for him, being tracked down on social media? If the shoe was on the other foot, Nadia wasn't sure how she'd respond. She'd discovered him in an innocent enough way, but explaining that, even to herself, sounded a bit too *Fatal Attraction*. She didn't want him to think she'd boil bunnies to get his attention. He was cute, but not *that* cute.

Emma had once taught her about 'The Secret'. It was based on the Law of Attraction, and Emma had tried to tell her that if a person changed their thoughts, they could change their life. Emma had been utterly convinced that's why she'd been given the restaurant review column in the paper – that she had visualized it, and made it come true. Nadia had written it off as mumbo-jumbo before, but in this new context – the context of desperately wanting a cute man she'd talked to for five minutes to cross her path again – she chose to believe. All day she told herself, *I am going to see this man again. Soon. This week.* She tried to picture it: bumping into him at the gym, or on the train to work. Maybe that was a hangover from when Train Guy wrote to her. She still half-heartedly thought there was something staggeringly romantic about meeting somebody on the underground: two people coming from different places, going to different places, chance putting them in the same place at the same time for mere minutes.

She wished she could tell Emma about it all. Especially when she walked into the gym space for her class that night, just as a friendly looking blond man left the changing rooms at the other side of the doors, and they both reached for the door handle at the same time.

'Oh, pardon me, let me get that for you,' the guy had said. He pulled the door open and let Nadia walk on ahead. She picked a spot towards the back of the room – over her dead body would she enter a middle row, let alone a front one – and threw down her water bottle and face towel. She stood to queue at the weights section to pick up her bar and a few dumbbells when they were called for, queuing behind the man who'd just held the door for her. He looked up and around at her.

'Oh, hey again,' he said.

'Hey again,' Nadia replied, slightly puzzled at his friendliness.

'Can I pass you something?' he said.

Did he work here? she wondered.

'Oh, you're very kind. Yes. Sure. What about a pair of the sixes, and maybe of the eights as well.'

The guy wore a gym vest and as he leaned across to pick

up her weights his back muscles rippled and she stared too long. He caught her. He smirked.

'There you go,' he said, a pair in each hand.

Nadia's hands weren't as big as his so he offered to follow her back to her mat. She walked ahead of him, self-consciously, wondering: *was he flirting?*

'Thank you again,' she said, and he put down her weights beside her water bottle and stood up, pulling himself up tall, shoulders back and neck elongated, and smiled broadly.

'Any time,' he said, winking at her. And then he was gone.

Nadia had caught sight of herself in the studio mirror. She looked flushed and silly, and she was smiling. He walked in front of her to get to his own mat, smiling at her again, and Nadia felt self-conscious for the whole session.

'Have a good one,' he shouted across the room to her as she left, sweating and red-faced.

Nadia had taken that class at least once a week for a year and never been hit on, but suddenly with the spring in her step of having flirted the night before, another man had flirted with her today. She wanted to tell Emma, 'That was it! That was the law of attraction!' She'd probably have been deeply suspicious of the guy helping her even two days ago. But with a different mindset came different reactions to the world. She believed romance was imminent, and so everything seemed more romantic.

I'm going to see this guy again, she told herself, after she left the gym and walked halfway home before getting the bus, to get rid of her excess energy. *I am. I am going to see Waistcoat Guy again.*

She had to tell somebody what was going through her mind, so she texted Naomi to see if she was about and arranged to call her when she got home, after her shower.

'And I don't mean to sound like a total stalker or anything, but . . . I found him on Instagram.'

Nadia could hear Naomi raise her eyebrows. 'You found the mystery man from last night on Instagram?'

Nadia stretched out on her bed, wearing nothing but a towel. She'd got out of the shower almost an hour ago, but in between scrolling through @DannyBoy101's Instagram (again), staring out of the window, and now talking to Naomi, she'd got no further than moisturizing her legs.

'It was an accident! I was on the bus on the way to work, and I put up the photo of us, and tagged the location. And then I was bored, and so clicked the geo-tag thing, and it brought up all the photos of that night. And one of the top ones had him in it.'

Naomi's smirk was obvious even down the phone. 'Sure,' she said. 'Sure.'

'It's true!'

Nadia lazily lifted a leg in the air to examine it. She should have shaved them. They were overgrown and patchy: a crop of thick dark hair sprouted with impunity from behind her ankle.

'I just – well, because he was wearing that stupid waistcoat thing, it caught my eye when I fell down the Insta-hole.'

She stood up and made her way to stand in front of the mirror.

'I saw his arms before I saw his face. His friend had tagged him in it. So I clicked on his handle. And then . . . I had a bit of a look.'

She loosened her towel so she was naked and able to look at her reflection. She turned this way and that, examining herself, and then lifted an arm. She looked like Julia Roberts at the *Notting Hill* premiere: she'd forgotten to shave there, too. She wondered if she could pass it off as a political state-ment, not that anyone saw her armpits.

'Well, you can't message him,' Naomi shrieked. 'What would you say, "Hey! I eavesdropped on your private conver-sation and thought you were super emotionally mature and that's my love language, and then you picked up my phone after knocking it out of my hand and it turns out you're fit too. I tracked you down like Glenn Close to say: drink?"'?

Nadia shrugged. 'I mean . . . yes?'

'Okay, no. No way. You are way above this. There must be another way! He was cute, darling, but not so cute that you have to act weird about it. What would you do if he messaged you on Instagram?'

'I know,' said Nadia. 'I wondered the same thing. But also, hey! I literally cannot believe you are judging me right now. You don't know what it's like to be out there, single and looking! You've been with Callum for years. Don't forget how rare it is to feel . . . the thing.' Nadia lay back down on the bed. 'I felt like I knew him! When he looked at me, it was like you or Emma or Gaby looking back. Dead familiar. Nice.'

'Jesus. Calm down.'

'Come on. I need your support here.'

'Okay. So. You're going to bump into him, this week. Just like that! As if by magic.'

'No. Not by magic,' Nadia admonished. 'By the law of attraction!'

'Great plan,' said Naomi.

Nadia replied, 'Oh ye of little faith.'

She was still dissatisfied with Naomi's reaction after they'd said their goodbyes. Emma would have been much better at making her feel less crazy. She missed her. She played with her phone in her hands, turning it over and considering texting her. But to say what? Just hey?

Hey friend – how you doing? she settled on, hitting 'send'. She stared at the message, waiting to see if it was received, and then read. It wasn't. Nothing appeared at the top of the screen to indicate that Emma was online and getting the texts. Nadia put her phone in a drawer and pulled on her pyjamas.

'I'm going to see Waistcoat Guy again,' she said aloud. 'I just know it.'

44

Daniel

Daniel was in a great mood – not only had he taken matters into his own hands with Nadia (again), but right before he'd left work, he'd had an email to say that by this time next week, he'd officially be a home owner.

'I did it,' he told Romeo in the lobby on the way out. 'The flat – it's mine! We're a go!'

Romeo leapt up from where he sat behind the welcome desk.

'That's great, man – really, really well done!'

'Thanks, dude.'

Romeo looked wistful. 'I hope me and Erika get to buy a place someday,' he said. 'That would be pretty sweet.'

Daniel raised his eyebrows in shock. 'Moving in together? I didn't know it had got that serious!'

Since the summer Romeo had been seeing Erika, a woman he'd met at a sourdough-bread-making class, and Daniel knew Romeo had fallen hard, but he didn't know he was already planning a future with her.

'I think it's the real deal,' said Romeo. 'I could definitely put a ring on it. Not like, tomorrow, but for sure she's a lifer.'

'Well, damn, that's great,' Daniel said. 'I tell you what – bring her to the house-warming party. You'll love all my uni mates, and I can't wait to meet her.'

Romeo held out a fist.

'Done and done,' he said. 'You've got yourself a date.' He lowered his voice a little, for comedic effect. 'Speaking of which – any word on when your note might run?'

'No,' Daniel said, slipping on his gloves as he felt a freezing November wind gust through the open door. 'I've never known, though. They just sort of run it when they run it. It's out of my hands now,' he added, holding up his gloved hands in surrender.

'Well,' said Romeo. 'The flat, the girl, it's all coming up, Weissman.'

'It's all coming up Romeo and Weissman,' Daniel corrected him.

'That sounds like a pretty sweet double act,' Romeo said.

'It does, doesn't it?' Daniel replied.

Daniel headed across the road to the tube, so he could bounce across the city to get to one of the City Professionals networking events. He'd been fifty-fifty on whether he should go, but since his great day he decided he should. If good luck came in threes, he was open to what Good Luck Number Three might be. He actually didn't have a contract lined up for after he finished at Converge at Christmas, although he suspected they might keep him on to establish the next part of the project. It wouldn't hurt to mingle with some new faces and hand out a few business cards.

'Daniel!' came a voice, not long after he'd hung up his coat and headed to the bar. There was always the awkward entrance when arriving somewhere alone, especially at a work event, that meant the safest bet was to do a lap of the room and then get a drink, figuring out where the friendliest faces were. He was relieved to have been commandeered by someone. The first conversation opener was always the hardest.

'Gaby!' Daniel said, turning around with his small glass of red. 'The woman, the myth, the legend.'

Gaby leaned in and they kissed both cheeks. 'I owe you an apology,' she said.

Daniel wafted a hand. 'Bygones,' he said, presuming she meant to apologize for leaving him stranded at her work's summer party a few months ago.

'Your email back to me was so kind, but I just wanted to say again that I am mortified that I cajoled you into coming to that party and then abandoned you without even explaining that Nadia wasn't coming. The whole thing was a mess. And you were very gracious about it.'

Daniel's body jolted at the name Nadia. He knew, of course, that Gaby couldn't be alluding to *his* Nadia, if he could call her that, but the name was so rare, really – he'd never met a Nadia before the Nadia on his train – that he couldn't help but have a reaction to it.

'Oh god, did I say something wrong?' Gaby asked.

'No, no. It's just – Nadia. You don't hear of many Nadias around.'

Gaby shrugged. 'I've never thought about it, but no, I guess not.' She smiled at him. 'How are you enjoying Converge, anyway? I've actually heard really interesting things about the ways they're incorporating the use of cloud storage in data expansion . . .'

And so the night went on. Fancy people talking fancy talk, with surprisingly good red wine and waiters dressed in bow ties serving tiny Yorkshire puddings with roast beef on them.

Daniel couldn't shake the fact that Gaby had brought up a Nadia, and as she caught him before he left, delayed by searching for his gloves that he could have sworn he'd put in his pockets, he couldn't help but ask: 'Gaby, weird question. But your friend Nadia – what's her surname?'

'Fielding,' Gaby replied. 'Why?'

Daniel shrugged. 'No reason,' he said. 'I just wondered if it was the Nadia I knew. Small world and all.'

'And is it?' she asked.

'No,' Daniel said, actually having no idea if it was or it wasn't. He'd never known what 'his' Nadia's surname was.

'Okay, well. Goodnight. See you at the February party?'

Daniel nodded. 'See you at the February party. Let me know if I can help with anything?'

'Will do,' Gaby said, turning her attention to another departing guest she wanted to say goodbye to.

Daniel googled NADIA FIELDING as soon as he stepped outside, his fingers bitterly cold, but the task at hand too important to delay. A series of photographs came up of the Nadia he knew – the Nadia from the market, and the train, and who he'd seen last night. He had a surname now, and from that he had a LinkedIn profile that confirmed she worked at RAINFOREST. He could hardly believe his luck. Gaby knew her! He was supposed to have been introduced to her months ago! All the signs pointed to the fact that he was absolutely supposed to meet her. It seemed their fates were unavoidable.

I feel it, he thought to himself. *This time, I won't mess it up.* He couldn't wait for the ad to run – he was so excited to finally, at last, meet her. They were meant to be! He couldn't believe he'd almost missed the love of his life.

45

Nadia

'Shit. Shit, shit, shit.'

Nadia Fielding launched down the escalator of the tube station, her new winter boots hitting the steps with force. Coffee held precariously in her hand, bag slipping from her shoulder, beret beginning to move from the top of her head down to the side, Nadia was a mess – but she'd be damned if she wasn't getting the 7.30. Today was a do-over on The New Routine to Change Her Life. She was getting on that damned train, she was going to have a superb day, and she was going to be a woman in charge of her own life. The air was different, today. She was different, today. Possibility for the adventure of her own life splayed before her. *I'm going to meet Waistcoat Guy again*, she continued to tell herself. *I see it. I feel it.*

She made it onto the platform, into her usual spot, before the train pulled up, and was thrilled she did because, amazingly, perfectly, OH-MY-GOD-I-CAN'T-ACTUALLY-BELIEVE-IT-EXCEPT-THIS-IS-WHAT-I-VISUALIZED-LY

– and there HE was. @DannyBoy101. The guy from the cinema event. The man she'd stalked on Instagram and willed to cross her path again.

Shit, Nadia thought. *It really is him!* He was cuter than she remembered. She had literally been on his Instagram only that morning, sneaking a peek to see if he had uploaded anything since the movies. He hadn't. Nadia had been frustrated, wanting a titbit about his life to fuel her interest in him, but his mysterious online ways gave her nothing.

She took a breath.

She looked across to the left as the train slowed to a stop.

The train doors opened.

@DannyBoy101 looked up.

Their eyes met.

'Hello,' he said, and as people pushed around her to board the train, she walked towards him, slowly, relieved that he seemed to recognize her.

'Hi.'

They stood and smiled at each other like they had done the other night, until the forward movement of the train forced Nadia to stumble slightly. As a knee-jerk reaction, @DannyBoy101 held out his arm and she grabbed it, waiting for the train to pick up speed before trusting herself to regain her centre of gravity. His arm was rock solid. She didn't want to let go.

'I almost didn't recognize you fully clothed,' she smiled, and @DannyBoy101 laughed.

'Yeah, I tend to save the leather waistcoat for when I'm not about to meet with my boss, and my boss's boss, and my boss's boss's boss.'

Nadia made a big demonstration of being impressed. 'Big day for you then.'

@DannyBoy101 swallowed and, holding her gaze and without blinking, said, in a voice that felt all loaded and heavy and deliberate: 'Apparently so.'

The way he said it was so laden with meaning that she felt her nipples get hard as her cheeks flushed. She smiled, willingly herself to rise to the occasion of the moment. She didn't want to be shy, or let this pass her by. She had to be brave. She was securing the name and telephone number of this man, confidence wobbles be damned.

Nadia was vaguely aware of the intrigue from the people around them. The London Underground was famed for being notoriously unfriendly. Several campaigns had been instigated over the years, typically from people Not From Here, to encourage chit-chat and smiles, including but not limited to badges that said 'Talk to Me!' in the red, white and blue colours of Transport for London (ostensibly not, in fact, issued by them) to buskers asking people to sing along, to American tourists trying to drum up conversations with locals only to be met with a stony silence and a pointed seat change. But – Londoners had a nose for romance. They loved a 'Tube Meet'. Nadia was quite sure one young woman had even taken off her headphones to listen in to them more closely.

'Where do you get off?' Nadia said eventually, her voice a little high-pitched – but at least she'd used it.

'There's a joke in there somewhere,' @DannyBoy101 smiled.

'Very funny.'

'I try my best.'

'I'm sure you don't have to try at all.'

Another loaded silence. Nadia knew, without a shadow of doubt, that he felt what she felt. He couldn't not. She couldn't explain what was happening, but she knew, understood implicitly, that this guy was going to be something mind-blowingly meaningful to her.

The train slowed down as they approached London Bridge.

'This is me,' said @DannyBoy101.

'Oh – me too,' said Nadia.

@DannyBoy101 held out his hand to indicate that Nadia should lead the way, and they walked side by side in the mass of people heading to the escalator, where Nadia got on first. She turned around, and being on the higher step meant she was now eye to eye with @DannyBoy101, at about the same height. She was close enough to smell him: cloves and sandal-wood and maybe cedarwood too. He had the tiniest speck on red blood at the side of his face, down on his jaw. Nadia thought it must have been from shaving, since his stubble was cropped close to his face. She could smell his mouthwash. Peppermint.

Nadia wondered to herself if she'd seen him before – before the cinema event. She must have seen him on the train, if this was where he worked too – though to be fair, she normally had her nose in her phone. @DannyBoy101 looked at her, leaning forward a little bit, and she almost closed her eyes and tilted her chin to receive his kiss before he said, pan-faced, 'You're staring at me, you know.'

She burst out laughing.

'Oh my god – I'm sorry.' She covered her face with a hand, and then dared look at him again, searching his eyes. Palpable electricity passed between them.

'It's just . . .' she began, but he interrupted her.

'Watch out!' he said, gesturing. He held on to her elbow and spun her around in time for her to realize they were at the top of the escalator. A moment later, and she would have been on the floor, no doubt taking out double figures of commuters with her. They walked side by side and she felt it again: the pull. *Ask me if I want get coffee before work*, she silently willed him, forgetting that she was more than capable of asking him if he wanted coffee. *Ask to see me again.*

'Well,' @DannyBoy101 said, as they reached the exit. 'I'm this way. At Converge.' He indicated left.

'And I'm this way,' said Nadia, indicating right. 'At RAIN-FOREST.'

Ask him for his number, Nadia thought. *Don't be a pussy, come on!*

'Well . . .' @DannyBoy101 said.

'Well . . .' Nadia said.

Come on! she thought.

'Do you . . .' Nadia said, as @DannyBoy101 said, 'I thought that maybe . . .'

They laughed.

She insisted he speak. He insisted she speak. They talked over each other and then neither said anything and Nadia decided she would ask him – she'd tell him she was getting coffee and that he should join her and—

'I really want to ask you for coffee,' he said, finally.

'I was just thinking the same!' Nadia said. 'Yes! Do you know Pete's coffee cart just around the corner? He does great coffee, I think it's the blend he has, something about Arabica beans with Robusta too? His hazelnut-milk flat whites are to die for. To die for!'

'I was going to say,' @DannyBoy101 continued, 'I really want to ask you for coffee but I have my meeting – the big one? With all the important people?'

Nadia felt really fucking stupid. Surely not. Surely she hadn't misread this. Surely!

'Your meeting, yes. Go. Go impress.' She gave a hollow and awkward laugh, and then felt even more stupid. 'Good luck.'

'Can I, maybe, erm, can I take your number?' he said, holding out his phone to her. 'Will you put it in here? I'd like to take you out. On a date. If you'd like that too.'

Nadia felt relief flood through her. 'I would like that very much,' she beamed, taking his iPhone and typing in her number under the name 'Girl on the Train'.

'Okay then,' he said, as she gave it back.

'Text me,' she said.

He nodded. 'I will.'

He walked away, turning around not once but twice to grin at her, widely. He almost walked into a man with a briefcase. It made Nadia laugh. She stood and watched him go with a little wave, butterflies dancing in her stomach. She felt as though the whole train ride had been a rollercoaster, going up and up and up towards the peak, and the moment she was suspended in now was the moment before the free-fall, when everything blurred and went fast and she lost control.

Her phone beeped. Unknown number.

I'm glad we didn't miss our stop today, it said. She presumed it was from @DannyBoy101, but Nadia didn't get it. Miss their stop? Huh? Why would they have missed their stop?

She tossed the thought around in her mind, trying to unpick it. *Their stop.*

How did he know they had the same stop? Is that what he meant? That they could have kept talking on the train and missed their stop?

I'm glad we didn't miss our stop.

Was it a saying she didn't know about? That like, when you met somebody you fancied you got off at their stop?

No. That didn't sound right.

I'm glad we didn't miss our stop.

Didn't miss our stop.

Our Stop.

The Twitter hashtag.

#OurStop

Miss our stop? thought Nadia. *Why would we—*

'OH MY FUCKING GOD,' she said into her phone, holding down the record button to Emma. 'I think I just met him. Train Guy! I think I just met him! Fucking call me!'

46

Nadia

Fifteen minutes later her phone lit up with a message, and Nadia grabbed her phone quicker than she ever had before in the hope that it was @DannyBoy101 again – though she supposed she could now think of him as Train Guy. She surprised herself by being just as excited to see Emma's name, who'd sent a link to a tweet. God, she missed her friend. She hoped they could get back to normal soon. Nadia opened it.

I think I just stood behind the #OurStop couple at London Bridge station – they were talking to each other! I think they might be dating! I need somebody to be as invested in this as I am! it said. There was a fuzzy photograph of the back of @DannyBoy101's head, almost totally obscuring the back of Nadia's. But it was them. It was them not even a half-hour ago, on the escalator, when Nadia felt her tummy lurch and pupils dilate and like she should note the date, and time, and location, because she'd never want to forget when she knew she had finally met her person.

Aside from the fact that it was weird somebody had invaded their privacy that way, Nadia's stomach did a little flip. If *she* thought he was Train Guy, it this woman on the internet thought he was Train Guy, it was all looking increasingly likely that the @DannyBoy101 was Train Guy.

Holy shit, she thought. She added it all up in her mind: Train Guy had stood her up, and she'd tried to put him to the back of her mind, and then she'd met @DannyBoy101 at Secret Cinema, deciding she fancied him even before he had turned around, and now it turned out that they were the same person.

'Fuck me,' she said to Emma, deciding to hide in the company bathroom and call her. 'I met Train Guy!!!!!'

She didn't open her conversation with a hello, or a 'We've not spoken in ages'. Nadia got straight down to business.

'I found him!'

'This is so cool,' Emma said, down the phone. 'Like, I'd given up on him! But now he's here!'

'I can't believe it,' Nadia said. 'He's so cute. Like, you'll die he is that cute.'

'Amazing,' Emma said. 'Totally amazing. This is just perfect. So, what now?'

Nadia was thankful there were no awkward pauses or needless explanations of why they'd both been absent from each other's lives. She was just glad they were talking.

'Well, I put my number in his phone, and he texted straight away. That's how I know it was him. He basically told me as much. So now I . . . text back? Oh god, I just can't believe it's him!'

'And we're very sure he doesn't seem like a psychopath?'

'Emma, he is so normal and cute and a bit geeky and quite handsome. He's like . . . fucking *it*. He didn't even have coffee breath!' As soon as she said it, she realized she probably had done. Oh well.

'Emma,' Nadia continued. 'I know things have been weird between us lately, but will you meet me for lunch? I need you.'

'Of course I will,' Emma said. 'Just tell me where.'

47

Daniel

You're Train Guy! her text message back read. *You're the one who wrote to me in the paper in the summer!*

Daniel fist-pumped the air. *Bingo.*

Oh thank god, Daniel thought to himself, before realizing, *Oh shit. So it* was *Nadia I stood up that time.* He hoped he had been forgiven. Presumably, if she was texting him back, he was. His phone beeped again.

You stood me up, you bastard!

Perhaps all had not been forgiven.

I have a totally legitimate explanation, he typed back.

And I have your bank card, she replied.

You were very good not to order the Dom Pérignon with it, Daniel said.

I almost did, she texted back.

Daniel was pacing up and down in the lobby at work, waiting for Romeo. He couldn't wait to tell him. He'd freak!

'Where've you been, man?' Daniel said, as he saw him turn the corner in his uniform.

'Woah, brother, relax,' Romeo said. 'We've talked about this before. 8 a.m. is when I get a little rumble in the jungle, you know what I'm saying?'

Daniel did not.

'Poop, Daniel. About 8 a.m. is when I take my morning poop.'

Daniel wished he didn't have to know that.

Romeo continued: 'What's the trouble?'

'Nadia. I saw her. Talked to her. And then got her number. I basically told her I'm the one who's been writing to her.'

'Well, that's great! Well done!'

'No! You don't get it! I should have . . . Told her properly. In a grander way, maybe. I want to do something big for her,' Daniel concluded.

'Okay . . .' said Romeo.

'I have to do something. I have to do something, now. Today. Strike whilst the iron is hot.'

Daniel was a little bit manic, with his eyes wild and full of half-formed plans. He looked at his watch. He needed to prep the last of some slides before a breakfast meeting to highlight the progress he'd made these past few months, ensuring the partners that he was leaving them with the formula for success.

'I mean, okay. If you're sure you're not being a little dramatic here. You have her number. So, just text her back and ask her out.'

'No,' Daniel said, with certainty. 'No, I want it to be bigger than that. This is going to be the last woman I ever ask out. This is going to be her last ever first date! It has to be memorable. I want her to understand that this is it.' He reflected on what he'd just said and added, a little more measuredly, 'You know, not to freak her out or anything. I mean, I just want to do her justice.'

Romeo understood. 'Okay, okay. What can I do to help you? I'm here, man.'

Daniel looked around the lobby, like the answer might present itself there. 'Wait here,' he told Romeo.

'It's my job to wait here!' Romeo said. 'Literally, I am paid to wait here. In this lobby. All day.'

Daniel ran across the road to the florists at the train station, and paid eighty-five pounds for a bouquet of sunflowers and gerberas and green feathery stuff. He jogged back across the road and handed them to Romeo.

'Okay, can you go deliver these to Nadia Fielding at RAINFOREST, around the corner? Will you do that for me? I've got this meeting . . .'

'If I can get Billy to cover for me for a minute, then yes.'

'No. Not maybe, mate. You'll deliver them, right?'

'Of course, mate. Yes.'

'Okay, excellent. Make sure they let you take them up to her. Don't just leave them at reception. She needs to get them now. In fact – fuck. Erm,' he said, looking towards the desk to see if there was something he could use to write on the blank notecard the florist had attached to the bouquet. His energy was nervous and untamed. He grabbed the biro and pulled off the lid with his teeth. When he was done scribbling he put the notecard into the envelope.

'There,' he said. 'For Nadia Fielding, yes?'

'I gotchu, mate,' said Romeo, taking the flowers. 'I will deliver these personally.'

48

Nadia

'Right then. Both of you, at the burrito place, at half past noon. No excuses. I need to talk to you.'

Nadia hit send on her voice note, sent to a new group she had made for her, Emma and Gaby. She got immediate responses from both of them.

Emma: *Okay x*

Gaby: *Okay!!!!!!*

Nadia carried the bouquet of flowers downstairs with her as she left for her early lunch. She didn't want to leave them behind. She wanted them with her, evidence of the romance unfolding in front of her. They'd been delivered by the strangest man, who'd handed them over and said, 'Oh, I see. I understand what the fuss is about now.' And then he had disappeared. There was a card with the flowers.

Tonight? it read. *I'll send a clue about where later . . .*

She was excited. She was over the moon. She wanted to show off – and to her best friends. She didn't care what had happened, or what was happen*ing* with them. She missed her friends and needed them to share in this joy she was experiencing in real time.

'Ohmygod – who are they for?' said Emma, standing up to hug her. She'd cut her hair and was wearing more eyeliner than usual. It suited her.

'They're beautiful!' said Gaby, standing up to kiss her too. They'd chosen a booth, and had both sat at the same side so that Nadia had to slide in opposite them, looking at them both – being looked at by them both.

'They're mine. From Train Guy.'

Gaby narrowed her eyes. 'He knows where you work already?'

'I must have told him this morning when we were talking,' Nadia said. 'And I mean, if you Google "Nadia" and "RAINFOREST" my surname must come up. I found him on bloody Instagram, for crying out loud. I don't think finding out about people is a hard thing to do when the internet exists.'

'Oh my god!' said Emma.

Nadia replied, 'I know. It's very cute.' The three of them paused for a moment, nobody knowing where to take the discussion next. Nadia didn't want to talk about Train Guy until she knew everything was okay.

'Listen – have you two got something you want to tell me?'

They looked at each other. Their stare held for a split second too long, making it obvious that there was indeed something that needed to be said – but Nadia knew that. It was just a case of who would go ahead and say it.

'Yes,' said Emma. She put her hand on Gaby's. 'Don't freak out, but . . .' She looked at Gaby. Gaby looked at her. Both of them smiled. Nadia felt like she'd witnessed something very private pass between them.

Gaby stepped in, turning to look at Nadia again. 'Well, you know we hit it off when you introduced us last year.' She looked back to Emma.

Emma continued, 'And it was really cool that like, I liked your work BFF.' Emma looked from Nadia to Gaby, and Nadia felt it again – like she was bearing witness to a really private moment between them, just in a glance.

'And I was so happy to be your work BFF when you obviously had great taste in real-life BFFs,' said Gaby.

'But, almost right away it felt like . . .' continued Emma.

'More,' Gaby supplied, stealing a look at Emma again, who smiled at her in encouragement.

'More,' Emma repeated.

Nadia nodded, and they dragged their gaze away from one another back to her.

'So you're . . . dating?' said Nadia, trying to get them to say the words.

The pair beamed.

'We should have told you,' said Gaby. 'It was just all so . . .'

Emma completed her sentence. 'Unknown. And at first it could have been nothing, but then . . .'

'It became something,' said Gaby. 'And by then, it was like we had to protect it. Give it a chance to grow.'

'We didn't want to tell you before we knew,' said Emma, and Nadia got the measure of them in the way they finished each other's thoughts and words – she could tell they were two halves of each other, and marvelled that she'd not seen how perfect a union that could be before. 'I almost did – at Soho Farmhouse. You asked me so many times what was up and –'

Gaby interjected: 'We'd had our first fight that weekend.

If she was horrible to be around, it was my fault.' She winked at Emma, playfully.

'You could have trusted me . . .' Nadia said.

'We trust you!' said Emma. 'But it happened so slowly, I don't think we kind of knew we'd crossed a line until . . .'

'. . . Until we had really crossed a line.'

'We wanted to tell you.'

'Eventually.'

'But also like, you know. What if it was a mistake?'

'How do you know it isn't?' Nadia asked. And then, 'I'm sorry – I didn't mean that how it sounds.' She didn't. It was a reflex, a hangover from romantic scepticism. She was just relieved they were telling her everything now. That it was all out in the open.

Gaby said, 'Well. To clarify. I'm gay. I think I always was and it wasn't until Emma that I realized it.'

'And I'm . . . into everyone? Bi? Pansexual? I don't know. Whatever. I just . . . really fancy Gaby. Sorry.'

The three of them laughed.

Gaby said, 'And I never want to even think about a man naked, ever again. I've seen the light, and baby she is female.'

Nadia put her hand over theirs across the table. 'I'm glad I know now,' she said. 'I'm glad you can stop hiding from me. I saw you, in Soho one night. I knew, guys. I've known for a while.'

Gaby and Emma nodded. 'We figured that you'd figured it out,' Emma said. 'And once we knew that you knew, but hadn't heard it from us, we didn't know how to bring it up. I'm sorry.'

'I'm sorry too,' said Gaby. 'I've missed you!'

'Me too!'

'Me three!' said Nadia. She felt instantly lighter. She hated that they'd had secrets, and that she'd had secrets. She liked everything being out in the open. 'Okay, okay – come on then. What are we going to do about this mystery man?'

'What does he look like?' said Emma.

'Oh, well – I can show you a photo, actually!' said Nadia. 'I found his Instagram profile before he spoke to me today. I feel like it was all meant to be, in a weird way.'

Nadia unlocked her phone and typed in his handle to Instagram.

'NO. Way!' said Gaby, pulling the phone from her hand. 'Do you know who this is?'

'Train Guy!'

'Well, Train Guy is also the cute guy I tried to set you up with at the summer party! Daniel Weissman!'

'That's the guy you met at work?'

'It is!'

'The guy you met at work is Train Guy who is also Secret Cinema Waistcoat Guy? This is . . . wild! All the times I've missed him . . . our paths must have been almost crossing for months. Wow.'

'Well, kid, let me just tell you: he's lovely. Didn't I say I knew your perfect man? Daniel Weissman! Shit the bed!'

'Well, I've got a date with him tonight. I don't know where, yet – I think he's going to text me specifics. Finally, we're going to have that drink.'

'No emergency call needed, presumably?'

Nadia shook her head. 'No emergency call needed.'

49

Daniel

Daniel saw Lorenzo's name flick up into his inbox as he sat in his meeting – a meeting where he was asked to stay on at Converge for another six months. Daniel was thrilled to say yes: having just got a mortgage, it was nice to think he could just enjoy his new place and afford to decorate, rather than interviewing for his next consulting gig. It really was all coming up Weissman.

He didn't get to read the email until lunchtime, with one thing and another, and he was glad he'd waited to give it his full attention.

Hey mate,

Listen, bloody congratulations on the flat. I'm made up for you – I really am. End of an era! It's been great living with you. Thanks for putting up with all my shit. Your next chapter is going to be amazing. I'm really happy for you.

I just want you to know that I accepted a redundancy package at work last week, and I just found out, yesterday, that my leave can start immediately. I'd been there ages, so the payout is enough money to travel for a bit and get my head straight. I know things were never the same after what happened with Becky, but I want you to know I've never been sorrier for anything. I've really had to face some truths about myself, and I've got a lot to answer for. I feel so lucky I didn't hurt anyone, but the truth is I wanted to have sex with her, even though she was so drunk she didn't know her arse from her elbow, and you knew it, and it's been hard to forgive myself, really. If I'd have slept with her it would have been rape. That's . . . It makes me really ashamed.

I'm writing you this from the flat, where I've come to pack a bag because I said fuck it and bought a train ticket to Portsmouth. I'm leaving first thing tomorrow morning. Apart from you, all my mates are cokeheads and reprobates and I need some space. I read about a retreat in Portsmouth for men who want to, like, get more in touch with their feelings or whatever, so I'm going to see what's happening there. I've sent you enough money for two more months' rent, and if there's any left because you leave early, or we get our deposit back, just whizz it back over to the same account.

My life was on a bit of a downward spiral, to be honest with you, and I really do think when you threw that left punch you knocked some sense into me. I just wanted to say bye, and sorry for putting you in the position I did.

I'll drop you a text when I'm back, if you don't mind.
For now, good luck, man. Oh, and my mum is going to
come and pack up my room for me. I've got rid of the
drugs and porn.

All the best,

Lorenzo

Daniel sat at his desk and reread what Lorenzo had written.
He could understand why he wasn't saying goodbye in person
– the brief interactions they'd had for months now had been
stilted. Daniel didn't know how to treat him. He couldn't just
forget what had happened, but he didn't know what he
expected from Lorenzo to make it better.

This, I guess, Daniel thought to himself, *this is a good step*
for him.

He wrote back: *I'm proud of you, mate. Make sure you stay*
in touch.

Life really was moving on, for everybody.

His phone rang.

Percy told him: 'I've got Gaby from RAINFOREST for you.'

Daniel smiled, knowing exactly what it must be about.

'Put her through,' he said.

'YOU'RE TRAIN GUY!' she yelled down the line.

Daniel said, 'Yes I am.'

'What are the chances . . .?' she marvelled.

Daniel nodded. 'You said I was perfect for her. You called
it.'

He could hear Gaby smiling too. 'Well, yes. But I also have
to let you know that if you fuck her over I will hunt you
down and kill you, okay?'

'Message received,' Daniel said, laughing.

There was a pause. 'So, what now?' Gaby said.

'I sent her flowers,' Daniel said. 'And tonight we're finally going to have that date.'

'You had better show her a good time,' Gaby said.

Daniel thought about it for a minute. 'Gaby,' he said. 'Do you want to help me?'

50

Nadia

Nadia steadied herself in front of the mirror in the loo at work. This was just like last time. Well, just like last time except she hadn't gone to all the effort of getting her hair done and wearing an outfit she'd actually ironed. Tonight's date had taken her by surprise but, in many ways, that was infinitely better. *Go to the lobby when you're ready*, his last text had said. She'd only had an afternoon to build it up in her head. Just a few hours to deal with the clammy forehead and dry mouth. She riffled through Gaby's toiletry bag: typical Gaby, always prepared. She gave a spray of deodorant and a sweep of pressed powder on her chin. She picked out a piece of gum, topped up her lipstick, and rearranged her boobs in her bra, so that her chest looked a little perkier.

Here we go, she thought, throwing on her coat.

51

Nadia

In the lobby, just like before her first first date with Train Guy, Nadia saw Gaby.

'I can't stop!' Nadia said. 'I can't be late!' she trilled, thinking of how her conversation with Gaby was the thing that had held her up last time.

'You won't be!' Gaby said, reaching out for her wrist.

Nadia spun around and looked down to where her friend held her.

'Listen to me,' Gaby said. 'Daniel wanted me to tell you something. I'm here as your first clue on where to go.'

Nadia balked. 'You spoke to him?'

'I did. He said to tell you to stop in front of anyone wearing a yellow rose.' Nadia suddenly realized Gaby was wearing a yellow rose, clipped to the top of her dress. 'There are things he wants to say, before you get to where you're going. The first one is that you are clever and kind and smart and he promises this: that this time he won't waste your time. He'll be there.'

Nadia didn't know what to say. 'Okay . . .'

'He promises he'll be good to you, Nadia. Now, go. Wait outside. Look for the yellow roses.'

Nadia looked at her friend.

'Go!' Gaby said, smiling.

52

Nadia

Nadia walked out of the office, and immediately her eye was drawn to a man in a security uniform, wearing a yellow rose in his lapel. He looked to her immediately. She recognized him as the man who had come up to her lab earlier that day with the flowers – the one who had stared at her and said the thing about understanding what all the fuss was about.

'Hi,' he said. 'Nadia.'

Nadia nodded. 'Hi, again.'

'I'm Romeo. I didn't introduce myself before, but I work with Daniel, and I hope you don't think this is strange, but I wanted to tell you, before you met him – he's a good guy. He was telling the truth about why he had to leave that night, when you had your first date. His mother needed him. But then, he's just that kind of guy . . .'

Nadia nodded again. She looked in the direction of the road, wondering who else she'd speak to and where he was hiding.

'I'm supposed to tell you that he's regretted it since it happened. He regretted standing you up. He's thought of you every day since then, and I can vouch for that because we've talked about it.' Nadia smiled. 'He said to take note of all the details you can, because you'll never have another first date again. He's going to do this one right.'

Nadia raised her eyebrows. 'That's confident of him,' she said.

Romeo laughed. 'He's confident about you, I think,' he said. And then: 'Okay. Go in that direction, across the road. Find the next person. Enjoy!'

Nadia smiled at him, and kept walking.

53

Nadia

'Nadia!' she heard, a voice she recognized. Across the street was Emma, wearing a yellow rose around her neck. 'Come here!'

Nadia shook her head, as if to say, 'What the hell?' Emma laughed. Nadia knew she must look confused, and that Emma laughed hardest when she looked like a fish out of water.

'He's wonderful!' she said, as Nadia reached her.

'You met him?' Nadia said.

Emma nodded. 'He's so wonderful, and I just wanted to tell you – don't worry. Just enjoy it. Enjoy him, okay? He's . . . I really like him.'

Nadia didn't know what to say. Her heart swelled and beat faster, her breathing speeding up to match.

'I have something I am supposed to tell you, though. Hold on.' Emma unfolded a piece of paper, where she'd scribbled something down.

'Ready?' she asked. Nadia nodded.

'*Coffee Spill Girl. Time to put our money where our mouth is and finally have this date. We're only about four months behind, but I have no doubt you're worth the wait. I can't believe I didn't say hello to you the first time I saw you. I promise not to make a habit of being so stupid. See you in a minute, Train Guy.*'

Nadia rolled her eyes. 'I was an idiot too,' she told Emma.

'Nah,' Emma said. And then: 'Okay. Head down that alleyway there. Go. Fall in love.'

54

Nadia

Nadia walked down the back alley as instructed, seeing, in the distance, a handsome man with a yellow rose in his hand.

'Hello?' she said, uncertain.

'Nadia,' the man replied. 'Are you Nadia?'

'Yes,' she said, reaching him.

'Lorenzo,' he said. 'I'm Daniel's . . . I know Daniel.'

Nadia waited for him to continue.

'He's been nuts about you ever since he heard you talking to your boss one lunchtime,' Lorenzo said. 'And I thought he was over-egging it a bit. Thought he was crazy to get so excited about a woman he hadn't actually talked to himself.'

Nadia smiled.

'But, that's who he is. He gets a read on people. Knows people. He's waiting around the corner for you, at The Old Barn Cat. Where you should have met last time. He wanted me to tell you how excited he is, and to ask if you saw the paper today? He wrote another advert, but – well, I don't suppose it matters now.'

'I don't suppose it does.'

'He was always going to find you again.'

Nadia smiled. 'I think we were always going to find each other,' she said, before thanking him and turning the corner to the bar.

55

Daniel

Daniel had gone straight into the bar this time, no dilly-dallying outside. He'd ordered a bottle of cava, some tap water, and a charcuterie board. The place was dark and peppered with candles, and the cold outside but warm air inside had forced condensation up the windows, making it feel cosy and like winter had almost arrived. His jacket was hung under the bar, on one of the hooks, and his phone was face-down in front of him. He waited.

56

Nadia

'It's you,' she smiled.

'It's you,' he smiled.

Nadia stood before Daniel, her flowers cradled in the nook of her arm. Her cheeks were flushed and she felt jittery and coy, like a schoolgirl. Her heart thumped.

He leapt up, remembering himself, and gave her a hug.

'Thank you for these,' she said, as they stood facing each other, nodding at the bouquet she held. 'And for the trail of people . . .'

'All the people that knew about you and me, before there was a you and me to know about . . .'

Nadia and Daniel sat next to each other at the bar – the same place they should have met the first time. The same guy was behind the counter. As he approached them he said, 'Hey! You guys found each other!' and they all laughed. Daniel poured them both a glass of cava, explaining that it was dry, like champagne, and Nada told him that she'd read something about that, maybe in *The Times*.

They had so much in common, and so much yet to learn.

'You know what?' Nadia said. 'Do you mind if we move to go and sit over there, at a table?'

Daniel cocked his head at her. 'Not at all,' he said, and Nadia explained: 'This is where I waited for you last time. When you didn't . . .'

'Say no more,' Daniel nodded, understanding. When he didn't show up.

The barman gave them a little bowl of olives with tooth-picks and a bowl for the pips, and said their charcuterie would be on the way. Once he'd gone and the polite chit-chat was over, Nadia finally stole a peek at Daniel and decided it was too far away to sit opposite him, so moved her chair around so that she sat on the corner of the table, next to him, her knees knocking into the side of his legs.

She said, 'Tell me from the beginning. Tell me what happened.' She raised her glass to his, and they said a small 'cheers'.

'Tell you what happened,' Daniel repeated. They were both doing that grinning thing again. They were both just so damn happy to be there.

'Well,' he said. 'I got a new job, and so hadn't been doing this commute very long.'

Nadia dropped her jaw, playfully. 'Oh wow, okay. You really are going from the beginning, beginning.'

Daniel's face dropped, disappointed. 'You said to!'

'I was just kidding,' Nadia said. 'Sorry. I'm . . . nervous.'

'You are?'

She shrugged. 'A little. Maybe.'

'Well, I'm glad you said that,' Daniel said. 'Because I am too.'

Nadia wanted to remember every detail of what was happening, like he'd said to. The shadows of the candles across his face and the taste of the bubbles against her throat and the way he half smiled when he was unsure and needed encouraging. She wanted to frame the smell of the place, pine cones and orange, and see herself from above, flicking her hair back off her neck.

She smiled at him. 'Go on,' she said. 'The commute.' He was so handsome – and so polite too, always making sure she was comfortable and topping up her glass without asking.

'Well. I saw you by the market one day, not long after I had started my job. Before the summer – maybe in May? You were with some slick, corporate guy, talking so passionately about, like, artificial intelligence? And laughing, and being smart, and I just knew you were a woman I wanted to know.'

'Slick corporate guy? I mean – if that was with Jared, that really was months ago! I got the go-ahead on that in . . . May, I think. April, even!' Nadia wanted to know everything about this man who had spotted her in a crowd so long ago. Why hadn't she seen him then?

Daniel looked down at his lap, where he fiddled with his hands. 'Yeah. I felt so stupid for not approaching you then, but what was I gonna do? You were working, and—'

Nadia realized something: 'And if you had tried to say hi I would have totally blown you off.'

Daniel laughed. 'Exactly. Let the woman have her lunch meeting!'

Nadia laughed too. Now she thought about it, it was pretty rare to have a guy randomly strike up conversation. Maybe that was why she'd stayed and talked to Eddie when he did, on that fateful night. It was important not to be hassled on the street, but on reflection, she hardly ever spoke to somebody she didn't already know. Like Eddie had said, it just didn't happen.

'But then I saw you,' he continued, 'on the train. My train. And over a couple of weeks I figured out that on a Monday you always got the 7.30, and sometimes on a Tuesday too.'

Nadia laughed from her. 'Ha! That's hilarious to me. I always have the best intentions at the start of the week, and it never lasts. I'm just not a morning person!'

'Noted,' Daniel said. 'I'll bear that in mind.'

Nadia smirked.

Daniel blushed.

'But I panicked then too. What was I supposed to do? Talk to you on the underground like a psychopath?'

He took a long sip of his drink. The condensation cooled on the outside of his glass, leaving a little wet mark on his chin. Nadia wanted to lean over and wipe it for him. She wanted to straighten his collar and touch his neck and pull him in close.

'Again, I would have told you where to go.' It's true. She'd never spoken to another human on the tube in her life, except to maybe say 'Excuse me' or 'Can you move your bag, please?'

'So I wrote to you. And then you wrote back. So I wrote again. It's funny, but I actually sent another *Missed Connection* after the cinema, and it ran today. But then I saw you on the tube and you recognized me and the adverts . . . didn't matter anymore.'

'This is so weird, but my friend Gaby tried to set me up with you. Didn't you go to the RAINFOREST summer party?'

'Yup. Gaby. Gaby asked me to. But you never showed.'

'And then the night at the bar? I showed up then!'

'My mum . . . she's just widowed. My dad died earlier this year. She was so upset . . .'

'Oh gosh,' Nadia said. 'That's so awful. I'm so, so sorry.' She could see the sorrow flicker across his face. She could see the traces of grief in his expression.

'It's okay. She had this huge meltdown that night and I think it was a relief for both us, to be honest – it stripped away a bit of the trying-to-be-strong and made us a bit more honest. She goes swing-dancing now, and got a karaoke machine for the living room so she can have a bit of a sing-along without anyone in the house to tell her she carries a tune like a strangled cat.'

Nadia reached out and slipped her hand into his, on his lap, playfully nudging him. The tenderness of it sent pulses through them both. He continued, encouraged: 'That's why I left that night – she was so upset. And then the next day I saw you with your boyfriend and thought maybe it wasn't you I'd been writing to after all. I mean – I meant it to be for you, but . . . Oh, I don't know!'

'Do you know when I met that guy?' Nadia said, understanding he meant Eddie.

'When?'

'The night you stood me up.'

'No way.'

'Way.'

Daniel stroked her hand with his thumb. 'Shit! I thought you'd been together for ever!' He knew leaving would have cost him, he just didn't account for how much.

'And then the cinema thing . . .' Nadia continued. She figured Daniel had been pretty honest and vulnerable with her, so she would give him something of herself in return.

'I have a confession,' she said.

'What?'

'I found you. On Instagram. After that. I was on the

geo-tag and your friend had uploaded a picture and tagged you and . . .'

'Oh shit,' he laughed. 'How far back did you scroll?'

'Pretty far.'

'Ooooooh. There's some dodgy filter usage in my past.'

'I saw,' said Nadia. 'A little sepia on those sunsets.'

He cringed. 'Guilty as charged, your honour.'

'I wanted you to ask for my number that night. I was so mad when you disappeared!'

Daniel laughed. 'You're telling me! I spent the whole night trying to find your face in the crowd!'

Nadia stared at him, earnestly. 'You did?'

Daniel shrugged. 'Maybe. Yeah.' He looked at her. She wanted him to kiss her.

'That makes me happy,' she said, uncrossing her legs and inching forward in her seat. 'Because I looked for you too.' She tilted her face upwards slightly, being brave enough to make it clear what she was doing. Daniel smiled. His voice dropped low and he leaned forward himself.

'So all these near-misses,' he said, his mouth centimetres from hers, his head tipped to the right. 'And only now do we get to be in the same bar . . .' He tilted his head the other way now, delaying the inevitable moment, making Nadia's breathing shallow and heart race and she swallowed, daring to push forward the tiniest bit. '. . . at the same time.'

'Apparently so,' she said softly, their noses touching now. 'It's quite the build-up.'

'Isn't it just.'

And with that their lips met, and they kissed. Slowly, gently, magically. And then, faster and more passionately – and a different kind of magic.

'Well,' Nadia said, grinning, eventually coming up for air.

'Nice to meet you, anyway.' She pushed her forehead against his. 'I'm Nadia Fielding.'

Daniel laughed, his hand firmly on the back of her neck, pulling her in for more kisses.

'Daniel Weissman,' he said. 'It's very nice –' his mouth kissed her cheek, her neck, near her mouth '– to meet you.'

57

MISSED CONNECTION BECOMES
CHARITY UNION

Two lovebirds commuted beside each other every day but never spoke, and then fell in love by writing to each other via this paper. Now they're launching an initiative as close to their hearts as each other.

They say love strikes when you least expect it, and for artificial intelligence worker Nadia Fielding, a warm July morning seemed a day like any other. But then an advert in this very paper changed the course of her life – and her heart.

Nadia, 29, didn't know about engineer Daniel Weissman, 30. She didn't know that two weeks into his new job in London Bridge he'd overheard her talking to her boss in Borough Market, and been captivated by her. She didn't know that he then saw her frequently on his new commute, where he was desperate to catch her attention.

'I knew, though,' laughs Daniel, perched on the blue and red velvet of the Northern line carriage, 'that I had to be clever about it. I knew Nadia wasn't a woman you made a pass at on a busy tube journey. I'd heard her talk, and knew that if I was only going to have one chance to get her attention, that I had better put some thought into it.'

An offhand comment from Daniel's housemate prompted him to reach out via *Missed Connections* – the famous Lonely-Hearts-style section of our newspaper, designed for commuters of TfL to get a second chance at a connection if they don't have the nerve or opportunity to ask out a commuter crush.

'He was absolutely right,' agrees Nadia, beaming, sat next to her unmissed connection as they ride into work together. 'I don't think I would have given a bloke cracking on to me at half seven in the morning the time of day. But I am obsessed with *Missed Connections* – not that he could have known that.'

She pauses to smile at him again. The pair are attentive to their interviewer, but constantly look to the other to share their attention, making it clear they are a firm partnership.

'My best friend and I would send each other our favourite adverts sometimes, but then one day she sent one and said it sounded like me. I couldn't believe it! It suddenly made my mornings so much more interesting!'

She wasn't 100 per cent convinced it was meant for her at first, though:

'It said something about being on the last carriage of the Northern line tube that goes through Angel at 7.30, and that's the one I try to catch, but I thought lots of women must! It was my best friend who sent back the first response to him.'

'Nadia's best friend Emma definitely deserves to take a lot of the credit for this, then,' Daniel says, bumping his shoulder against Nadia's in a display of what is obviously an established joke between them. 'Because from then on, throughout the summer we'd send notes back and forth, in the newspaper – which feels odd to say, but it didn't feel odd. It felt fun and exciting, although also a bit like having your private Tinder messages read by half of London.'

And half of London did, indeed, read them: the hashtag #OurStop trended on Twitter, with invested fellow commuters desperate to see the pair finally meet.

'But then he stood me up for our first date,' deadpans Nadia, before laughing at Daniel cradling his head in his hands, obviously mortified. Nadia continues: 'When we'd finally arranged to meet up, he had a family emergency and left me waiting for him at the bar. I was furious!'

Furious she might have been, but Nadia was, in spite of herself, also determined to know who the author of her letters was. 'Even though it killed me to admit it,' she adds.

'In the meantime I dated, but I always wondered if he was still on my tube carriage sometimes. I wanted to at least get a look at the guy with enough imagination to write me letters in the bloody paper.'

But a chance meeting at London's Secret Cinema saw them meet face to face for the first time.

'And not long after that, it was officially love,' says Daniel, with Nadia tipping her head up towards him for a peck on the lips. They're easy in each other's company, and very openly affectionate.

That was six months ago. 'But we're in no rush,' says Nadia. 'Daniel just moved down the road from me, so we see each other a lot, but we're happy to make sure this all unfolds naturally. We both know falling in love isn't a happy ending – it's just the beginning.'

Just the beginning is a theme for them, then, as they join forces for their new charity venture, Future Connections – a play on their own connection, and their love for shaping the work culture in their industries of technology and engineering.

'It's about training people who would normally get left behind by the tech revolution,' explains Daniel.

'I work in AI,' says Nadia, 'and, shamefully, build robots making people technically unemployed. This is my way of giving back.'

Daniel is quick to leap to his girlfriend's defence. 'Not that she shouldn't be doing that: lots of jobs are done better by robots. But people always come first, and with our training programme they can hopefully gain skills and opportunities to develop.'

'Our biggest focus is getting older people into STEM, and even more women too.'

Launching tomorrow, anyone is able to apply for the month-long programmes, which take the form of downloadable modules, meaning students can work at their own pace.

'And then they can stop by the studio on a weekend for real-life demonstrations and advice,' says Daniel, referencing their Newington Green office area, paid for through a donation from Nadia's employer RAINFOREST.

'There's no judgement or expectation of what anybody "should" know,' adds Nadia. 'We just want to help. And we're so proud that we can do that together.'

As we pull up to London Bridge tube station, Nadia whispers to Daniel, 'Babe, it's our stop.'

The pair say their thank yous and goodbyes, and walk out into their Future Connection, together.

Acknowledgements

Thank you to:

Ella Kahn, Phoebe Morgan, Katie Loughnane, Sabah Khan, Bella Bosworth and Cherie Chapman – what a dream team of women without whom this book would quite literally not exist.

And.

My family, who told me I could do this all along and reminded me when I forgot. I am living out my dream so that I might do your faith in me justice.